EVER MARKED

MARY H. AKERS

ISBN: 9781698532165

Book Design by TeaBerry Creative

For Jamie.
My husband, my partner, my friend.
Thank you for helping me make this dream a reality.

CHAPTER 1

She could hear it. The whisper of leaves rustling in the wind. The gentle creak of branches weaving and swaying as they danced in the breeze. The undulating waves of sound filling her ears, calling to her soul. She lifted her face to the sky and breathed deeply, filling her lungs with air that had been cooled in the shade of a thousand trees. The scent of moist earth and growing things filled her nostrils. She slowly exhaled, basking in the tranquility of the moment. Never had she felt so grounded and at peace. It was as though her feet had sprung roots, as though she were a part of the very forest itself.

Through her eyelids she could sense the beams of light breaking through the shadow of the canopy overhead. How she longed to open her eyes! She fought the urge, taking another deep breath and drinking in the sensation of being alone in a place that she loved. The secret refuge to which she could escape. A break from reality.

What was that? Her brow wrinkled as she listened more intensely. There it was again. It was her name. It was muffled by the wind, but it was definitely her name, being called by a voice she didn't recognize. It was the voice of a man. She held her breath, staying perfectly silent so that she could hear him. Who was he? Did he know her? Could he see her?

"Elora!" Over and over he called to her, louder and clearer each time. "Elora!" He was coming closer! She could feel her pulse quicken as excitement, tinged with fear, began to well up in her throat. Still she battled the urge to open her eyes. She could hear his footsteps now, the crack of twigs beneath his feet as he neared her. "Elora!" His voice was rich and deep. "Elora!" He sounded frantic as he searched for her. And then suddenly the footsteps ceased. "Elora." There was relief in his voice. A few purposeful footsteps followed, and then silence. Her breath caught in her throat, knowing how close he must be. She suddenly felt his fingers slide across her palm as he took her hand and with a gasp, she opened her eyes.

He was gone. As were the peaceful forest and the cool breeze. In their place was a hot, smothering gust of wind and the stone wall she had been leaning against when she'd closed her eyes. Elora squinted, momentarily blinded by the light of the sun beaming down from a cloudless sky. She took a moment to gain her bearings, disoriented by her sudden change in surroundings. She looked down at her hand, rubbing her thumb across her palm, his touch still fresh in her mind. The warmth of his voice still hummed in her ears.

She had visited the forest many, many times in her daydreams but never before had she encountered someone else there. She felt a pang of disappointment that she hadn't been able to see his face, but then, she'd never actually seen the forest either. At least, she thought it was a forest that she escaped to in her daydreams. She couldn't be certain, having never actually been in a forest before. There were no forests in the Grasslands. There were scrubby little bushes and an occasional tree, but the wind and the soil in this place made for wide open plains, not mighty forests.

Elora turned and began walking over the hard, rocky ground along the stone wall. It was about 20 feet high in most places and stretched for nearly 3 miles, surrounding the entirety of Windom, protecting the citizens of the small town from the wilderness beyond. She took slow, absentminded steps as she puzzled over her daydream. It hadn't really felt like a daydream. The sounds and the sensations had been so vivid, had seemed so real! It was always that way when she escaped to the forest. But why couldn't she open her eyes when she dreamed of that place? She could only remain in the forest dream if she kept her eyes closed. And she only ever dreamed of the forest when she was awake.

Perhaps they weren't dreams. She stopped and propped her shoulder against the trunk of a small tree. Maybe they felt real because the place she escaped to actually was real! Could they be some kind of vision and not just a creation of her imagination? Could the man she just encountered in the forest truly exist? That last thought thrilled her.

But she quickly checked herself for even entertaining such a foolish notion. She couldn't be having supernatural visions. That was the stuff of fairy tales and legends, not the reality of a simple girl from the Grasslands. Sure, she'd felt a little different all her life, but that was only because her arrival in Windom as a child had been so unusual. There was nothing extraordinary about her, and honestly, she was comfortable with that fact.

Elora was a typical and utterly normal young woman. Aside from a somewhat unique birthmark, there was nothing singular about her. Which is probably why she was nearing her 19th birthday and had yet to be seriously courted. True, she had only been eligible for a year and it was hardly uncommon for people her age to remain unbound, but her best friend Alysa had received no fewer than 4 letters from hopeful suitors on her 18th birthday.

It can be quite humbling, friendship with an exceptionally beautiful person. Fortunately, Alysa was both sweet and kind as well. The girls had always adored each other with equal fervor, and so jealousy had never gained a firm foothold between them. Though Elora's lack of suitors did sting a bit.

"Everything alright down there?" Elora looked up to find a member of the Guard peering down at her from atop the wall. The Guard was tasked with keeping

Windom safe, both from outsiders and from citizens alike. Ordinarily Elora would have felt intimidated being called upon by a Guardsman, but when she recognized the face of her childhood friend she smiled.

"Hi Trig!" she called. "I'm fine, just got a bit lost in my thoughts. How's the view from up there today?" she asked.

"Nothing too exciting. I saw a wagon nearing the North Gate earlier though. I'm guessing it came from the Highlands by the looks of it."

Trig's deep baritone voice still seemed foreign and ridiculous to her, coming from the mouth of the boy she'd known since they were both in diapers. She still had trouble seeing him for the man he'd become. But there he was, tall and muscular and assuming one of the most dangerous occupations in the settlement.

"Where's Alysa? Aren't you two attached at the hip?" he asked with a conspicuous amount of interest.

Elora grinned. "You are so transparent Trig Davenport! Have you written her a letter yet?"

"No," he admitted dejectedly. "I was afraid it would get lost amongst the heaping pile of other proposals. How many letters has she received now?" he asked with a miserable sigh.

"I think she's up to 8," Elora answered with a wry smile. "It really is an impressive pile."

Elora laughed at the grimace on his face. She did enjoy tormenting him, but she'd been waiting a while for just such an opportunity to put her two friends out of their misery and she wasn't going to miss it. She stopped laughing and looked up at him earnestly. "You should write her, Trig." She held his gaze unwaveringly and willed him to stop being such a daft idiot. Slowly a hopeful smile spread across his face.

"Really?" he asked, struggling to believe her.

"I promise she wouldn't lose your letter, Trig."

Elora smiled happily at the surprised and then elated expression on his face. She wasn't one for meddling, and matchmaking certainly wasn't her calling, but she couldn't help herself. Those two had been completely smitten with one another for the past three years but too terrified to admit it.

"Really?" Trig asked, needing to hear her say it one more time.

"Really," she said with conviction.

"Wow!" he whispered, a bemused smile playing on his lips.

He took an absentminded step toward the edge, likely preoccupied with thoughts of Alysa she presumed, and Elora cringed.

"Hey Trig," she called, waiting for him to look down at her. "Don't fall off the wall."

"I won't," he said, laughing and shaking his head. "Thanks Elora."

"No problem," she replied. "I probably should have told you when you were on the ground anyway. This stops being fun for me if you end up crippled."

"No. I wasn't going to fall off the wall, you silly girl," he said, chuckling. "I'm not even close to the edge! This thing is like, 10 feet wide. I meant thank you for cluing me in. I wasn't even going to try for her, you know."

"I know you weren't," she said, shaking her head. "Why do you think I told you, you idiot."

"Hey!" he laughed, in mock outrage.

Elora laughed along with him, giddy at the prospect of having helped her friends towards happiness.

"Did you say you saw a Highland wagon earlier?" Elora asked, an exciting thought popping into her head. "I should go check out the market and see if they brought anything good to sell. Maybe they brought something from the Woodlands!"

"Well, you'll have to hurry. There are some ugly clouds heading our way. Looks like a pretty decent storm," Trig warned.

Elora turned to leave but then she hesitated. The height of the wall made for a great vantage point and Elora had heard that the Grasslands were beautiful from up there. This seemed like a good chance to see for herself.

"Hey Trig? Do you think I could come up there?" she asked timidly.

She had never been atop the wall. Citizens were forbidden from being up there. And as unpleasant as spending a night in the Confines might seem, it was actually less frightening than the specter of her father's wrath. Jonas Kerrick was kind and gentle, but he brooked little in the way of disobedience. They were rule followers, the Kerricks. They stayed within the lines, followed the law, and avoided attention at all costs. Elora didn't quite understand her parents' paralyzing fear of the limelight, but they had made it quite clear from an early age that their privacy was precious and the consequences were harsh for putting it in jeopardy.

Thus having a dear friend standing guard on the wall presented a very tempting opportunity to finally see the wilderness beyond. It was an opportunity too tempting to ignore.

"Please?"

"Sure," Trig shrugged. "It's the least I can do" he said with a grin.

He put down his rifle and dropped the pack he'd had slung over his shoulder, pulling out what looked like a jumble of rope. Elora glanced down at the brown pants and tan tunic she wore for working in the gardens, glad that they were well suited for climbing. A knotted rope slapped the ground in front of her. She squinted up at Trig who was peering down at her. The top surface where Trig was standing extended beyond the wall itself to create a lip, making the wall nearly impossible to scale. The rope dangled in front of her and she reached out to grab it, inhaling apprehensively.

"I'm nervous," she admitted, laughing uneasily. "I hope I can do this."

"It will be worth it," he encouraged.

She took a firm hold of the rope and jumped, clamping her feet above the lowest knot. Carefully she pulled herself up, pushing against the knots tied every few feet.

"This isn't so hard," she thought to herself.

In what felt like hardly any time at all she reached the top, throwing first one leg, then the other up over the edge of the wall. She felt Trig's hands on her arms to steady her as she turned to sit, with her feet dangling over the edge. She rested her hands on her knees and paused to catch her breath.

"Elora Kerrick, you've done that before!" Trig exclaimed in an accusatory tone. "I hope I can do this" he pantomimed in a high-pitched voice, imitating her. "I can barely climb that fast myself and I've been guarding this wall for nearly a year."

"I have not!" she cried. "Really!"

"Right. Well, I'm impressed either way." He said, shaking his head in amazement.

The wall extended about 5 feet higher on the outer edge, creating a protective barrier for the Guards. As Trig had told her, the platform was actually very wide. There were metal loops protruding from inside the outer edge of the wall at intervals, which is what Trig had used to secure the rope.

"Do you always carry a rope?" she asked.

"We all do. One of the first tools they give new Guardsmen is a rope like this with a metal hook braided onto the end," he explained, pointing to the hook attached to the wall. "Sometimes we need to get off the wall in a hurry."

Elora nodded quietly, soaking it all in as she stood and walked the few remaining paces to the outer wall. Standing on her toes she peeked over the top of the wall.

She gasped. Brown and green stretched as far as the eye could see, the blades of grass swirling in the wind like waves in the ocean.

"Here, let me help you," Trig said, bending down and putting his hand out for her to step in before boosting her up to sit on the outer wall. "Don't fall off the wall, Elora," he said, mimicking her earlier comment in some good-natured teasing.

"Thank you for this," she said, smiling at him from her perch on the wall. I know you won't believe me, but I've never seen the Grasslands like this before. I've never been on the wall, or even beyond it actually. The view is incredible."

He looked at her in disbelief.

"You've never left Windom?" he asked, shocked. "Not even just to explore? Your whole life? Why?"

"I don't know," she replied, shrugging self-consciously. "I mean, you know my parents."

"They always have been very protective of you," he agreed. "Come to think of it, you really didn't go on any school outings beyond the wall, did you."

Elora shook her head.

"Maybe someday, when I'm not in their house anymore, I'll work up the nerve to venture out there," she said, nodding to the wide open plain. "But as long as I'm in their house, it's their rules."

"But why wait? What's the worst that could happen?" he challenged. "You're 19, now. You're not a child, even if you're living in their house."

"I know. But their fear of the outside world has always been so genuine," she said. "I guess I kind of inherited it."

She looked out at the Grasslands, a vast wilderness stretching beyond the horizon. Clumps of tall shrubs and bushes dotted the landscape. A herd of grazing animals were off in the distance. The land was so flat and open, she could see for miles.

"It goes on forever," she whispered.

"Not really forever, but the Grasslands are rather huge," he agreed.

He crossed his arms on top of the wall and rested his chin on his hands.

"I've heard it takes weeks to reach the mountains of the Highlands and who knows how long to reach the Woodlands beyond that," he said. "I wouldn't want to make that trip. It's rife with snakes and drifters and wild animals out there, not to mention the storms. I mean, you've seen the merchants who arrive here. Those people have been through something."

Elora nodded. She had definitely noticed the hard edge on the Highlanders who traded wares in the market. No wonder their goods were so expensive. They had risked a lot to bring them to Windom.

She could see riders on horseback trotting along the road toward the North Gate, returning from a hunting expedition. She noticed the workers who had been harvesting wheat from the fields that surrounded the town also making their way back to the gate.

"They're hurrying home to beat that," Trig said, nodding his head at the dark gray clouds swirling in the far-off sky.

"Wow! Is that rain?" Elora asked, pointing to faint blurry bands stretching from the clouds down to the ground. "I've never seen it like that before. It's magnificent!"

"It really is pretty amazing." Trig agreed. "But that storm is going to be here before you know it. You better get on home, Elora," he said, patting her knee affectionately.

He held her hand to steady her as she hopped off the wall.

"Oh God, I have to climb back down, don't I," Elora realized belatedly.

"Actually," Trig smiled sheepishly, "there's a ladder not too far this way. I'll walk you."

Elora smacked his shoulder.

"Trig! Why'd you make me climb that rope?" she shouted.

"I wanted to see if you could do it! If I'd known you would be so good at it and make me feel like an amateur, I might not have." he said, laughing.

He walked her the short distance to the ladder and unlocked the grate used to block access from below. As she grabbed hold of the railings and put her foot on the rung, he stopped her.

"You're braver than you give yourself credit for, Elora," he said. "Not many people would scale a wall like that just to see the view."

“Thanks Trig. It really was worth it” she said, smiling as she started down the ladder. “Wait!” she cried, pausing as a thought occurred to her. “Are you staying up here during the storm?” she asked, concerned.

“I’ll be alright,” he said nonchalantly. “If it gets really bad, I’ve got the rope, remember?”

“You really have turned out all manly and tough, Trig. When did that happen?” Elora mused as she climbed down.

“Such flattery! Why Elora Kerrick, I think you might fancy me! Should I write you a letter instead?” he teased.

“Very funny,” she chided. “But I saw you kiss Lizbeth Ganther behind the schoolhouse when we were 12, remember? No, thank you!” Elora said, laughing.

“Hey! That was years ago! I’ve improved a lot since then,” he cried.

“For Alysa’s sake, I certainly hope so!” she shot back as she reached the ground.

Trig chuckled. “You’re a good friend, Elora!” he called, as she started off towards home.

“Write that letter!” she shouted back, a smile on her lips.

Elora opted to skip the market for today having seen the storm for herself, but she intended to search out the Highlander merchant tomorrow. Sometimes amongst the stone and metal goods from the mountains, there were also carvings and trinkets all the way from the

Woodlands. They were far too expensive for Elora to ever consider buying, but she could touch and look at them, at least temporarily satisfying her fascination.

She had, for as long as she could remember, been enchanted by the Woodlands. She doubted she would ever see them in person, particularly in light of the fact that she never intended to leave Windom, but she was enthralled nonetheless. That's probably why she had those vivid daydreams.

As she made her way home, her mind drifted back to her latest visit to the forest. More specifically, to the moment he had touched her hand, the man who had called to her with such familiarity. Her hand tingled and her stomach flipped as she remembered the sensation of it. She tried desperately to recall the sound of his voice, replaying her dream over and over. She remembered how rich and deep and intoxicating it had been, but the sound itself was lost. Oh, what she wouldn't give to hear that sound again! She smiled, hoping that her next daydream would be as exciting.

Elora, at long last, finally reached the small plot of land that belonged to her family. It was bordered by a low fence made of mortar and stone. Elora swung open the wrought iron front gate and paused to admire the flowers lining the walkway to the front door. Her mother could make anything grow.

The storm clouds were already overhead, blocking the last remaining rays of the light from the setting sun. Elora could see the glow of candlelight in the cracks around the front door. The window flaps were already tied down in preparation for the storm and she could hear her parents laughing from within the house. The comforting feelings of home settled around her as she reached out to open the latch. She paused, taking a deep breath and closing her eyes as she let all the concerns of the day fall away.

"Elora."

She heard her name spoken gently in the low, rich tones of the voice she longed to hear. Her eyes flew open and she gasped, looking around her. But there was no one. She sighed. "If only my real life were as exciting as my daydreams," she thought, unlatching the door and walking inside as the first raindrops began to fall.

CHAPTER 2

The next morning Elora rose early so that she could visit the market before heading to the interior gardens for work. She had been tending the gardens for nearly a year and with her mother as a mentor, she excelled at it. Her mother had worked in the gardens for as long as Elora could remember. Watching her nurture the plants with skillful hands, knowledge and instinct, Elora had naturally inherited a love of horticulture.

The air was muggy and hot after the storm over night. Elora walked carefully on the path toward the town square, slipping through muddy patches and dodging puddles along the way. The market was relatively quiet this early, though most vendors had already set out their goods. She walked along the rows of familiar merchants, thinking that perhaps Trig had been wrong about a Highlander wagon. But just as she was about to abandon her pursuit, she noticed an unfamiliar man wheeling a large trunk towards an open space among the last row of vendors. Behind him was a light haired young man carrying a small table. The two set to work, laying out a fine linen cloth and carefully displaying the contents of the trunk.

Elora felt giddy with the anticipation of seeing something new. She feigned interest in a horse bridle on a table nearby, stalling so as not to seem too eager. The table's merchant, Thomas Wiggins, looked at her curiously, knowing that she didn't have a horse, and began opening his mouth to say as much. She dropped it quickly, smiling sheepishly at him, and decided to abandon any semblance of restraint and give in to her curiosity. As she neared the Highlander's table, she had to surreptitiously cover her mouth with her hand to hide her smile, such was her excitement. There were gorgeous trinkets with various stones and gems that had been mined from the Highland mountains. There were rings and bracelets; necklaces and pins; a beautiful wooden pen with a sharp metal nib. She saw pelts from animals she'd never known existed. He had so many amazing things on display. At last her eyes fell on a necklace the likes of which she'd never seen before. The merchant had been absentmindedly watching while she surveyed his goods, but as she lifted the necklace for a closer look, he froze and his gaze shifted to Elora's face.

"What is this?" she asked.

"It's a necklace," he replied stoically.

"No, I know that much," she sighed. "I mean this charm. It looks like a seed of some sort," she suggested.

"It's just a seed. Came from one of the trees in the Woodlands," he replied.

He was watching her very carefully and it made her acutely uncomfortable. He was an intimidating figure, rough and ruddy from days in the sun. He was large and burly, with long brown hair tied back at his neck. His thick beard was short and peppered with gray, and he rubbed it subconsciously as he appraised her.

"How much?" she asked.

Elora rarely purchased such novelties, but something about this necklace called to her. The charm was a small brown seed, oblong and shaped almost like a teardrop, slightly bigger than her thumbnail. It was pierced by a small ring on one end and threaded onto a simple chain. That seed was so familiar somehow. She needed to have it.

"10 dollars," he replied gruffly.

He watched her, gauging just how much she wanted the necklace.

She couldn't pay that. She only made 5 dollars a week working in the gardens. How could she justify spending two weeks' wages on a seed attached to a chain? But she couldn't seem to put it down.

"Will you take 5?" she asked, hopefully.

"I'll take 7," he countered with a sigh.

Still so expensive! Was this small trinket worth more than a week working in the hot sun, on her knees, her hands in the dirt, sweat dripping from her brow? She could hardly believe it when she decided that yes, it really was.

"I'll take it."

She reached into the coin purse tied to the waistband of her pants and pulled out her hard-earned money. She felt guilty handing it over, thinking of what her father would say, but she couldn't muster an ounce of regret.

The merchant nodded, taking the money.

She unhooked the clasp and bent her head to fasten it behind her neck as she turned to go. The merchant still had his gaze fixed to her. She smiled uncomfortably and walked quickly away, fingering the small seed that now rested below the hollow of her throat. She tucked it beneath the neck of her tunic, putting it safely out of view lest her mother notice. They disapproved of her fascination with the Woodlands and she certainly didn't want to own up to how much she had paid for it.

She made her way out of the town square, heading toward the interior gardens on the far side of Windom. The fields would be a muddy mess today. It was time to harvest the last of the vegetables and she was making a mental checklist of things that needed to be done. The sun was already high in the sky and her steps quickened as she thought about the misery before her if she didn't get her work finished before the heat of the day reached its peak.

The oppressive humidity started taking its toll and sweat began dripping from her face. She could feel it trickling down her back, tickling her skin. She reached behind her to rub away the itch and briefly recalled the birthmark located in just that spot. She'd been self-conscious about it ever since becoming aware of it as a child. Fortunately, Windom culture encouraged more conservative attire and so only her parents even knew of it. Occasionally her father would affectionately brush his hand over the spot in passing. Elora couldn't really see the birthmark, as it was located over her spine midway up her back, so she rarely thought about it. But as she rubbed at the itch it suddenly dawned on her. That's where she'd seen that shape before. She saw it every time she turned her back to the mirror. The seed on her necklace was identical to her birthmark.

The day continued on, uneventful and just as muddy and uncomfortable as Elora had imagined. As the sun finally began its downward path and the heat became truly unbearable, Elora's mother Winifred Kerrick, who managed the interior gardens, finally rang the bell for dismissal. Elora stood and stretched her back, working out the tension in her muscles and breathing a sigh of relief that the work day was over. Walking over to the supply barn to wash up, she smiled at her mother who was ringing the giant bell a second time to ensure that everyone heard.

"I don't think anyone missed it, Mom. We've all been waiting for you to ring that thing for hours now," she teased.

Her mother laughed.

"It really was a miserable day, wasn't it?" she said, reaching out to adjust Elora's braid, affectionately running her hand down the silky length of it. "Are you reconsidering your choice in occupation, dearest? Would you rather be indoors sewing dresses like Alysa?"

"Not in a million years." Elora replied with conviction. "I just wish it didn't always have to be so hot!"

"You'd think after 19 years here I'd be used to the heat, but it really is just awful," her mother agreed.

"It wasn't like this where you come from?" she asked.

Her mother almost never mentioned her life before Windom. A fact that made Elora desperately curious.

"No," she smiled, her eyes unfocused as she remembered a far-off time and place. "There are beautiful places that are nothing like the Grasslands," she waxed nostalgically, before quickly checking herself. "But this is our home and it has its own beauty about it," she said gently.

Elora smiled to cover her disappointment. She knew that was as much information as her mother would give away and truthfully, even that little lapse was more than she usually revealed. Her parents were very committed to leaving the past behind them for some reason. After 19 years of trying Elora still hadn't plied the truth from them and she doubted she ever would.

"I don't think this basin of water is going to make much difference considering how enthusiastically you threw yourself into work today, Elora," teased her mother.

Elora laughed. She really was filthy.

"I suppose you're right," she admitted. "I'll head home for a proper bath and some clean clothes. Do you need me to start supper?"

"I wouldn't mind if you'd peel some potatoes," her mother replied.

"See you in a while?" Elora asked.

Winifred smiled and nodded.

Elora turned to go but halted when she heard her mother call out to her.

"Hey Elora! Why don't you dust off your pants a bit. We need some of that dirt to grow the vegetables!" she said, chuckling at her own joke.

"You're hilarious!" Elora laughed back.

But looking down at her pants, she groaned as she realized that there were huge clumps of mud stuck to each knee. She brushed off her legs as best she could, casting her mother an irritated look which only made her laugh harder. She hadn't decided yet if she loved or hated working alongside her mom.

She slowly trudged home along the roads, carefully picking her way through the ruts created by the wagons as they had struggled through the mud that morning. She fingered the seed on her new necklace absentmindedly as she walked. She hadn't stopped thinking about it all day. She felt connected to it somehow.

"What kind of tree did this seed come from?" she wondered.

A movement in her peripheral vision caught her attention and she looked to see a young man with light blonde hair. He quickly turned and headed out of view down a side road. She paused, staring at the intersection where the man had disappeared. She had seen him before.

He had been working for the Highlander merchant this morning. He certainly had wandered far from the market. She felt a sudden uneasiness in the pit of her stomach. Was he following her? Had he been watching her all day?

"Hey!" she called, walking back a few paces to look down the road, but he was nowhere to be seen.

She shook her head, puzzled and a little nervous. Being alone on a country road suddenly didn't seem like such a good idea. Elora decided to jog the rest of the way home, looking back every few minutes to see if she had company. The man never reappeared and she breathed a sigh of relief when the front gate to her house finally came into view.

She took off her muddy boots on the porch and quickly went inside. She slid the bolt on the door and slumped back against it, panting and wiping the sweat from her face. She quietly chuckled at herself, dismissing her nervous feelings as yet another instance in which she let her overactive imagination run away with her. Shaking her head, she stood and made her way back toward the bathroom to wash away the evidence of her muddy day's work.

Slipping out of her pants and tunic, Elora paused a moment in front of the mirror in her underclothes. She reached behind her neck, unlatching the clasp of the necklace and then held the seed up to examine it more closely. It was exquisite. There were ridges curling an intricate design across the entire surface of the seed, almost as though someone had carved into it. It looked nothing like any seed she'd ever seen before. Turning, she lifted the back of her chemise until she had revealed her birthmark. She held the necklace so that the seed dangled just next to the mark. They were identical, at least in shape and size. Her birthmark was simple and plain, while the seed was delicate and elegant. It thrilled her for some reason she couldn't grasp and she smiled.

Placing the necklace on her dresser, she grabbed her favorite sage green dress and fresh underthings and hurried to the bathroom to clean up. She was due to meet Alysa in the square before dinner and she was anxious to know if her meddling had done any good.

A long while later, a clean Elora with her long wet hair twisted into a braid came rushing in to slip on her sandals and hastily fasten her necklace. She ran down the short hall to the front door but slid to a stop when she noticed her mother sitting at the kitchen table, quietly reading.

"Oh! I didn't hear you come in!" she exclaimed, trotting back to drop a kiss on the top of her head. "I'm so late! I lost track of time."

"You and your long baths," her mom replied with a knowing smile. "I take it you didn't peel any potatoes."

Elora gave her a sheepish smile.

"I forgot," she admitted. "I'm sorry,"

"It's alright. Go on," her mother said indulgently. "Give Alysa a hug for me."

"Thanks! Love you! See you for dinner!" Elora shouted, accidently slamming the door behind her as she took off at a run.

But she didn't run for long. It was late-summer and the days were at their longest. The sky was still bright despite the fact that evening was fast approaching. The heat was oppressive. Elora didn't want to sweat through her clean clothes, so she slowed to a brisk walk. She peeked up at the clock tower in the middle of the square. She was so late. Alysa probably wouldn't care, but Elora felt awful anyway. She hadn't meant to linger so long in the bath, but she'd closed her eyes for just a moment and found herself transported to the forest again. She couldn't resist waiting and hoping for the mysterious caller to make an appearance. Sadly, he hadn't and by the time she realized how long she'd been dreaming, she was already 20 minutes late. The whole thing was disappointing in so many ways.

Alysa lived near the center of town, perhaps a 20-minute walk from Elora's house. She was quickly rounding the corner to Alysa's street, looking up at the clock once again, when she ran straight into the hard chest of a man hurrying in the opposite direction. She would have fallen had he not grabbed her arms. Startled, she looked up to find Trig peering down at her with an expression of concern.

"Is your face okay?" he asked. "I think you stabbed me with your nose!" he teased, rubbing his chest where they'd collided.

She laughed, gently touching her nose, which, truth be told, hurt a little.

"I'll live," she said. "Sorry about that. I'm late to meet up with Alysa and wasn't looking where I was going."

"It's ok. It was my fault too," he admitted. "I was walking pretty fast myself."

Elora looked up at him quizzically and then peeked behind him at Alysa's house.

"Trig Davenport, are you running away?" Elora cried.

He hung his head, embarrassed, and shrugged sheepishly.

"I'm scared to see her," he confessed. "I left a letter with her father earlier, which was terrifying in its own right I'll have you know. And then I saw her arrive home just a few minutes ago. So now I'm getting as far away as I can. I don't think I can handle it if she rejects me, Elora," he said, a desperate look in his eyes. "I'm so pathetic," he sighed, rubbing his hands over his face.

Elora put a comforting hand on his arm and smiled reassuringly.

"She's cared for you for a long time Trig," she said. "Don't worry so much."

Just then, the door to Alysa's house flew open. Trig jumped behind Elora, ducking his head.

Seeing her friend, Alysa started running.

"Elora! Elora! He proposed!" she nearly screamed, waving the letter in the air as she flew down the steps.

Trig lifted his head, stepping out from behind Elora his eyes wide. Alysa stopped dead in her tracks, startled.

They stared at one another for a moment as they struggled through their shyness and fear. Elora held her breath as she looked back and forth between her friends. Alysa's face slowly stretched into a jubilant smile and Trig letting out a chuckle of relief. She took off running again towards him.

"I accept! I accept!" she shouted.

Trig closed the space between them and she launched herself into his embrace, wrapping her arms around his neck, his proposal letter still fluttering in her hand. After a moment, he released her, gently lowering her until her feet touched the ground. They stared into each other's eyes, basking in the joy of love requited. He reached up to brush a strand of hair from her face. She closed her eyes and released a shuddering breath.

"I accept," she whispered.

"Thank God," he sighed.

With a gentle thumb beneath her chin, he lifted her face to his and placed a tender kiss on her lips. She opened her eyes, smiling joyfully up at him as she tightened her arms around his neck and kissed him again in earnest.

Elora slowly turned and walked away, giving her friends the privacy they needed. Not that they were aware of her presence anyway. She smiled as she looked back, overjoyed that they had at long last found their way to one another, and a bit smug that she'd played a part in it.

As she walked through the town square, she wandered toward the market, curious to see if the man who had been following her was actually the one she'd seen that morning with the Highlander. She wasn't entirely sure what she would do with that information, but she felt compelled to know, nonetheless. She made her way past the rows of merchants packing up their goods for the day until she came to the place where she'd bought her necklace. The spot was empty.

"I suppose he's already packed up for the day," Elora said dejectedly to Sam Tegan, a merchant she recognized in a booth nearby.

"He left a while ago actually. Right after he sold you that chain," he nodded to her necklace. "Packed up and rode out of town quick as that," he said, snapping his fingers. "Craziest thing I've ever seen."

"He's gone?" Elora asked in surprise. "But he'd only just arrived! He surely didn't make enough off of me to make the journey out here worthwhile!"

Sam shook his head and clucked his tongue, clearly baffled.

"Did you happen to see a young man with him? Blond hair?" Elora inquired.

"I know who you're asking about," he nodded. "I saw him helping out this morning too. But he wasn't on the wagon when that Highlander drove off," he said, shrugging his shoulders.

Elora bit her lip, uneasy with all this puzzling information. She smiled at the merchant. "Thanks Sam," she said, turning to go.

Sam reached out to touch her arm, stopping her.

"If you don't mind my asking, what's so special about that chain that you paid $7 for it?" he asked, his brows furrowed.

Elora blushed. Apparently not much went unnoticed in the market.

"I mean, it's nice enough, but Angus Port would have sold you something much finer for half that," he stated, referring to the town silversmith a few rows down.

"I didn't really buy it for the chain. I bought it for the charm" Elora said, fingering the seed that dangled above the neckline of her dress.

"What charm, dear girl?" he asked, leaning in for a closer look.

Elora looked him in the eyes, confused. She lifted the seed to show him better.

"It's a seed," she explained. "From the Woodlands."

He stared closely at her hands and then looked her in the face, squinting his eyes in a doubtful expression.

"Are you playing with me?" he asked.

"No!" Elora replied, startled.

"There's no charm there, Elora Kerrick!" he said, exasperated. "What are you getting on about?"

Elora looked down at the seed grasped firmly in her fingers. What was going on?

"You don't see it?" she asked, her brow wrinkled in confusion.

"Well of course not! There's nothing there, you daft girl!" he answered, throwing his hands in the air, clearly finished with whatever game they were playing.

He shook his head and turned his back on her, returning to his booth to finish packing for the night.

Elora stood still a moment staring after him, her mouth open but nothing to say. He couldn't see it. Obviously he was telling the truth because he was very clearly annoyed with her. How was that possible?

Elora left the market, wandering aimlessly as she digested everything that had just happened. There was something so strange going on and it all seemed tied to the beautiful seed she wore around her neck.

The sun finally began its descent and Elora turned her feet towards home. She smiled as she walked, thinking of Alysa and Trig and the excitement they must be feeling tonight. It was the beginning of a whole new world for them. She wondered how long they would wait until they had their Binding Ceremony. Surely not long, based on what she'd seen between them earlier.

What does it feel like, she wondered, knowing you've found your match? And how amazing when that person chooses you too. Would that ever happen for her? She felt a brief pang of jealousy that she hadn't found even a glimmer of that kind of happiness yet. But she shook her head, trying to dislodge the sadness that was threatening to steal the joy of seeing her friends united. It would happen for her. Surely it would. If only waiting weren't so hard.

CHAPTER 3

Alysa was sitting on the short stone wall around the Kerrick yard, a smile stretched across her beaming face when Elora opened the door the next morning. Elora laughed at the sight of her, amused and delighted at the unabashed joy of her dearest friend.

Alysa leapt off the fence and threw her arms around Elora's neck.

"Thank you," she whispered. "You are truly my best friend."

Elora smiled and hugged her back.

"Well someone had to do something!" she said, taking her friend by the hands. "I couldn't handle the longing glances anymore!" she teased. "Besides, I was afraid you were starting to consider accepting that proposal from Phillip Rawlings."

She shook her head and scrunched her nose in disgust.

'Hey! Phillip isn't so bad," Alysa gently scolded.

"You're right. He's not bad at all," Elora conceded. "But he's no Trig. And I wasn't about to watch you settle for someone you didn't want. Especially when it was so obvious that Trig is desperately in love with you too."

"I had no idea! How could you tell?" Alysa exclaimed, smiling and shaking her head, bemused.

"Oh my gosh, Alysa! How could you not?" laughed Elora, holding her head in her hands and looking up at the sky in bewilderment. "Thank God I was here to save you two lovely idiots from yourselves."

"Yes. Thank God for that," Alysa said, laughing joyfully.

Elora's heart swelled to see her friend so radiantly happy.

Putting her arm around Alysa, she said, "I have to get going. Will you walk with me a bit? You are a delight to be around today and I want to soak up as much of that joy as I can. Maybe it will help me forget what a lonely old maid I am."

They turned and headed out the gate, arm in arm.

"Well, Phillip Rawlings is available, you know," Alysa said, giggling.

Elora nudged her with an elbow and Alysa jumped aside, laughing merrily.

"So did you two actually do any talking last night?" Elora teased her shy friend, shamelessly enjoying the instantaneous blush that appeared.

"Yes!" Alysa exclaimed. "Lots of talking," she said defensively.

"Well I don't know why," Elora said bluntly. "You waited a long time to kiss that boy! Oh please, don't be embarrassed around me!" she pleaded. "I'm living vicariously here and I want to know everything!"

Alysa laughed, raising her hands to cover her pink cheeks.

"Alright. Alright. There was a healthy mix of talking and ... not talking," she admitted.

Elora threw back her head and laughed. "Good for you! Was it everything you'd imagined?"

Alysa smiled, staring at the ground clearly lost in memory.

"It was so much better than I imagined. All butterflies and tingles. I don't know what you saw when you were twelve Elora, but that Trig Davenport can kiss," she gushed.

"Well thank goodness for that!" Elora cried, laughing. "So I guess you won't want to wait too long for the Binding then."

"Two weeks."

"Wow! That's soon! I half expected you to say 'tomorrow' though, to be honest," Elora said, chuckling.

"Trig did float that idea," Alysa giggled. "But everyone is busy with the harvest right now and probably will be for a few more weeks. So we figured two weeks sounded more reasonable."

"I'm not sure 'reasonable' is the word Preacher Woodward will use when you tell him," Elora said, raising an eyebrow sarcastically.

"Probably not," Alysa agreed with a laugh and Elora couldn't help but join in.

Alysa's happiness was infectious and Elora was enjoying every moment of it.

"We really don't want a big ceremony, but even then there is still so much to do!" Alysa said, throwing her hands up in exasperation. "You should have seen my mother last night when we talked about our plans. I've never seen her more excited and more panicked. I hadn't realize how much she'd been looking forward to this and I guess two weeks is a little less time than she anticipated."

"Maybe a little," Elora teased. "What did your dad say?"

"He was too busy staring at Trig to say much of anything," she said, laughing.

"Poor Trig. I think your dad nearly scared him out of leaving you that letter in the first place. He must be truly besotted to face Michael Scott, Head Guardsman. I'd actually forgotten that your dad is his boss. That's pretty brave," Elora said, nodding in admiration.

"I know!" Alysa beamed with pride.

"Of course, he was hiding behind my skirt when he saw you come out the door yesterday ... so clearly his bravery has its limits," Elora joked.

"Oh hush! I can't wait to see how you handle falling in love. It's almost as terrifying as it is thrilling!" Alysa cried.

Her words called up the memory of the man in the forest and Alysa's hand tingled as she recalled his touch. Terrifying and thrilling was exactly how it had felt. She shook her head to clear her thoughts, surprised once again at how real the sensations seemed when it was all just a silly fantasy. She really needed to meet someone soon if a mystery dream man was the closest she could get to imagining love.

"He's been brave when it counted. I'm actually pretty pleased if I'm his one weakness," Alysa grinned. "That's to my advantage!"

"That is true!" Elora laughed.

They were nearing the edge of the developed section of the settlement, where cobbled streets gave way to the dirt roads leading out to the gardens. While Elora was dressed in boots and pants for another day of weeding and harvesting, Alysa had on a soft blue frock and slippers better suited to her job in the dress-maker's shop. This was as far as she could venture.

"Before we go, I have something I'd like to ask," Alysa said earnestly, turning to look Elora in the eyes. "I'd like for you to stand beside me for the Binding, as my Witness."

Elora beamed.

"I would be honored," she said breathlessly.

"Perfect!" Alysa cried, clapping her hands excitedly before throwing her arms around Elora's neck for a quick hug. "Can you come to the shop on Saturday? I need to measure you. I have such an amazing dress in mind for you!"

"Will you have time to make me a dress? Don't you need to work on yours?" Elora asked.

"My mother has been working on a dress for me since the minute I turned 18," Alysa said shaking her head in amusement.

"Be grateful," Elora laughed. "I'll probably be wearing my field clothes and mud boots for my Binding if it's left up to my mother," she joked.

"But the flowers will be amazing!" Alysa asserted, pointing her finger in the air.

"True," Elora smiled.

"Alright! I've got to run!" Alysa said, turning to head towards her mother's dress shop.

"Congratulations Alysa! I'm so happy for you!" Elora said in parting.

Alysa turned back with a radiant smile and waved once more before rounding a corner and slipping out of view. Elora stood looking at the spot where she'd last seen her friend feeling both elated and envious, wondering if perhaps it would soon be her turn to find love too.

A movement in the corner of her eye caught her attention and Elora turned just in time to see a young blonde-headed man disappearing down an alley. A chill went up her spine and she gasped. Could that have been the same boy from yesterday? Suddenly the prospect of walking out to the gardens by herself made her acutely uncomfortable. She looked around nervously, wondering what to do. Was she being paranoid?

"Elora! You left ages ago! I figured you'd already be knee deep in dirt by now."

Elora breathed a huge sigh of relief at the sound of her mother's voice. Turning, she smiled and fell into step beside her as they made their way to the agricultural area within the settlement.

"I'm happy you came along, Mom," she said earnestly.

"Oh really? Everything alright?" she asked.

Elora considered telling her about the blonde haired young man, but seeing him only twice, no matter how strange it seemed, was hardly convincing evidence that she was being followed. Her uneasy feelings were probably just another result of an overactive imagination. She shook her head, mentally chastising herself for tending to jump to such wild conclusions.

"Everything's fine mom. It's just nice to have company," she said, slinging her arm up onto her mother's shoulder affectionately.

Winifred wrapped her arm around Elora's waist, enjoying the camaraderie of her daughter.

"It really is nice," she agreed, smiling.

But as they ventured down the road, Elora couldn't help sneaking a quick backward glance. Just in case.

It was so hot. The growing season was nearly over and soon the wind would be bitterly cold and ruthless as it rushed over the wide-open plains. But today, it was still miserably hot.

It was barely past noon and already Elora was so exhausted she could hardly summon enough energy to trudge the short distance to the supply barn for a drink of water. Pumping the well handle, Elora filled her canteen beneath the spout and took a long swig. She walked back to the barn and slid down the wall to rest a while in the shade. Taking off her hat, she looped it over her knee and raised the hem of her tunic to mop her brow. She dropped it in disgust when she realized it was soaked through already.

"Why did I choose this job?" she quietly asked herself.

Leaning her head back against the rough stone sides of the barn, Elora closed her eyes, attempting to relax despite being so uncomfortable. She tried to take a deep breath but a hot gust of wind tried to smother her instead and she sighed, utterly resigned to her misery.

She was nearly asleep when she felt the tingle of a cool breeze brush across her skin. She was no longer surrounded by the sounds of trowels shifting dirt and the chatter of familiar voices. The soothing rustle of leaves and the soft call of birds filled her ears. Elora sighed as she realized she had escaped the prairie and was once again lost in the refuge of her forest.

She breathed deeply, taking in the fragrance of decaying leaves and moist earth. She felt through the fabric of her shirt that she no longer leaned against the hard round stones of the barn, but the rough bark of a tree. She was so relieved to be free of the oppressive heat, she didn't even care if her mystery man made an appearance this time.

"This is heaven," she thought.

But the air was brisk and she was soon shivering in her damp shirt. She was just about to open her eyes when she heard her name shouted in the distance. Her heart lurched with excitement and she sat up. She heard it again.

"Elora!"

But then she heard it again in a different voice. And then again. And again. This wasn't her mystery man. This was a group of people and their voices weren't rich and deep and lovely. These men sounded furious.

"Open your eyes! Open your eyes!" she shouted in her mind.

But the voices were getting louder and she was paralyzed in fear. Her heart pounded in her ears and she struggled to catch her breath.

"Elora!"

Over and over they shouted her name. She could hear the crunching and crackling of the forest floor beneath their feet as they came ever closer.

Suddenly she heard a familiar voice among the chorus.

"Elora!"

She felt a hand jostling her shoulder, startling her eyes open. She gasped as the heat and brightness of the day crashed down upon her. She shook her head to clear her thoughts and looked up into the worried gaze of Danny Jenkins, a fellow gardener.

"That must have been some bad dream," he remarked.

Elora nodded in reply, still trying to get her bearings.

"How long were you sleeping girl! It looks like the grass has grown up around your lazy self while you sat there in the shade," he teased.

Elora smiled and looked around, surprised to see that he was right. She didn't remember the grass being this tall when she'd sat down. The blades rose above her shoulders and were brushing against her cheeks in the hot wind.

"Why did I pick to sit here?" she wondered, seeing that the grass was short and recently trimmed just a few feet away.

Danny reached down and took her hand, pulling her up out of her grassy nest.

"Hm. I suppose Robert missed a spot when he cut the grass yesterday," he mused, shrugging his shoulders before turning to fill his canteen from the well.

Elora took a few steps toward the field, intending to return to work, when she noticed her mom standing rigid in the midst of her crop, staring past her with wide eyes. She turned to see what her mother found so startling and gasped. The area around the supply barn was well-tended and the wild grasses were trimmed frequently. All looked as it should except for the spot surrounding where Elora had been. There was a semi-circle of knee-high grass extending 5 feet from the place where Elora has been resting.

She turned back to find that her mother was no longer staring at the grasses, but at her. There was a look of anguish on her mother's face and it sent a chill down her spine. Elora quirked her head, confused and uneasy.

Her mother quickly averted her gaze and dropped back down to her knees, returning to work as though nothing were amiss.

Elora walked slowly back into the field and resumed her work harvesting the bean crop. Occasionally she would peek at the tall grasses, baffled. By the end of the day she had convinced herself that the grass must have been that tall all along. What other explanation could there be?

After the dismissal bell rang, Elora gathered her tools and stored them in the barn. She waved to her mother and started the long walk home, utterly exhausted. Before the barn was out of sight, she glanced back for one last look. What she saw made her stop and catch her breath. There was her mother, alone, frantically hacking the tall grass down. The task finished, Elora watched as her mother paused to wipe at her eyes before gathering up the clippings and walking away to the compost pile. Scared and mystified, Elora turned and slowly hiked the rest of the way home.

CHAPTER 4

The week dragged on until at long last, it was Saturday. Elora awoke in the morning with a delicious feeling of freedom, languidly stretching her arms as she lay in bed, enjoying the prospect of a day without sore muscles and sweaty hair. She took a deep breath, loathe to leave her comfortable spot but anxious to meet Alysa for their dress making appointment.

It had been a few days since she'd had an opportunity to spend any significant time with her friend. It was unusual for them and left her feeling out of sorts. Alysa had been busy with Trig and the preparations for their binding ceremony all week. Elora knew it was just a precursor to how life would be once they were bound to one another and she couldn't help the sadness that tugged at her heart. She tamped down her negative feelings and threw her legs over the side of the bed, determined to be happy and excited for her dearest friend. Besides, she would have Alysa to herself for a while today and she desperately needed to talk to someone about the odd things happening around her lately. She scurried around the room, quickly pulling on her clothes for the day.

A short while later Elora emerged with her chestnut hair neatly braided and wearing her sage dress, the seed necklace safely hidden beneath the modest neckline. She slid her feet into her leather slippers and made her way down the hall. She found her parents sitting at the kitchen table enjoying a cup of coffee, still dressed in their nightclothes.

"Good morning!" Elora said, greeting them with a smile.

"Good morning, sweetheart," her father said, rising to wrap his arms around her in an affectionate embrace.

She turned to look at her mother, who gave her a small smile. Ever since the incident at the barn, her mother had been different. Her normally cheerful demeanor was muted. She barely spoke to Elora, barely spoke to anyone actually, and she always seemed preoccupied. It was confusing and truthfully, was starting to scare Elora.

She walked over and leaned down to give her mother a hug. "Momma, are you sick?" she asked quietly, looking her in the eyes.

"No, dear girl," she replied, her face softening as she looked lovingly at her concerned daughter. "Everything is fine. Don't worry about me."

"She's fine!" her father chimed in boisterously. "She's just worried some fine young man will come snatch you away like Alysa," he teased. "I can't believe how quickly this is all happening!"

"I know!" Elora agreed. "Though if you'd seen all the moony looks and romantic angst I've witnessed the past few years, you might not be so surprised," Elora said with a laugh, walking to the stove to pour herself a cup of coffee.

She turned in time to see her father looking at her mother with reprimand in his eyes. Her mother dropped her gaze to the table and her father quickly returned to the jovial expression he'd worn only moments before. Elora knit her brows. They were hiding something from her. Uncomfortable and suddenly desperate to leave, she took a gulp of coffee and winced as the hot liquid scalded her throat. She put down her cup, no longer interested in finishing it.

"Well, I have to run! Alysa wants to make me a dress and needs to measure me," she said.

"I can't wait to see it, sweetheart!" her father said with a bit too much enthusiasm.

"Me too!" Elora replied with a smile, waving as she hurried out the door and closed it firmly behind her.

She paused on the doorstep and took a deep breath, shaking her head. Something just wasn't right. Her parents had always been very private and sometimes even secretive, but she'd never seen her mother so worried before. She couldn't help but feel uneasy.

Elora took a deep breath and mentally tamped down her negative feelings. She forced a smile and set out towards Alysa's house. The day promised to be full of laughter, and Elora intended to savor every moment.

She walked at a leisurely pace, trying desperately to think happy thoughts. She plucked a leaf from a nearby bush and played with it absentmindedly as she strolled. She wondered if anyone would be traveling to Windom from afar for the wedding. The prospect of meeting a handsome new stranger made her smile. But could she have a future with a foreigner? That would mean someday leaving Windom and her parents and everything she'd ever known. No. Nope. She immediately dismissed the possibility and decided she might as well steel herself to a life with Phillip Rawlings or the like, because she would never leave Windom. She frowned at the idea, suddenly depressed with her options.

Reaching up, she fingered the seed dangling beneath the hollow of her throat and her thoughts shifted to the Woodlands. What might it be like to actually visit her forest someday? Would it be the way she imagined it? Her last daydream had truly frightened her and she'd been hesitant to even venture a thought of her forest refuge ever since. But she couldn't seem to help herself. The forest called to her. It filled an emptiness in her soul. The idea of leaving Windom terrified her, but she wondered if perhaps she could overcome that fear if it meant actually experiencing the peace and contentment she only found in her daydreams. Could she overcome that fear, she thought, if it meant perhaps finding the man she'd encountered there. She felt ridiculous for thinking so often of someone who was obviously a figment of her imagination. But the dream had felt so real. It haunted her. She knew nothing about him but the sound of his voice. And yet the memory of it made her stomach flip and the back of her neck tingle.

Lost in thought, she had walked nearly the entire distance to Alysa's house when the snap of a twig jolted her out of her reverie. She looked up just in time to see a young blond man disappearing around a bend in the road. She gasped and froze. It was the Highlander again. She just knew it. He must be following her!

Looking around, she realized just how vulnerable and alone she was on the road. What should she do? Her heart was pounding out of her chest, her pulse throbbing in her ears. She stared at the spot where he'd been, frightened and panicking. What could he want with her? She had no idea how long she stood there, too afraid to move, when she suddenly felt something brush against her arm. Startled out of her panic, she jumped and bolted a few steps before peeking back to see what had touched her. She gasped.

It was a rosebush. Except this was unlike any rosebush she'd ever seen. Most roses were already long past flowering by this point in the season but somehow this bush was still covered in vibrant blooms. It was magnificent. Every branch was covered in giant, bright red roses. She reached out to touch a flower, gently stroking the velvet petals.

How had she not noticed this before? How had she walked near enough to brush up against it without seeing it? She stood, bewildered, staring at the most beautiful plant she'd ever seen, knowing in her heart that she could never have missed it. It was as if it had appeared out of nowhere. As if it had grown in an instant. She immediately thought of the tall grass near the supply barn and subconsciously started shaking her head in denial.

"You're crazy. That's crazy," Elora chastised herself. "You cannot make plants grow."

She slowly backed away from the rosebush, disconcerted. She felt a sudden urgency to get to Alysa's house and leave the bizarre happenings of this morning behind her. Picking up the skirt of her sage dress, she took off running. As she neared a bend in the road, she couldn't help but look back once more before it was out of sight. She stared with wide eyes at the glorious rosebush growing on the side of the road, it's branches reaching out towards the place where she had stood. She shook her head and ran even faster.

Alysa was patiently waiting on her front porch steps when Elora came sprinting around the corner. She smiled happily upon seeing her and stood, ready to embrace her friend. Elora slowed to a walk, struggling to catch her breath after her frantic run. She made a weak attempt to return Alysa's smile as she walked into her arms. Alysa frowned in concern as Elora hugged her tightly and let out an audible sigh of relief.

"Did something happen, Elora?" she asked.

"I don't think you would believe me if I told you. I hardly believe myself," Elora said with a bemused laugh.

"I would believe you!" Alysa replied indignantly, leaning back to look Elora in the eyes. "You know I would!"

"I'm not sure even you, my devoted friend, would be able to set aside common sense enough to believe the absurd things I've been thinking," Elora said, shaking her head. "I'd rather just go inside and get started. I've been looking forward to spending time with you all week."

"Me too. I haven't seen you in days!" she exclaimed.

She looked with concern at Elora. After all these years as friends, she was able to sense the anxiety that Elora was determinedly trying to downplay.

"Are you sure you won't tell me what's wrong?" she asked, her brow furrowed.

"Very sure," Elora nodded, looping Alysa's arm through hers and turning to walk up the front steps of the house.

No matter how fervently she wanted to talk to someone about the strange things happening around her, now that she had the chance, Elora was too embarrassed to give voice to the ridiculous ideas swirling around in her head.

"Let's get to work!" she exclaimed.

"Alright, well, that's probably a good idea since there is literally not a second to waste," Alysa said. "Can you believe it? This time next week Trig and I will be standing in front of everyone, our arms wrapped in the Binding Cord, making our promises!" Alysa gushed, letting out a little squealing of excitement and drawing a laugh from Elora.

"So you're sure about this? Because I'm just not sensing any enthusiasm, Alysa." she teased.

Alysa giggled, poking her in the side good naturedly.

"Any more enthusiasm and I think I would explode," she said with a laugh.

She grabbed Elora by the hand, pulling her hastily through the front door and into the small sewing room off the foyer. She turned to block Elora's view of the room for a moment and stood grinning shyly at her. Elora looked back with a confused and expectant smile. Alysa let out an excited giggle before stepping aside to reveal a dress form in the middle of the room.

Elora gasped. The mannequin was draped in the most gorgeous gown she'd ever seen. It was a light, earthy green color embroidered with intricate ivory vines. A modest sweetheart neckline rose into wide, delicate lace straps. It was a slender A-line cut, flowing from a form fitting v-shaped bodice into a generous skirt that was hemmed a bit shorter in front than in back.

"It's exquisite, Alysa! Your mother has outdone herself! You will be stunning in it," Elora gushed.

"Oh no! This isn't my dress," Alysa said, breaking into a smile. "But I can't even tell you how thrilled I am that you thought my mom made this. I must be getting pretty good."

Elora's mouth fell open.

"You made this? I had no idea you could do something like this!" she whispered in awe.

"Well, lucky for you I can! Go ahead and undress behind that screen over there and I'll bring you the dress when you're ready," she said, pointing to the corner of the room.

Elora stood stunned for a moment.

"This is my dress?" she asked, shocked.

"Made especially for you, my sweet friend," Alysa smiled.

"It's too much," Elora said, her voice catching with emotion. "I don't deserve it. This must have taken you months!"

"It did. I was making it to practice my embroidery and also because I love you, of course. But it works out perfectly that you can wear it as my Witness! And you do deserve it, by the way. Now don't ruin my fun by making a fuss. Go get behind that screen," she ordered, shooing her across the room to the shoulder height panels of stretched fabric where she could undress in privacy.

"How do you know it will fit?" she asked, pulling her dress over her head.

"I snatched one of your dresses a few months back to get your measurements. I expect I might need to make a few adjustments though. And you wear that sage dress all the time, so I figured green was your favorite," Alysa chattered as she gathered the dress and draped it over the screen.

"I can't believe you did this!" Elora exclaimed as she stepped into the dress.

The fabric was cool and soft as she gently pulled it up and slid her arms though the straps. Holding the lace up to her shoulders, she stepped out from behind the screen.

"Can you fasten the back?" she asked.

"Of course! It's a little different, Elora. I hope you don't mind. I was feeling inspired," she said with an anxious look. "I designed it to be open in the back, with just a bit of lace stretching across your shoulder blades to hold the straps in place. I know how modest you are, so don't worry, it's not terribly low cut. There's a small button just here," she said, fastening the delicate fabric at the nape of Elora's neck. "Let's take a look!" she said, her excitement bubbling over.

Both girls turned to the full-length mirror leaning against the wall.

"You are so gifted, Alysa," Elora whispered in awe.

"And you are so beautiful," she replied, a satisfied smile on her lips. "Truly, Elora. I bet you'll have a letter or two waiting for you after the ceremony once the town gets a look at you like this."

"I do look rather pretty," Elora admitted. "It must be the dress."

"You're crazy. You've always been lovely, with that thick chestnut hair and those sparkling green eyes," Alysa admonished, clucking her tongue. "Not to mention your long neck and creamy skin, which I've accentuated perfectly with this dress, if I do say so myself," she gloated, knotting Elora's braid into a hasty updo.

Elora turned to see just how revealing the back of the dress was and couldn't help but frown. Her eyes immediately focused on the birthmark in the middle of her back. It was almost as though the dress had been designed to specifically draw attention to it, the one part of her she had always sought to keep hidden.

"I guess there's no hiding my birthmark in this dress," she remarked with a nervous laugh.

"What birthmark? Your skin is flawless!" Alysa replied, a confused expression on her face.

"Right there," Elora said, pointing to the mark. "It's impossible to miss it. Please don't pretend you can't see it."

"Are you playing with me?" Alysa asked.

"No! Really? You don't see that?" Elora asked, bewildered.

"Oh, stop it Elora! There is nothing there. You are so silly sometimes," she said, dismissing her with a wave of her hand.

Elora looked at Alysa for a long moment. She really couldn't see the birthmark! Elora reached for the seed at her neck. Her testy exchange in the market the other day with the merchant came to mind. He had insisted that he couldn't see the seed on her necklace either. She shook her head, refusing to believe the strange things that were going on around her. She was holding the seed between her fingers. It was very real. She'd hated that birthmark her entire life. It was definitely there. Why couldn't people see them?

She turned to regard her back in the mirror again. Her eyes widened in surprise as she stared at the light brown seed shaped mark. It was different. It had changed. There was a short, fine line extending upwards from the mark along her spine. She took a step closer for a better look. It really had changed! She quickly turned away from the mirror, a pebble of fear settling in the pit of her stomach. What was happening to her?

Alysa brushed her hand against Elora's arm and she jumped, startled out of her private musings.

"You seem very distracted Elora," Alysa said, her face lined in worry. "Are you sure you don't want to talk about it?"

"I really don't, but thank you for being so concerned," she replied, her features settling into a genuine smile. "I can't believe you did this for me," she said, lifting the skirt of the dress to admire the delicate leaves and blossoms embroidered on it.

"Do you like it? Really?" Alysa asked, relishing the praise after all her months of hard work.

"I love it. I really do. It's the most beautiful dress I will ever own," Elora gushed. "But please tell me your mother has created a masterpiece for you to wear, because I will be mortified if I come to the ceremony wearing a finer dress than the bride."

"Oh, you know my mother. This dress is my best work yet, but my skills are nothing compared to hers. And she's outdone herself from what I've seen. I will outshine you, don't worry," she laughed.

"As you should, my sweet friend."

"You know, I actually don't really see any need for alterations Does anything feel uncomfortable to you?" she asked, walking a circle around Elora.

"Besides the gaping hole in the back?" Elora joked.

"Oh Elora! Be brave and daring!" admonished Alysa. "It's elegant and really does flatter you. Besides, there's no time to change it."

"I'm kidding. It's perfect Alysa. Perfect. Especially since my birthmark appears to be invisible," she joked, trying to make light of her concern.

"You're ridiculous, you know that?" Alysa replied with a laugh.

"I know," Elora sighed. "I really am," she whispered, looking at the seed dangling in the hollow of her throat, perfectly framed by the lacey neckline of the dress. "Hey Alysa," she said, lifting her hand to toy with the seed. "Do you think the necklace I'm wearing will do for the ceremony?"

"It's nice, but it might be a little plain. I think it would be prettier if you added a charm to it. I have something that would look perfect actually. Wait right there!" Alysa said, scurrying from the room to retrieve the jewelry.

Elora stood quietly watching herself in the mirror. Her expression remained stoic, but she couldn't keep the disappointment from her eyes. Alysa couldn't see the seed either. She was beginning to think she was crazy, except for the fact that the Highlander who had sold it to her could obviously see the seed too.

She was suddenly uncomfortable wearing the mysterious and extraordinary necklace. She reached back to unclasp the chain, pulling it from around her neck. She cupped the seed in her hand, looking at it for a moment. Furrowing her brows, she leaned in for a closer look. It had changed! A few of the intricate grooves in the surface of the seed were suddenly shiny, as though embedded with strands of silver. Elora's eyes widened in surprise and she closed her hand around the seed. This was magic. There was no other explanation. She quickly ran behind the screen and tucked the necklace into the pocket of her sage dress. Something unexplainable and bizarre was happening and she wasn't sure if it was exciting or terrifying.

She emerged just as Alysa returned, holding a lovely silver necklace with a delicate flower pendant.

"Here! Try this on," she said.

She fastened the necklace around Elora's throat and stepped back.

"It's perfect! Oh Elora, the whole thing suits you so well! The color and the vines and the flower pendant. It really is the perfect dress for you, my dearest friend who makes the flowers grow," she smiled, squeezing Elora in a one-armed hug as they stood before the mirror.

Elora's smile faltered for a second as Alysa's words summoned a vision of the rosebush on the roadside. She laughed at herself, pushing thoughts of the morning from her mind, and returned the hug.

"Phew! I'm so glad I don't have to make any alterations! One less thing on my list," exclaimed Alysa.

"Well, let me take off this gorgeous dress and I'll help you tackle that list. What's up next?" asked Elora as she turned and motioned for Alysa to help her with the button.

"I need to finish weaving my part of the Binding Cord but I want to do that myself. If you don't mind though, we could go check out the church courtyard. There hasn't been a binding ceremony there in a while and I'm sure it needs some tending. And since you're a professional weed picker, I bet you'll be handy!" Alysa teased.

"I really am an expert," Elora called over the screen as she stepped out of her gown and slipped back into her clothes. Her favorite sage dress seemed pitiful compared to the beautiful gown she held in her hands.

Elora walked around the screen and handed the gown back to Alysa, who gently draped it over the dress form. "Why don't you leave it here and let it be a surprise to everyone. We can get dressed together before the ceremony," she said enthusiastically. "Plus, I just like to look at it. I'm a little proud," she admitted, blushing.

"It's gorgeous, Alysa. You *should* be proud," Elora encouraged. "I can't wait to wear it for the ceremony."

"It's going to be a really good day for so many reasons," Alysa gushed. "Are you ready to go?"

"Ready when you are," Elora nodded, following Alysa back into the foyer. "What's your parents' Binding Cord look like? I've never seen the one my parents used."

"Really? My mom has had theirs displayed front and center for my entire life," Alysa said. "Maybe she's more sentimental than yours."

"I don't know if she's more sentimental, or just more domestic," Elora laughed.

Alysa took a detour on the way to the front door, leading Elora into the family room instead. There on the fireplace mantle was a shadow box holding a coil of intricately woven cord with a delicate dried rose nestled in the center. The rope consisted of three braided strands, one comprised of strips of leather and faded gray fabric, one made of ivory silk and lace, a third made of gold twine. The three cords were woven together to make a single cord.

"It's lovely," Elora remarked. "You know, I actually don't really know much about the cord or the binding ceremony. My parents never talked about it and I've never been to one."

"Oh, Elora! You're going to swoon. It's such a romantic tradition," Alysa gushed, reaching out to lovingly touch the glass of the shadowbox. "That strand represents my father and is made of strips from his first Guardsman uniform. The other strand is for my mother and was made of scraps left over from the dress she wore that day. The thick gold thread represents God. They are braided into a single cord to symbolize the way their lives are intertwined and to represent the idea that their union makes them stronger. The gold thread represents the way that God has joined them together and is a part of that union. The cord is wrapped around their joined hands during the ceremony to signify that they are bound to one another."

Alysa wore a dreamy smile and a pink blush across her cheeks as she finished her explanation. Elora could tell she was envisioning her own ceremony.

"That really is romantic," Elora whispered, quietly studying the cord.

She couldn't hide the longing from her voice and Alysa gave her a sympathetic smile. Embarrassed and eager to divert Alysa's pity, Elora pointed to the dried flower resting in the middle of the rope.

"Is the flower significant to the tradition too?"

"It's not really part of the tradition, but it's a sweet part to my parents' story," she shrugged. "My father picked that rose and snuck into my mother's room to give it to her the morning of their ceremony. She wore it in her hair that day."

"I never would have guessed your father to be so romantic," Elora mused. "Does Trig know how high the bar is set?" she laughed.

"He knows and is up to the challenge."

Both girls jumped at the sound of Trig's deep voice coming from the doorway. He stepped into the room, pulling a gorgeous bloom from behind his back and presenting it to Alysa with a grin. She laughed, taking the rose from his hand and walked into his waiting embrace.

"Wow! It's gorgeous! Thank you," she said, smiling shyly up at him.

"I couldn't walk past a rosebush and not pick one for you, love. Especially when I didn't even have to step off the road to do it," he said, utterly besotted.

"You mean you didn't even break a sweat retrieving this for me? Perhaps I shouldn't be so grateful then," Alysa teased.

"I think I still deserve a little gratitude," he chuckled, leaning down to steal a kiss. "Besides, I most certainly did break a sweat. It's ridiculously hot out there!"

Elora stared at the rose, a plastic smile stretched across her face to conceal the sick feeling in the pit of her stomach. She knew exactly where Trig had found that flower. She had managed to convinced herself over the past hour that she'd imagined the entire thing, or maybe hadn't seen things accurately due to her panic. But she couldn't very well deny the giant bloom in Alysa's hand.

"Where on earth were you walking that you passed a rosebush in bloom?" Alysa asked. "All the rosebushes I've seen are long past blooming. I've been disappointed, actually, because I had hoped to wear one in my hair, like my mother did. Now maybe I can! This is wonderful!"

"It's just a quarter mile down the road between my house and yours. I can't believe I never noticed it before," Trig replied. "It's incredible. Come on, I'll show you!"

Taking her hand, he led Alysa through the house and out the front door. Elora followed hesitantly behind them, nervous to be confronted again by the evidence of her impossible ability. The two lovebirds laughed excitedly and discussed the impending ceremony with enthusiasm as they walked. Elora listened halfheartedly, quietly walking alongside Alysa.

"This is absurd," she thought. "Unbelievable."

As they rounded a curve, they noticed a small crowd of people gathered on the side of the road.

"I guess I'm not the only one who noticed," Trig said. "I hope they haven't stripped the bush bare already."

"It's alright, Trig," Alysa soothed. "I already have one and hopefully it will keep until the ceremony."

"I'm glad to hear you say that," Trig nodded. "But still, it was magnificent. I wanted you to see. Oh look, most of the blooms are still there!"

As they neared the crowd, Elora could feel her heartbeat quickening. Even from this far away the vibrant red roses were breathtaking.

"Oh my goodness Trig! There are so many of them and they are huge!" Alysa cried in delight. "Elora, you have to go tell your mother about this!"

It was even more incredible than Elora had remembered. She reached out to touch the soft petals of the bloom nearest to her. Lost in her own thoughts, it took a moment for the conversations around her to penetrate.

"Where did it come from? I walk here every day and I've never noticed it before!" said one person.

"Why is it blooming this late in the year? It's so strange!" said another.

Elora suddenly became painfully self-conscious and tried to swallow the lump of panic rising in her throat. She took a deep breath, willing herself to calm down as her pulse pounded in her ears.

"No one would think that this has anything to do with me," she reassured herself. "That would be absurd. And besides, maybe this really *doesn't* have anything to do with me" she thought hopefully.

Then right before her eyes, a small bud formed on the tip of a nearby branch, and quickly grew in size. Her mouth dropped slightly open in shock. When the bud suddenly burst and spread into a gorgeous bright red rose, she gasped and jumped away. She looked around to see if she had been the only witness and was unfortunately greeted by a number of wide-eyed expressions from the crowd.

"That was unbelievable!" exclaimed Alysa who had sidled up next to her.

"Yes," Elora whispered with a shaky voice. "Unbelievable."

She backed away from the rosebush, turned and started running toward home.

CHAPTER 5

Elora gripped the front gate to her house, leaning over to rest her forehead against her hands as she tried to catch her breath and gather her senses. Hopefully she hadn't made a spectacle of herself running away as she had. At worst they would think she was scared of a plant, but at best maybe they believed she'd just ran to fetch her mother, a well-known lover of flowers. That would be the rational reaction of a reasonable person, after all. Elora wouldn't classify herself as either rational or reasonable at this moment, but she took comfort in thinking that perhaps she had at least appeared so.

Her breathing finally under control and her pulse slowed, she pushed through the gate and quietly made her way inside. She could hear the muffled sounds of her parents talking in their bedroom. She quickly tiptoed to her room and closed the door, sighing with relief to finally be alone and unobserved. Falling back onto her bed, she rubbed her hands over her face and threaded her fingers into her hair.

"What on earth?" she mused, shaking her head and letting her arms fall to the bed on either side of her head.

She lay that way for a long while, silently considering all the extraordinary things that had happened.

"This is real," she thought. "All of it. The seed, my birthmark, the grasses, the rosebush, all of these strange things have really happened. It doesn't make sense. I don't understand it. But it all really happened and I'm not crazy."

It was somehow comforting to accept it, to allow herself to believe it. The seed was magical. And somehow, despite a life that had been heretofore utterly average, she was magical too. She still questioned how those two facts related to one another, but she could finally acknowledge them without completely losing herself in panic. She was slowly shifting from a state of fear to one of curiosity.

"Nothing bad has happened, after all. In fact, the ability to grow things is a rather useful talent for a gardener" she thought with a chuckle.

A knock on the front door jolted her from her thoughts. She moved from her bed and quietly cracked her bedroom door so that she could eavesdrop.

"Elora's not here?" she heard Alysa ask. "I thought for sure she came to tell you about the rosebush."

"What rosebush?" asked Elora's mother.

"It's the most incredible thing, Mrs. Kerrick. This giant rosebush in full bloom just appeared out of nowhere overnight! It's just a half mile down the road. You need to go see it. It's gorgeous!" Alysa gushed.

A silent moment passed and Elora leaned closer to the opening, listening for her mother's response.

"Is everything alright Mrs. Kerrick? Did I say something to upset you?" Alysa fretted, her voice much softer and unsure.

Clearly the news of the rosebush was an unwelcome surprise. Elora thought back to her mother's reaction to the tall grasses and a chill settled in her spine.

"Oh, no! Everything is fine, dear. I've just been struggling with a headache this morning. I'll be sure to check out that rosebush later today," her mother replied quickly, recovering from her obvious surprise and distress.

"I'm so sorry to hear that! I'll leave you alone then. But I do wonder where Elora could be," Alysa mused aloud in question. "Maybe she went to start weeding the church courtyard. Though I don't know why she'd be in such a hurry to do that! I guess she enjoys gardening even more than I thought!" she laughed. "Feel better soon, Mrs. Kerrick," she said over her shoulder as she turned to leave.

"I'll tell her you're looking for her if she comes home. And let me know if you need anything for the ceremony," Elora's mother called out warmly before closing the door.

The house was still for a moment before her father's voice broke the silence.

"It's happening."

Elora gasped at her father's words and quickly covered her mouth.

"No!" sobbed her mother. "Not yet. She's not ready. I'm not ready."

"It's not up to us," he replied.

Elora heard her father's footsteps as he moved to embrace her mother.

"And she *is* ready," he reassured her softly.

Elora could hear the muffled sounds of her mother's tears as she cried into his shirt.

"Wipe your tears, Winny," he gently urged her. "She was born for this. We've known it her entire life. Now, let's go see what our amazing daughter has done."

Elora heard the thud of the front door closing behind them as they set off to see her rosebush. She closed her door and leaned her forehead against it, finally releasing the shuddering breath she hadn't realized she'd been holding. She sat down abruptly on the floor, as her legs suddenly felt too weak to support her. They knew. They had known all along. And they had kept it from her.

"I was born for this," she repeated her father's words.

Born for what? The way her mother had been crying, it certainly didn't seem like anything good. But her father had actually sounded proud. Perhaps even a little excited.

She felt deceived. She felt curious. But mostly she felt scared. Her hands trembled and tears stung the corners of her eyes as she looked around, trying to regain her bearings. She gripped the ledge of her bedside table to steady her as she pulled herself back onto her feet. As she rose, her eyes settled on the small potted lavender plant she kept there. Her breath caught and her eyes widened as a lavender bud grew and bloomed into a cascade of purple flowers in a matter of seconds. Without thinking, she swung out her hand, sending the pot flying across the room where it smashed again the wall. The sound jolted her out of her panic and she stared at it wide-eyed, dismayed at what she'd done. Closing her eyes and taking a deep breath, she plopped down onto the bed.

"I can't keep letting my emotions take over like that," she admonished herself, shaking her head. True, her world seemed to be tipped on its side at this moment and it was difficult to make sense of all the strange things that had happened, but this was unlike her. She was usually steady and calm and grounded. But she'd been frightened and flustered so many times in the past week between her scary daydream, being followed by the Highlander, and her life-changing self-discovery. She needed to get a hold of herself.

"Wait," she whispered, cocking her head to the side. "That's it!"

All those times when she'd lost control of her emotions, when she'd been driven into a panic, the plants around her had reacted. She'd awoken from her frightening daydream to find that the grass had grown up around her. The rosebush had appeared after she'd encountered the Highlander and had panicked. And just now, she had made the lavender bloom while trying to recover from the shock of her parent's deception.

"I can control this," she thought hopefully. "Or at least predict it," she reasoned.

Relief rushed over her as she claimed a degree of ownership over her powers and she felt her world sliding back into order.

Standing, she walked over to where the lavender plant lay on the floor and picked it up. Cradling the clump of roots and soil in her hand, she took a deep breath and tried to focus. She stared at the plant, replaying the memories of those panicked moments in her mind, attempting to summon an emotional response. But there was nothing. She closed her eyes, dejected and exhausted.

Suddenly a cool breeze brushed across her skin. The scent of the forest filled her nostrils and she was surrounded by the sounds of the woods. A sense of dread came over her as she remembered the last time she'd visited here. Keeping her eyes closed, she turned her head from side to side, listening. Reaching around, she felt the trunk of a tree behind her and she slowly leaned back until she was resting against it. The forest was quiet and still, and she began to relax, letting her hand fall to her side. The snap of a twig jolted her upright and she turned towards the sound.

"Elora."

It was him! Her heart jumped into her throat.

His voice was gentle and calm. There was a lilt to it, an accent she'd never heard before. She held her breath, willing him to say more.

She gasped as she felt a rough hand caress her cheek.

"Wait for me, Elora."

Her eyes flew open and she was jolted back to reality. She was panting for breath as a torrent of emotions swirled in her mind. She didn't know whether to be thrilled or terrified. Her brain was firmly telling her to be scared, but her heart was singing!

"He's coming for me," she whispered.

She lifted her hand to touch her face where his had been but drew back in surprise at the grainy texture against her cheek. At the sight of the soil covering her palm, she was suddenly reminded of what she had been doing and realized that she must have dropped the plant. Looking down at the floor, her mouth fell open. What had once been her small lavender plant with a single bloom was now a small bush so covered in vibrant purple flowers that it took her breath away.

"Well, that answers that," she said aloud quietly.

Kneeling, she lifted the considerably larger plant, holding it up to better appreciate the extent that it had changed.

"Amazing," she whispered under her breath.

As she turned the plant in her hands, a small smile crept across her lips. She had done this! Slowly the fear of her incredible ability slipped away and was replaced by pride. She felt empowered. True, she would have to get her emotions under control, but this ability, while unexpected and unexplainable, was a gift. She should embrace it, not fear it. She ran her finger along a stalk of lavender and chuckled quietly as Alysa's words came to mind. "...my dearest friend, who makes the flowers grow."

Elora stood and walked through the house and out the backdoor, gently carrying the plant outside to the private garden behind the house. Grabbing a trowel, she found a clear spot beneath her bedroom window where she began to dig. Once the hole was big enough, she tucked the exposed roots of the lavender plant into its new home and firmly packed soil around it.

"Sorry for breaking your pot," she whispered, as she gave the dirt one last pat.

"I had better get to the church courtyard before Alysa comes looking for me again or before my parents come home," she thought as she rose and headed back inside.

She quickly swept up and discarded the broken flowerpot. Grabbing two sets of gardening gloves, she slipped out the front door and headed towards the church.

Elora had no desire to be there when her parents returned. She was simply not ready to face them. The idea of seeing them turned her stomach now that she knew they had kept such a secret from her. What would she even say to them? Should she tell them what she'd discovered about herself? Did she even want to know the secret they had kept from her? She just didn't feel equipped to handle any more than she already was at this moment.

She took the long route to the church so as to avoid passing the rosebush and more importantly, her parents. As she walked, she looked around furtively for any sign of the blond Highlander. Out of all the bizarre things happening in her life, the possibility that this man was watching her, following her, was the only thing that felt wrong. It was the only part that truly scared her.

As she walked, she replayed her latest vision of the forest and the man in her mind. How did these visions figure into her new reality? Could they be real? They certainly felt real. And after the events of this morning, Elora was coming to believe that literally anything was possible. It couldn't merely be a coincidence that after years of quiet, uneventful visits to the forest, the man appeared just as she discovered her ability. The forest had been her refuge, full of calm and peace and solitude, for her entire life. Why only now, as she found the magical seed and her birthmark was changing, did he suddenly appear. They were surely all related.

She stopped suddenly as an epiphany struck her. Could the Highlander be the man in her visions? Her mouth fell open at the thought and she subconsciously shook her head. No. He couldn't be. The man in her visions wouldn't lurk in the shadows. He wouldn't intentionally avoid her. The man in her visions called to her openly and searched for her with purpose. He approached her boldly and touched her with affection. True, their interactions had been few and fleeting, but she just knew. It was unexplainable and irrational, but in light of her new understanding of the world in general, she wasn't going to doubt herself. The man in her visions was coming, and she would know him when he did.

She was nearing the church courtyard and could see Alysa standing beneath the trellis arch looking around in a mixture of panic and confusion. This would be a good first test of her self-control.

"I will not make things grow," she whispered to herself.

She took a deep calming breath and stepped into view.

"Elora! Thank goodness! I don't even know where to start!" Alysa cried.

As she walked into the courtyard, Elora started to chuckle in disbelief. "Oh, Alysa. This is terrible! It will take forever to clean this place up!"

"I know! It's so much worse than I'd imagined. I'm debating whether to have it indoors instead and just abandon this idea entirely," she said dejectedly.

"But you've always wanted to be married here, like your parents and grandparents were. You must have told me that a thousand times," Elora protested.

"I know! I do!" she cried. "But it's been so neglected. Even if we pull all the weeds, it will still look pitiful."

"Why is it like this? Weren't Lorna and Robert Kincannon bound just a few months ago? How did it get this bad?" Elora asked, confused.

"They had their ceremony on the town square, remember?" Alysa said, frowning. "Two summers ago there was an unfortunate bee incident here during a ceremony and so no one has used it in a while. I'm so surprised how quickly the weeds took over."

"Bees?" Elora asked, looking around suspiciously. "It must have been a pretty bad incident to scare people away for two whole years!"

"It was bad. I'm not going to lie. But don't worry," she said, laughing at Elora's dubious expression. "Preacher Woodward nearly burned down the church with his exuberant extermination efforts. Those bees are gone."

"I don't know if should believe you," Elora teased. "Obviously no one else does or they would be having ceremonies here."

"Oh hush! I'm not sure I'm going to have it here either, honestly," she exclaimed, throwing her hands up in the air. "It just looks so awful, Elora!"

"Well, we have a week, right? I can do a lot in a week," Elora encouraged. "Especially if you and Trig help out."

"We definitely will," Alysa said nodding vigorously. "But are you sure it's even possible?"

"I am suddenly a big believer that all things are possible," Elora said quietly. "So let's get to work! I'll start over here in this corner pulling weeds and you start over there dragging brush out from under that desert willow," Elora directed, handing Alysa the extra pair of work gloves she'd brought.

The women set to work in comfortable silence. The flowerbeds were in terrible condition, but Elora was able to quickly identify the species that were planted intentionally and she ruthlessly weeded out the invaders. Satisfied that she was making good headway, she stopped to wipe the sweat from her brow and check on

Alysa's progress. The area around the desert willow tree was noticeably more clear. She smiled as she watched Alysa wrestle a dead branch from the clutches of the tall grasses and vines that had taken over the garden. The branch suddenly snapped free and Alysa fell backwards with a startled cry. Elora quickly covered her mouth to stifle her laughter but Alysa heard her and looked over, a smile on her lips.

"What a friend you are, Elora Kerrick! Laughing at my misfortune!" she teased.

Elora held up her hands in surrender.

"I'm sorry! I couldn't help it!" she cried. "Don't hate me. It's looking much improved already, if that makes you feel any better."

"Much improved, yes," she agreed, surveying their work. "But it's still ugly," she said, scrunching her nose.

"We have 6 more days to fix it. And I bet my mother has some flowers we can plant here to make it beautiful," Elora encouraged.

"Too bad we can't go dig up that beautiful rose bush on the side of the road. It would make any place beautiful. I think it's too big though," Alysa said shaking her head.

Elora felt her spine stiffen at the mention of her rosebush.

"Just breathe," she thought.

"Hey! I meant to ask you where you took off to in such a hurry earlier. I had figured you went to get your mom, but I checked for you at your house and you weren't there," Alysa asked curiously, her head cocked to one side.

Elora could feel her pulse quickening and panic starting to well in her chest. Her eyes widened as, to her horror, she watched the plant she'd been weeding around only moments before start growing and sprouting tiny purple flowers. She closed her eyes and took a calming breath.

"Sorry for leaving so suddenly. I remembered that I had left my gloves out in the tool shed by the gardens and ran to get them," she fibbed.

She opened her eyes and looked to see if Alysa had believed the lie.

"Well, I guess it's a good thing you ran, considering what a mess this place is," she said, laughing as she walked over to inspect Elora's progress. "Oh! How lovely! I didn't notice those pretty purple flowers before! Do you think there are more hidden under all these weeds?" she asked hopefully.

Elora gave a relieved laugh and nodded her head.

"I'm sure there are."

Alysa clapped her hands happily and turned to resume her work.

"Maybe this will work out after all!" she said with renewed optimism.

Elora reached out to touch the flowers that she had caused to grow and bloom in only a moment. She looked around at the courtyard and a smile slowly stretched across her face.

"This will definitely work out," she said softly.

CHAPTER 6

Elora rose from bed early the next morning. She and Alysa had worked for hours in the courtyard yesterday and while they had made some headway, there was still an enormous amount of work left to do before it would be fit for the ceremony. They had agreed to meet there again the following day after the church service with reinforcements.

As Elora walked around her room quietly primping for church, she wondered and worried about how her parents would react to seeing her. She had arrived home late in the evening and had gone to bed without running into them, thankfully. Thus they hadn't spoken since the rosebush incident and the revelation of her ability. Truthfully, she was dreading their reaction and was scared of what they might tell her. But she needed their help with the courtyard.

Grabbing a satchel, she stepped over to her dresser and retrieved a pair of work pants and a tunic, shoving them into the bag. She planned to change after the service and get right to work. There really was no time to spare.

She then gave a furtive look around before opening the top dresser drawer. She picked up a folded handkerchief that had been tucked into the corner and gently pulled the corners apart to reveal the seed necklace. She had hidden it there last night. Now that she recognized how special and precious the seed was, it felt foolish to leave it out in the open. She ran her thumb over the intricate grooves of the seed as she lifted it for a closer examination. It seemed as though even more of the grooves were lined in silver this morning.

"I wonder if I'm doing this too," she thought.

It couldn't be a coincidence that the seed began changing right as her ability began to manifest itself.

She unclasped the necklace and reached behind her neck to fasten it before tucking it beneath the collar of her dress. She patted it one last time with her hand before walking out of her room in search of her parents.

The house was unusually quiet. She walked into the kitchen expecting to see them sharing breakfast as they typically did every morning, but they were not there. The door to their bedroom was open and she walked over to peek inside. The room was empty and the bed already made. Turning back to the kitchen with a perplexed look upon her face, her eyes settled on a sheet of paper resting on the kitchen table. Surprised and curious, she moved quickly to read the note they had left for her.

Elora,

We had some errands to run this morning. Sorry to miss you. Have a fun day with Alysa!

~ Mom and Dad

Elora slumped down into a chair with a sigh. She had been fretting about this confrontation since the day prior and now they weren't even here. Were they avoiding her too? She lifted the paper to read it again. How unlike them to miss the church service. What could they be up to? And this note was as vague as it could possibly be. They could be gone the entire day for all she knew! She had really hoped they would be able to help in the courtyard today. This was her last day off of work before the ceremony and there was so much to do.

"I can still do this without them," she said, lightly tapping her fist on the table in encouragement.

After grabbing an apple from the bowl of fruit on the counter, she walked out the back door into the garden. She munched on the juicy piece of fruit as she wandered around, considering which of her mother's flowers would work best in the courtyard. She paused to admire her lavender plant as she walked past, a smile on her face. Finished with her breakfast, she threw the apple core into the compost heap and moved to gather the tools she would need for the day. She picked up a bucket and loaded it with her gloves, a trowel, a cultivator, and a pair of pruning shears. After fetching her work boots, she was finally ready and set off around the side of the house and out the front gate.

It was early still and her journey to the church was uneventful. She was the first person to arrive and so she spent some time appraising the courtyard, plotting her course of action. They really had accomplished quite a lot yesterday but there was still half the courtyard left to be weeded. Once the overgrown grass in the middle of the yard was cut down it would look much more manageable. Perhaps she could recruit Trig to handle that. He was pretty handy with a scythe if she remembered correctly.

"Hey there Elora!" came a familiar baritone voice.

She turned to see Trig walk into the courtyard arm in arm with Alysa.

"I was just thinking of you!" Elora said, smiling.

"Well you better stop that. I'm already taken, Elora," he replied with a wink.

"Oh stop it!" Elora cried, swatting his arm. "I was just thinking about how often you used to have to trim the schoolyard grass."

"You really did have to do that a lot," Alysa nodded.

"It was Teacher Howard's favorite punishment, that old sourpuss," Trig said, grimacing at the memory. "I got pretty good with that scythe though!" he remarked, puffing out his chest.

"Yes, you really did," Elora agreed.

She smiled at him expectantly.

He looked at her and cocked an eyebrow in question. He then looked around at the courtyard and sighed.

"I see where this is going," he said with a grimace.

"It's your ceremony too, big guy," Alysa reminded him.

"Does it really need to be here in the wilderness?" he asked beseechingly.

"Well, it won't be wilderness if you cut the grass, my love," Alysa cajoled.

"Alright. Alright," he relented. "Just stop looking at me with those big eyes. I haven't figured out a defense against those yet."

"Let's hope you never do!" Elora cried, threading her arm through Alysa's other elbow and turning them toward the church entryway. "We better get in there before the last bench gets filled. We wouldn't want to be stuck at the front!" she said with a laughed as they rounded the corner, nearly bumping into Preacher Woodward.

Elora's hand flew to her mouth.

"Elora," he said reproachfully, shaking his head.

"Preacher," she replied, with an apologetic smile.

"We were just planning how to set up the courtyard for the ceremony!" Alysa told him exuberantly, attempting to draw attention away from her friend. "It's going to be lovely!"

"Are you sure you want to have it here? There are no bees, I can assure you, but it's been very neglected Alysa," he replied with concern.

"Oh, Elora can make it happen! I have faith," she said, wrapping an arm around Elora's shoulders.

"For that kind of miracle, perhaps you should be sitting in the *front* row, Ms. Kerrick," Preacher Woodward remarked, chuckling at his own joke before turning to welcome another congregant.

Elora laughed good-naturedly as they walked into the church before turning to Alysa with a mortified expression on her face.

"I can't believe that just happened," she moaned, pressing her hands to her hot cheeks.

Alysa giggled and hugged her affectionately.

"You do keep life interesting, Elora," she teased.

"So, wait, do we have to sit in front?" Trig asked.

The three friends looked at each other and burst out laughing.

"You two decide. I'm going to be hiding in the outhouse," Elora joked.

They opted to sit on a bench in the middle and took their seats as the rest of the congregation started filing in.

"Are you saving some seats for your parents?" Alysa asked looking around at the quickly filling rows. "It looks like there will be a crowd today."

"Oh, I seriously doubt they're going to be here," Trig chimed in and Elora looked over in surprise. "I had the sunrise shift guarding the wall and saw them leaving out of the East Gate at first light," he mentioned casually while making googly eyes at the toddler seated in front of him.

Elora stared at him in shock and confusion. They had left Windom? Her parents had always been so adamant about staying within the town walls. What were they doing? How many more secrets were they keeping from her? She shook her head in disappointment and looked off out the church window as she tried to gather her thoughts.

"Did you not know?" Alysa asked, sensing her displeasure at the news.

"They left me a note about errands, so I kind of knew," Elora said, cocking her head to the side. "But I didn't know how big an errand it was. There's no way they will be around to help out today."

"It'll be okay. Trig and I can help. I bet I can even talk my dad into pitching in," Alysa said encouragingly.

Elora smiled in return. But then Preacher Woodward caught her eye as he walked past their bench on his way to the front of the church and her embarassment was inflamed anew. She blushed and gave him a halfhearted little wave. He shook his head in amusement and continued on to the pulpit where he opened the service with a prayer about worshiping with eagerness and enthusiasm.

"...Let us come to You with passion, ever seeking a front row seat in Your house."

Elora's mouth fell open and she looked over to see Alysa and Trig struggling to stifle their laughter. She sighed, closed her eyes and said a silent prayer that Preacher Woodward wouldn't torment her forever. Hearing a collective creaking of the benches as the congregation stood, Elora opened her eyes and rose. She joined in as they began to sing a familiar hymn and fell comfortably into the habit and ritual of the church service.

Her mind soon wandered back to her parents and their persistent secrecy. She'd lived with it her whole life, but it no longer seemed bearable. She felt completely betrayed by them. But then again, had they really betrayed her? They wouldn't intentionally hurt her. They were her parents and loved her more than anyone. They only ever acted in her best interest. Surely they had a good reason for keeping her in the dark. She recalled the way her mother had sobbed yesterday and she shuddered. Perhaps the dark was a good place to be.

"I don't think he's ever going to stop talking," Trig leaned over to whisper.

Snapped out of her thoughts, Elora chuckled and looked up to see Preacher Woodward pacing back and forth on the altar, delivering an exuberant but utterly boring sermon.

"Hush! That man has ears like a bat" she warned. "And you're sitting next to me. I don't need any more of his attention this morning."

Trig elbowed her good naturedly and then gave a huge sigh of relief as Preacher Woodward finally raised his arms to indicate they should stand for the closing hymn. But before leading them in song he held up his finger to make an announcement.

"It will be my honor to preside over the Binding of our dear Alysa Scott and Trig Davenport next Saturday afternoon. Let us all come to share in their joy. The ceremony will be conducted in the church courtyard at 10 o'clock next Saturday," he said, gesturing toward the courtyard.

There was a murmur among the congregation as people looked at one another, some shaking their heads. The word "Bees" was buzzing in the air like the insect itself.

"There are no bees," he stated emphatically, his annoyance obvious.

Elora leaned over to make eye contact with Alysa.

"Exactly how bad was this bee incident?" she exclaimed in a whisper.

Alysa gave a small smile and shrugged, turning her gaze back toward the preacher as the opening notes of the hymn rang out.

The day was hot and humid. Elora, Alysa and Trig worked diligently in the courtyard, mowing, weeding and trimming the unruly vegetation. Though they started in good cheer, with laughter and lively conversation, after a few hours in the sweltering heat they were exhausted and nothing seemed quite as funny anymore.

"I don't think I can pull one more weed," cried Alysa, collapsing onto one of the old wooden benches that radiated from the center of the courtyard.. "How do you do this every day, Elora?" she asked as she wiped the sweat from her neck.

Elora was on her knees, elbow deep in dirt as she uprooted a dead shrub.

"You get used to it," she said, sitting back on her feet as she wiped her arm across her brow.

She rose and turned back to grab the dead bush she'd just dug up before dragging it to the back of the courtyard and chucking it over the stone fence. Trig had promised to come by later in the week to take care of all the weeds and clippings that they'd piled up back there today. She walked over to lean against the desert willow near Alysa.

"It is particularly hot and miserable today though," Elora admitted.

"Does that mean you won't judge us if we call it quits?" Trig asked, collapsing onto the bench next to Alysa.

"I've been judging you all day, Trig Davenport," retorted Elora jokingly.

"Ordinarily I would have a witty response to that, but I'm just too tired," he replied.

Elora looked around at their progress and smiled. The desert willow had been pruned, the dead bushes had been removed, and the flowerbeds were mostly cleared of weeds. The tall grasses had been cut back, revealing rows of rustic benches in a semi-circle surrounding a trellis beneath which they would conduct the ceremony. It was hardly recognizable as the same space they had entered that morning.

"We did a lot today!" she exclaimed. "I'm feeling really optimistic!"

"Really?" asked Alysa, surveying their handiwork. "It does look a lot neater, but it's still a far cry from what I'd envisioned."

"Yes, really," Elora nodded. "I can definitely get the rest of this weeded by tomorrow. And then I'll start transplanting some of my mother's flowers from our yard."

"Too bad we can't move that gorgeous rosebush," Alysa lamented again.

"I've actually seen quite a few rosebushes in here that might put out a few blooms now that they aren't being strangled by vines. Who knows? I do have a fairly green thumb," Elora said encouragingly.

"So, what you're saying is that we can leave?" asked Trig hopefully.

"Yes," Elora said laughing. "I can take it from here."

"Are you really sure?" Alysa asked skeptically.

"What are you doing, woman?" Trig cried, jumping up with renewed vigor and grabbing Alysa by the hand. "We are nearly free! Don't question it!"

"I'm sure!" Elora shouted, laughing as Trig dragged Alysa toward the courtyard gate.

"You are the best!" exclaimed Alysa. "The absolute best! Thank you!"

"Yep! The best!" agreed Trig, walking backwards for a few strides so he could give Elora a wink and a smile before turning and hurrying though the gate.

Once they were out of view, Elora plopped down onto the bench and sighed. It really was hot and her energy was sapped too. She reached up to rub a kink from the back of her neck and in doing so felt the chain from her necklace.

She tucked her fingers beneath the chain and lifted the necklace from beneath her tunic. The tiny silver fibers in the seed glinted in the bright sunlight. She looked around cautiously to make sure she was unobserved. Confident that she was alone, Elora walked over to one of the spindly, barren rosebushes she'd found smothered in weeds earlier that day. Reaching out, she touched one of the thorny branches.

She thought back to the lavender plant in her bedroom. Just remembering the feelings of being scared hadn't worked. Her ability only seemed to be triggered by a genuine emotional reaction. She needed to focus on something unsettling.

She immediately thought of her parents. Where had they gone today? They were keeping secrets. They had lied to her. But they loved her. Perhaps they were protecting her. She was confused, angry, frightened. But she still loved them more than anything. She felt a lump rise up in her throat and tears prick her eyes.

Her fingertips began to tingle and through the blur of her tears, she saw splotches of yellow burst forth from the branches of the rose bush. She quickly swiped her hand across her eyes to clear her vision and stepped back in awe. She'd done it! The rosebush was suddenly awash in colorful blooms.

"Incredible," she whispered.

Walking to the next rosebush, she reached out her hand and closed her eyes. This time she summoned an image of her best friend standing beside Trig, their arms wrapped in the binding cord, their eyes locked on one another, joy radiating from them like beams of sunshine. Her chest swelled in happiness and she felt a gentle hum flow through her fingers. She opened her eyes to find the rosebush aflame with red blooms.

She moved back to the bench and sat down to consider her work. The rosebushes were gorgeous. They were shockingly beautiful, particularly amongst the drab and bare landscaping of the courtyard. She could make this place beautiful. She could give her friend the breathtaking event she'd dreamed of for her entire life. But it would draw attention to herself. Would people believe that a simple "green thumb" had allowed her to create a botanical masterpiece from an overgrown disaster in only a week? She might be revealing her secret if she did this. But then, did she want to live her life keeping such a secret?

She walked back to one of the unfinished flowerbeds and pulled on her gloves, digging her hands into the earth to pull up the weeds by the roots. A smile played on her lips as she worked. Visions danced in her eyes of the courtyard overflowing with flowers; of Trig and Alysa pledging their vows to one another, enveloped in the beauty of a thousand blooms. She would do this for Alysa. She would do this for herself. She didn't like secrets.

CHAPTER 7

Elora walked home from the courtyard five days later on the eve of the ceremony. Her emotions were waffling on a razor's edge. She was torn between feelings of euphoria and panic. As she approached the rosebush that had been her awakening, she paused to gather her thoughts and calm her fears.

The courtyard was stunning. She'd worked there for hours each evening all week after completing her harvest labor in the fields. She had asked for privacy, calling it her "gift" to the newly bound couple. Everyone had willingly complied, as they were busily preparing for the ceremony themselves. A "No Entrance" sign had been posted at the gate and since the courtyard had long since been abandoned anyway, no one had bothered her. She'd been free to work and experiment in solitude. And she hadn't wasted a moment.

In the hours spent cultivating the courtyard, she had honed her ability. It was no longer a struggle to summon the intensity that was necessary to awaken her gift. She'd discovered that her powers didn't require as much a heightened emotional response, as just a deep and singular focus. Although when that deep focus resulted in an emotional response, her ability became incredibly powerful. It hadn't take very long for Elora to discover that thinking of one thing, one person in particular was the most effective in bringing her ability to life. A man she'd never seen but somehow felt connected to intimately.

She'd spent the past 5 days reliving every vision she'd had of him. Her stomach still flipped as she remembered what it was like hearing his footsteps as he approached her for the first time. Her skin tingled at the memory of his touch. The memory of his voice stole her breath every time. Her heart clenched as she recalled his words over and over again.

"Wait for me, Elora."

She felt foolish to have such a response to something that possibly, probably, wasn't real. But seeing the plants burst forth from the earth and explode into color around her, it hadn't seemed so foolish after all. This was not the world she'd thought she had been living in her entire life. Anything was possible anymore. And oh, how she prayed that he was real, that he was coming for her, that he would be hers. Her hope was in every seedling, her heart in every bloom. The courtyard was a love song to the man in her dreams. And it was magnificent.

In fact, it was conspicuously magnificent. People would talk. Summer was at its end and fall was just around the corner. Most of the flowers had long since withered in Windom. Except in the courtyard. The courtyard which had been abandoned and neglected until only a few days ago. The transformation was nothing short of miraculous. And people would talk. There would be no turning back after tomorrow.

Elora took a deep calming breath and shook her head. This gift was a part of her now. It gave her meaning. It gave her purpose. It made her feel alive. Whatever would happen tomorrow, whatever people may say or think of her, she would not regret using her ability. She had spent her whole life hiding, avoiding attention, shunning the limelight. But she was done with that. To hide her talent would be shameful. She had no intention of shouting about it from the rooftops, but she could not hide it. She would not deny her gift.

She stepped back from the rosebush and turned to continue walking home, but paused as she suddenly had a thought. Reaching out to touch a barren stem on the bush, she closed her eyes and called up the memory of his hand in hers. The now familiar tingling sensation began coursing through her fingers. And then suddenly there was a cool breeze and the feel of his skin was no longer memory. She felt him next to her, his arm brushing against her. He gently slid his hand into hers. She gasped as their fingers intertwined. She was afraid to move, afraid to breathe lest the moment would end. How she wished this would last forever. And yet, it couldn't.

She slowly opened her eyes and he was gone. Before her on the once barren branch was a rose; a vibrant, gorgeous bloom; her love in a flower. She turned and walked slowly down the road, smiling at the thought of Trig stopping on his way to the church in the morning to pluck that flower. The flower that Alysa would wear in her hair.

As she neared her home, Elora was startled to see a man leaving through the front gate. In the fading daylight it was difficult to see him clearly, but he was tall and trim. His hair reached past his shoulders and was tied back at the nape of his neck. His features were concealed by the brim of a hat and the parts of his face that were visible were hidden beneath a thick beard. He seemed to falter momentarily at the sight of her but recovered quickly. Elora's curiosity overwhelmed any semblance of manners and she openly stared as he walked by, subtly nodding his head in acknowledgement as he passed her.

"Elora!"

Her father calling from the doorway jolted her out of her stupor.

"I feel as though I haven't seen you all week!" he exclaimed.

It was true. She hadn't spent more than a few minutes with her parents in the past 5 days. The avoidance had been intentional on her part however. She thought perhaps it had been on purpose for her parents as well, but she couldn't be sure. In spite of everything though, she had missed them.

Elora quickly closed the distance remaining between them and gave him a hug.

"Well, I'm not sure you actually have seen me," she said. "You all came home so late on Sunday and I've been working every spare minute in the courtyard."

"I know. Your mother and I have been busy too. Work is always hectic this time of year. But I am so looking forward to the ceremony tomorrow. I'm sure everything will be beautiful, sweetheart," he said. "Especially you."

"Alysa has made me quite the dress, so you just may be right," Elora laughed.

"You would be beautiful in a potato sack, Elora," Jonas Kerrick said, shaking his head.

"Said like a true father," she replied, hugging him once more.

"Are you hungry, honey?" her mother asked, coming around the counter to enfold her in a hug as well.

She was actually famished. She hadn't been home in time for dinner all week and her stomach growled audibly at the smell of a warm, home-cooked meal.

"I'll take that as a yes," her mother laughed, patting Elora's rumbling belly before turning to make her a plate of supper.

Elora bent to take off her work boots by the door.

"Who was that leaving just now?" she asked, looking up at her father.

She noticed a furtive glance pass between her parents before he answered.

"No one special," he replied. "Just a man new to town and looking for work. It's a good thing too. The South wall is crumbling in a few areas and we really need the help."

Elora nodded and looked down as she untied her laces. He was lying. She could tell. It was a convincing lie though. Her father managed construction and maintenance of the town facilities and the South Wall truly was in bad shape. But no one had ever come to their home in search of a job before, especially so late in the evening. What really gave him away though was the look that had passed between her parents. Considering they'd been hiding the truth from her for the entirety of her existence, it was surprising how terrible they were at lying.

Elora made her way to the bathroom to wash her hands and run a wet cloth over her face and neck. She was greeted by an awkward silence upon her return, disrupted only by the sound of her mother setting out a plate full of food on the table. Elora took a seat and smiled appreciatively at her. Her appetite wasn't what it had been a few minutes ago. She lifted a forkful of food to her lips and chewed slowly as the quiet stretched uncomfortably between them.

At last her father cleared his throat.

"I'm sorry, honey. I'm so tired. I think I'm going to turn in," he said, rising from his seat on the sofa.

"I think I'll join him," her mother said soon after. "I want to be well rested for tomorrow's celebration!" she gushed with forced enthusiasm.

Elora nodded and smiled at them as they retreated to their bedroom. She let out a disheartened sigh as their door clicked closed. This was miserable. They had run away to hide. They had been uncomfortable blatantly lying to her.

"That should count for something at least," she mused.

She sat quietly picking at her food, weighted down by the thoughts swirling around in her head.

"Who was that man really? Why did they lie about him?"

"What would her parents think when they saw the courtyard?"

"What would happen tomorrow?"

Her dinner turned cold before her, forgotten in the fog of worry, confusion, and exhaustion. She finally stood, carrying her dishes into the kitchen where she scraped the remains of her meal into the compost bucket. She washed her plate and put it away before heading to her own room. Giving one last glance at her parents' closed door, she turned and closed her own.

Too exhausted for a bath, Elora shed her dirty work clothes into a pile on the floor, trading them for the nightgown she'd left draped across the footboard that morning. She pulled back the sheet and was about to climb into bed when she remembered her necklace. Reaching up, she undid the clasp and gently gathered it in the palm of her hand.

The seed glinted in the light of her bedside lantern as she lifted it for a closer look. The silver strands that were embedded in the grooves of the seed had multiplied and spread during the course of the week. She had no doubt that this seed and her gift were related. The more she used her ability, the more the seed changed. The two were linked somehow. She closed her hand around the necklace and let out a deep sigh. How she wished she understood any of this. She pulled open the top drawer in her dresser and wrapped the necklace in a handkerchief before tucking it beneath a stack of underclothes.

Elora extinguished the lantern and climbed into bed, pulling the sheet up to her chin. She stared up at the ceiling as her eyes adjusted to the darkness and troubling thoughts churned in her head. She struggled to squelch her negative feelings and focused instead on an image of Alysa and Trig with their arms bound together, eyes locked on one another, joy written on every feature of their faces. Tomorrow was not about her. Tomorrow was about them. It would be a good day.

"Rise and shine Elora!"

Trig's boisterous voice pierced through the fog of her slumber and she jolted up, sitting amongst her covers and looking around in bemusement. She rubbed the sleep from her eyes and gathered her senses.

"Trig?" she asked confused.

"I'm out here," he called from outside the flap of her bedroom window. "I didn't want to wake up everybody just to get your lazy bones out of bed."

"It's barely sun up, Trig!" she exclaimed in irritation.

"I know," he said apologetically. "But my betrothed asked for me to fetch you on my way to her house this morning, and I'm not about to disappoint her today."

"Oh my gosh! How long does it take to put a dress on?" Elora groaned, falling back onto her pillow.

"Apparently it takes 4 hours," Trig replied bluntly.

"Considering it's Alysa, that actually sounds about right," Elora admitted with a chuckle. "Alright. Give me a minute," she called out.

She quickly pulled on trousers and a tunic, slid on her work boots, and tied her hair back into a messy bun. She didn't even glance in the mirror before slipping out of her bedroom and through the front door.

Trig gave out a low whistle upon seeing her.

"Looking stunning this morning Ms. Kerrick," he teased.

"Be quiet, you," she fussed. "If I'm going to be 'getting dressed' for 4 hours at Alysa's house, this is what she gets to start with."

"Fair enough," he conceded. "Shall we?" he asked, crooking his arm to escort her.

"We shall," she smiled, grasping his arm as he led them through the front gate.

They walked in amicable silence, enjoying the peacefulness of the morning. It was already warm despite the early hour and promised to be another hot day. The sun was quickly rising, burning off whatever remained of the morning dew as it turned the sky lovely hues of pink and orange.

"Thank you, Elora," Trig said earnestly, patting the hand that she had tucked in his elbow. "Thank you for being her Witness. Thank you for transforming the courtyard. Thank you for opening my eyes. Thank you for being such a true friend to both us. Just thank you. I can never repay you for the happiness you have brought into my life."

Elora couldn't squeeze any words past the lump in her throat. She looked up at him with tears in her eyes and smiled, placing her hand over his.

He shook his head in understanding, grunting to clear the emotion from his voice.

"Do you think there is one last rose left on that rosebush?" he asked. "I owe her a rose for today."

Elora nodded and then turned her head abruptly as a man entered the road ahead coming from the direction of the stables. Her eyes widened as he came close enough to make out his features. She had never seen him before. He was tall and trim, dressed in tan trousers and a clean but well-worn white button down shirt. His dark blond hair was cut short and his face was clean shaven. His eyes were downturned as he walked at a determined clip. Elora could feel her heartbeat quicken as he neared them. Suddenly he lifted his head and his eyes locked onto Elora's. They were light blue with a hint of green, like pools of water. She sucked in a breath involuntarily. Her brain seemed to stop working entirely. He was gorgeous.

His eyes widened slightly as though he seemed to recognize Elora. He held her gaze unwaveringly as he passed within a few feet of her, and nodded in greeting. She was vaguely aware that Trig had nodded back in reply. She had been incapable of reacting, completely stunned by her attraction to him.

"I'm betting you wished you'd primped a bit more this morning right about now," Trig teased, nudging her with his elbow after the man had passed out of earshot.

"What?" she asked, shaking her head in an attempt to restore brain function.

"That guy was a looker. If I hadn't already won over my Alysa, I'd be a bit panicked. Especially considering the affect he had on you," he said, chuckling.

"What are you talking about?" Elora mumbled, her cheeks flushing bright pink in embarrassment.

"I've never seen you so gob smacked, Elora. I think you might have even drooled a bit," he joked, leaning down to inspect her chin.

Elora shoved him away laughing.

"Oh stop it!" she cried, reaching up to touch her messy bun before cringing. "Am I a mess, really?"

"You didn't even look in a mirror before you came out of the house, did you?" Trig said, shaking his head with a smile. "How on earth are you and Alysa best friends?" he mused.

"We balance each other," she replied, shrugging. "So, you're saying I'm a total mess then," she said with a groan. "The most attractive man I've ever seen in my life walks by and I'm a disaster. I have such amazing luck."

"Hey! Don't say that," he said defensively. "It's not true. You've seen me nearly every day of your life."

"Oh my gosh, Trig! How is Alysa going to survive your terrible sense of humor?" she asked, looking heavenward in exasperation.

"First off, she loves my sense of humor. Second, I wasn't kidding. And third, you aren't a disaster."

He looked at her earnestly.

"You do look a little rough around the edges this morning, but it's really hard to hide your particular kind of pretty, Elora. I mean, you could be covered in mud and still somehow be attractive. Come to think of it, you usually *are* covered in mud," he said, his eyebrows raising wryly as he chuckled.

Elora punched his shoulder in mock outrage, but she couldn't help laughing because it was largely true.

"Thank you, I think," she said with a chuckle.

"Kidding aside, that guy couldn't take his eyes off you," he said encouragingly.

"Are you sure he wasn't like, staring in disgust?" she asked.

"Nope. I think I might have seen a little drool on his end too," he said.

Elora couldn't help but grin at the thought that there might have been a mutual attraction. She wondered if he would be at the ceremony. Suddenly primping for the next four hours didn't seem like such a bad idea.

They walked quietly for a few minutes while Elora replayed the moment in her head. That man was truly the handsomest thing she'd ever seen. Where had he come from? Why was he here? Oh, how she hoped she would see him again. Perhaps at a time when she had put forth a little more effort to look nice. She tucked some loose hairs behind her ear, thinking about how wild she must look this morning.

"I'm not really sure I believe you, Trig Davenport. I think my 'kind of pretty' is rather well hidden this morning," she lamented. "Alysa would never have left the house in this condition. Hence her stack of proposals."

"Let's not mention those," Trig muttered. "I adore Alysa and think she's the most beautiful creature on earth, as you well know," he explained.

Elora nodded and was about to voice her agreement when Trig held up his hand to quiet her.

"But," he continued, "you have a natural and earthy beauty about you Elora. Your kind of pretty is subtle and unrefined. You are pretty without even trying and apparently without even knowing."

Elora tucked her head to hide the blush his words had elicited.

"Don't compare yourself to Alysa. She is like a rose. You are like a wildflower. Both are beautiful in their own way. And that guy back there REALLY seemed to like wildflowers," he said, nudging her with his shoulder.

"Thank you Trig," she smiled as her heart swelled with newfound confidence. "Speaking of roses..."

They had rounded the corner and Elora's rosebush came into view.

"Oh wow," Trig whispered. "It's perfect."

He jogged forward and cupped the perfect bloom that had appeared the night before. He looked up at Elora with happiness and excitement in his eyes.

"It's almost as if the bush grew this rose just for her" he remarked.

Elora smiled and nodded.

"Perhaps it did," she whispered.

Trig laughed with joy as he pulled out his knife and cut the stem. He sliced off the thorns and gently twirled the flower between his fingers.

"Incredible," he said softly.

"A rose for your rose," Elora smiled.

"A rose for my rose," he agreed.

CHAPTER 8

Elora smiled at Alysa's reflection in the mirror as she tenderly tucked the rose into the tangled braids of her intricate updo. It had taken Elora nearly an hour to plait and arrange Alysa's thick dark hair just so. And another half hour to help her don the incredible dress her mother had sewn. Elora couldn't help but laugh at the number of buttons. Trig was sure to appreciate that. But looking at her dear friend, Elora could hardly breathe.

"You are the loveliest thing I've ever seen," she whispered.

"Don't make me cry," Alysa warned, shaking a finger at Elora.

"No! No crying. At least not yet," Elora teased, winking at her. "There's just no way either of us will make it through this ceremony without tears."

Alysa turned away from the full-length mirror and held up a hand mirror to see the reflection of her back. She touched her updo gently, admiring the rose in her hair.

"It's perfect," she breathed.

"It really is," Elora agreed.

Alysa set down the mirror, took a deep breath and smoothed her hands over the dress. "I'm ready. Is it time yet?" she asked anxiously.

"No, thank goodness," Elora said, chuckling as she looked down at the white bathing robe she still wore.

"Why? Oh!" Alysa's hand flew to her mouth. "Well, get dressed already!" she cried, laughing.

"It will only take a minute, don't worry. There's only the one button after all," Elora joked as she retreated behind the screen. "My husband will be grateful for that someday. I can't say the same for yours though! I think Trig might hold a grudge against your mother for that dress."

"There *are* an awful lot of buttons," she agreed. "I do happen to be an expert seamstress though. I can always sew them back on should the challenge be too frustrating for him," she giggled.

Elora stuck her head back around the screen with her mouth agape.

"Alysa! I never imagined such a scandalous thing would ever come from your lips!" she cried.

"Well, there are a lot of buttons!" she cried in self-defense, a blush rising up her cheeks.

Elora let out a gasp of surprise and collapsed into a fit of laughter.

"Oh Alysa," she said, wiping at the tears her laughter had wrought. "I will remember this moment forever! This day is just the best."

"It really is the best," Alysa agreed, a smile stretching across her face.

Elora came back around the screen wearing the beautiful dress Alysa had made for her. She slipped her feet into the delicate slippers Alysa had loaned her since she had none that were suitable. She walked over to the mirror to admire her reflection. Alysa came up behind her to fasten the single button at the base of her neck.

"You truly are gifted," Elora said softly as she fingered the intricate embroidery on her skirt.

"Wait! There's one more thing!" Alysa cried, walking out to the front hall.

She came back quickly clutching a small bouquet of wildflowers.

"Trig left these for you to wear in your hair," she said, holding up the flowers.

Elora smiled and a hint of tears glistened in her eyes.

"He's quite a person, you know," she said. "I don't think anyone else could deserve you."

"I know," Alysa said, smiling at Elora's reflection in the mirror as she began tucking the flowers amongst the chestnut braids of her loose updo. "There. Now you are perfect too."

Elora turned and wrapped her friend in a hug. "Thank you for letting me be a part of this special day."

"I couldn't imagine it without you," Alysa smiled. "Now, it probably really is time to go! I need to get my binding cord and then we can head over to the courtyard," she called over her shoulder as she hurried to retrieve the cord from another room.

While she was gone, Elora picked up the hand mirror and held it up to see the reflection of her back in the full-length mirror. She was touched by Trig's gesture and wanted to see the wildflowers in her hair. She smiled at the sight of them. They suited her. But as her eyes moved down her reflection, the smile slid from her mouth. She sucked in a startled breath.

Her birthmark had changed drastically. It no longer resembled a small brown seed. There was now a thin line extending from the seed several inches up her spine with what looked like a few delicate little branches extending from either side. It almost looked as though the seed were sprouting. She rubbed her eyes and blinked, trying to clear her vision. It couldn't be. It was impossible. Her birthmark had transformed. There was no denying it.

The markings were exquisite. They were beautiful. Elora stared at them, mesmerized with awe but also paralyzed with fear. How could she go out in public like this? Her heartbeat began thudding in her ears and she had to remind herself to breathe. What could she do?

Alysa hadn't said a word about it. It was impossible to miss and yet she hadn't noticed. Just as before, she still couldn't see it.

"It's invisible," Elora reassured herself. "No one can see it. Pretend it isn't there."

She could feel the panic welling up. Her breathing was rapid and uncontrolled, leaving her lightheaded. She was going to be sick. Putting down the mirror, she placed a hand over her stomach to try to quell a sudden surge of nausea. She looked around desperately for a solution, anxiously rubbing her forehead as she frantically searched the room. She could hear Alysa's footsteps as she came down the stairs.

Suddenly her eyes fell upon a scrap of white satin draped across the dress form in the corner of the room. Salvation! She rushed across the room, pulling the scrap free and held it up. It was a rectangle of fabric, simple and sheer, but long enough to serve as a wrap.

"This could work!" she thought, as relief washed over her.

She hastily pulled it across her back and draped it over her elbows. Then she ran over to the mirror and turned to see how effectively it covered her birthmark. It wasn't perfect but it definitely would obstruct anyone's view. She took a calming breath and tried to regain her composure before Alysa walked into the room.

"Smile. Breathe. Everything is fine," she silently told herself.

"Ready?" Alysa called out before stepping through the doorway, her binding cord looped around her hand.

"Yes. Yep! Ready," Elora replied with perhaps a bit too much enthusiasm.

The smile faded from Alysa's lips as she took in Elora's appearance and her eyes focused on the fabric covering her like a shawl.

"Oh Elora. Really? Are you truly that shy?" Alysa asked, the disappointment obvious in her voice.

"The dress is so beautiful Alysa," Elora gushed, trying to placate her. "I love that you are daring in your designs. Please, please forgive me. I'm just not quite daring enough to wear this one yet."

"Oh, it's alright. I knew when I was making it that it might be a little too much of a stretch for you. I want you to be comfortable. The satin is actually a really nice solution. And the dress is still lovely on you," Alysa conceded, wrapping an arm around Elora's shoulders.

"Thank you. Please don't be offended," Elora beseeched her as she turned to embrace her fully.

"Nothing is going to offend me today. Especially not you," Alysa replied.

Stepping back from the hug, she held up the cord for Elora to see.

"As my Witness, it's your job to hold onto this until Preacher Woodward asks for it," she said, handing it over.

Elora took the cord, admiring how creative and talented Alysa was.

"It's perfect. If you were a cord, this would be you," she said with a giggle, tucking it into the small satchel tied at her waist.

"Well, I tried. It's harder than you'd think. I can't wait to see what Trig came up with. Creativity isn't his forte," she said, laughing. "Now let's go see what you've done with that courtyard and get this binding ceremony done!"

"Okay," Elora said, smiling despite the sick feeling in the pit of her stomach.

"It's the start of my new life!" Alysa cried happily, and squealed in excitement.

"I hope I feel like that when it's my turn," Elora laughed.

"I certainly hope so! Everyone should!" Alysa replied as she grabbed Elora's hand and started pulling her toward the door enthusiastically.

Elora chuckled and followed. But she glanced over her should once more into the mirror at her birthmark as they left the room.

Alysa and Elora could hear the hum of a crowd inside the courtyard as they approached.

"It sounds like the entire town showed up!" Elora remarked.

"It really does," Alysa agreed nervously. "Would people think badly of me if I just sprinted up the aisle? It's stressing me out to think of all those eyes on me."

"People would definitely talk about it. But I'm in complete agreement about making this a speedy walk," Elora said, nodding.

"Just make sure you keep up," Alysa said, laughing.

They reached the gate and stopped at the entrance. Preacher Woodward noticed them from where he stood near the trellis in the center of the courtyard. The crowd went silent as he lifted his hands to mark the beginning of the ceremony. Trig and his older brother Nate, who was standing as his witness, both moved to stand next to the preacher. It seemed as if nearly the entire town truly had turned out for the ceremony, and they all shifted to watch the two girls process down the aisle.

"Running sounds like a really good idea, actually," Elora whispered, as she got a good look at just how full the courtyard was.

When Alysa didn't answer, Elora turned to find her gazing in awe at the courtyard, tears glistening in her eyes.

"Oh, Elora," Alysa sighed reverently. "I have no words."

The courtyard was overflowing with flowers. Every bed was awash in color, filled with roses, and hydrangeas, azaleas and rhododendrons. The preacher was standing at the front of the courtyard beneath a trellis that was dripping with purple wisteria blooms. Huge white lilies were planted at the end of each bench and a carpet of tiny pale blue flowers filled the gaps between the large stones of the walkway. It was breathtaking.

"Is it what you had imagined?" Elora asked, please by her reaction.

"It is so much more. So much more. I don't know how you did it! Thank you," she said wiping the tears from her eyes and wrapping Elora in a hug.

At that moment, Danny Jenkins played the opening cords of the traditional Binding Hymn on his guitar. Alysa pulled herself away, wiped her eyes once more and centered herself on the walkway. Clasping her hands in front of her, she took an encouraging breath, and stepped into the courtyard. Keeping her eyes locked on Trig, she took steady, measured steps in cadence with the song.

"So, no running then?" Elora whispered.

She heard a low chuckle from Alysa and smiled to herself as the congregation began to sing.

Dear Holy Father, to You we lift our song
We will sing Your praises our whole life long.

Elora clasped her hands and mirrored Alysa's steps a few paces behind her. She focused on the rose in Alysa's hair and attempted to ignore the hundreds of eyes that were watching her every move.

In Your wisdom, You have made us to be paired
In Your mercy, You have given us a love to be shared

A little past halfway down the aisle though, a hand reached out to touch Elora's elbow and she looked over to see her parents beaming at her. As she smiled back at them she stepped forward and the person sitting beside her father came into view. She drew in a breath as she recognized the man from the road earlier that morning. They locked eyes once again and he smiled. It felt as if her heart had stopped for a moment. She wasn't sure if she smiled back or not, she was so flustered. She nearly fell out of step with Alysa but jerked her gaze away and quickly recovered.

Two hearts You bind together to weather the unknown,
Two become one, for we're not meant to live alone.

As the end of the last verse hummed in the air, Alysa reached the trellis and took her place beside Trig. The smile they shared brought a lump to Elora's throat as she walked the few remaining steps to stand behind Alysa. The procession over, a gentle creaking filled the air as the congregation took their seats on the worn wooden benches. Preacher Woodward lifted his hands to begin the ceremony, welcoming the town to the joyous occasion and asking all those in attendance to bow their heads in a prayer for the couple.

Out of the corner of her eye Elora spotted Trig's young niece break free of her mother's arms and come toddling quickly toward them. Her eyes were locked on the beautiful lace train of Alysa's gown and her clumsy little hands were reaching out to take hold of it. Elora moved swiftly to intercept the child, scooping her up into her arms and onto her hip. She smiled and held a finger to her lips, trying to put the little girl at ease and remind her to be quiet. Elora quickly carried her back to her mother, who smiled gratefully as she took the baby.

No one seemed the wiser of the incident as nearly everyone had their head bowed in prayer. But as Elora turned to retake her position beside Alysa, she heard a gasp from behind her. She looked over her shoulder to see the handsome stranger on his feet, a shocked expression on his face, his gaze locked on her lower back. Her parents on the bench beside him were both wide eyed, their mouths slack. She realized that her wrap had slipped in the commotion and she hurried to adjust it. His eyes darted to hers and she quickly looked away, taking a few hasty steps to return to her place near the trellis. She looked around anxiously, trying to gauge who had seen the markings on her back. No one was looking at her, thank goodness. The congregation was instead staring with concern at the young man.

"Did he see a bee?" someone whispered loudly.

Suddenly the entire congregation was murmuring and looking around uneasily. Elora cautioned another glance at the young man. He was no longer staring at her, but was nervously scanning the crowd, obviously uncomfortable in the spotlight.

"Everything alright, young man?" Preacher Woodward asked.

"Yes, yes," he replied. "I just thought I saw a b—" he started, but as Elora began furiously shaking her head, he locked eyes with her and stopped short. "A wasp. I thought I saw a wasp, but it's gone now." He took his seat again, but his eyes remained on Elora. She gave him a weak smile and sighed in relief.

The crowd stilled and refocused on the ceremony at hand. Elora turned back toward Preacher Woodward, attempting to listen as he spoke to Alysa and Trig about the blessings and challenges of living life with and for one another. He spoke of the permanence and significance of being bound. It was beautiful, what little she actually heard through the torrent of thoughts and emotions swirling around her brain.

She remained acutely aware of the stranger among them and glanced over her shoulder a number of times to find his eyes on her. Obviously, he had seen the markings on her back. But he was neither disgusted nor frightened by them. He seemed to be in awe of them, as though he understood them, as though they meant something good. And the intensity of his reaction to seeing them was both thrilling and terrifying.

"And now, let us witness as these two people choose to bind themselves to one another. Do you have your cords?" Preacher Woodward asked, holding out his hand.

Elora snapped out of her reverie and fumbled to retrieve the cord from the small pouch tied to her waist. Gently, she pulled out the beautiful cord Alysa had entrusted to her. It was elegant and elaborate, consisting of bits of lace, intricately embroidered ribbons, and delicate white strips of satin from her dress all lovingly woven together in a representation of herself. Elora stepped forward and placed it in the preacher's outstretched hand.

Similarly, Nate placed Trig's contribution to the binding cord into the Preacher's hand. His was masculine in appearance and somewhat clumsily woven together, though obviously made with great care. Elora smiled as she looked at the cords and thought how beautifully they symbolized her friends.

Preacher Woodward reached into his own satchel, pulling out a simple twine woven of golden threads. He placed the golden thread between the cords in his hand and knotted them together.

"Elora, if you please," he said, holding up the knot for her to hold. She stepped beside him and took hold of the knotted end. He then began to speak as he wove the strands together.

"Both Alysa and Trig come to this union as whole people unto themselves. They have strengths and weaknesses and are capable of living a life of their own. This is represented by the cords they have created to symbolize themselves. Alysa has created something beautiful, but delicate," he smiled at Alysa. "Trig's cord is made of strong stuff, but is perhaps not as pleasing to look at," he said with a chuckle that spread throughout the congregation. "Alone, these cords are useful and complete. They are enough. But God intended more for Alysa and Trig. He brought them together to create something new, something greater and better than it was before. As their cords combine to create a rope that is stronger, fuller, and more beautiful, so they too will unite to form a life in which burdens will be shared and joys will be multiplied. In the midst of this union is a gold cord, which represents our merciful and loving God. And as this gold thread helps to bind their cords, so God will help bind them together. Their promise to God will stand firm should their promise to each other weaken. And so this gold thread will strengthen this cord through adversity. And as this gold thread magnifies the beauty of the cord, so will God bless the union of Trig and Alysa."

Elora couldn't help the tears that trickled from her eyes as she watched and listened to the beautiful symbolism playing out before her.

"Trig and Alysa, face one another and join hands," he said as he tied the final knot in their binding cord.

Alysa and Trig turned to one another, their eyes locked, radiant smiles on their lips. Trig reached out and took her hand, raising it to his lips for a brief kiss before turning his attention back to the ceremony.

Preacher Woodward draped the cord over their clasped hands. "Let us hear the vows you have prepared as you bind yourselves to one another from this day forward." He stepped back and looked toward Alysa, prompting her to go first.

"Trig, I have loved you and will love you my whole life," she said, softly but clearly as she slowly wound the cord around her hand and wrist. "I promise to bring you joy, to share in your sorrow, to be your comfort. I will be your companion, your friend, your partner, your love, no matter what life may bring. I am yours and you are mine, praise be to God."

As she completed her vow, she finished wrapping the cord around her forearm and looked up at Trig, who was beaming, his eyes glistening. Now his turn, Trig cleared his throat and took a settling breath before taking hold of the opposite end of the cord. He slowly began winding it around his arm.

"Alysa, I can't ever imagine being worthy of your love but I intend to spend the rest of my life trying to deserve it," he said, his voice thick. "I will cherish you, protect you, encourage you and support you. I promise with everything I am to love you and our children, may there be many," he winked slyly at her and Alysa couldn't help but laugh through her happy tears. He wrapped the cord once more as he looked solemnly in her eyes and said, "I am yours and you are mine, praise be to God."

Preacher Woodward stepped forward again and raised his hands.

"It is my great pleasure to announce the union of Alysa and Trig Davenport as they have bound themselves to one another on this day before God and these witnesses. Let us all rejoice as they celebrate the beginning of their new life together," he cried out, his voice exuberant.

The congregation rose to their feet, clapping and cheering in genuine happiness. Alysa laughed as she wiped the tears from her eyes. Still bound together by their cord, Trig wrapped his free hand around the nape of her neck and pulled her in for a sweet and lingering kiss.

Elora clapped and laughed with joy, completely abandoning any effort to stem the tears that were flowing freely down her cheeks. It had been more beautiful and romantic than she could ever have imagined. She was completely lost in the emotions of the moment until she happened to glance at her parents and the handsome stranger. They had ceased clapping and were staring, mesmerized by something behind her. She turned in time to see a new wisteria blossom cascade into bloom on the trellis near where she was standing. Her hand flew to her mouth in horror and she quickly looked around to see if anyone else had noticed. Thankfully everyone seemed to be enchanted by the young couple. Alysa was laughingly pushing away Trig as he stole a few more kisses from his new wife.

"Calm down. Breathe. Be in control," she thought, closing her eyes and focusing on slowing her heart and quieting her thoughts.

She opened her eyes and unconsciously sought out the gaze of the handsome stranger. He was watching her, a small smile dancing on his lips and excitement in his eyes. She cocked her head to the side, struck by his unexpected reaction. Looking over at her parents, she saw an unmistakable expression of pride on her father's face. Her mother, however, was biting her lip in an attempt to keep it from trembling and her eyes were glistening with the tears she was holding back.

At that moment, Trig and Alysa began to walk back down the aisle, their joined hands lifted triumphantly into the air eliciting another uproarious cheer from the congregation. Elora looked away from her parents just in time to see Nate step towards her and hold out his arm. She smiled as she took hold of his elbow and allowed him to escort her down the aisle behind the happy couple.

Their exit was not nearly as formal as their entrance, with people reaching out to touch and embrace them as they moved. Everyone was exuberant and joyful after having watched the emotional ceremony. The townspeople were enchanted with the newly bound couple and couldn't wait to express their excitement. But Trig hadn't given anyone a chance, charging down the aisle with a giggling Alysa in tow. His brother Nate, however, politely meandered down the aisle at a respectable gate. He and Elora smiled and acknowledged the kind comments that were showered upon them as they walked. She was uncomfortable with the attention and quickly grew impatient with their slow progression. Especially once she lost sight of her parents and the handsome young stranger.

Elora smiled awkwardly as yet another person touched her arm and remarked on her beautiful dress and how lovely everything had been. Her attention was suddenly diverted as she caught sight of something bizarre from the corner of her eye. The large bush that topped the wall in the corner of the courtyard was rustling vigorously. As Elora watched, a young man with long blond hair stepped out from the bush, briefly made eye contact with her, and then jumped down to the other side of the wall.

She froze, her eyes wide with alarm as she instantly recognized the man. It was the same one who had been in the market, the one she suspected had been following her. She hadn't seen him since the encounter a week ago that had resulted in a rosebush. She had hoped that perhaps she wouldn't see him again. But apparently, he was still here and still watching her.

She was jolted out of her shock by a gentle tug from Nate. He was looked at her concerned and followed her gaze up to the courtyard wall where the man had been hiding.

"Are you alright?" he asked, kindly.

"Yes. Yes," she said, trying to recover her wits. "Can we just hurry a bit?" she smiled.

"Of course! Just hang on," he said with a mischievous grin reminiscent of Trig.

He tucked her arm snuggly in his elbow, plastered a smile onto his face, and started taking big bold steps down the aisle. The people receded back out of the walkway as it became apparent that Nate was moving with purpose. Elora smiled, relieved to be escaping the scrutiny of the crowd. But while the seemingly endless throng of well-wishers had felt smothering, she also worried that her stalker was lurking beyond the courtyard wall. She held tight to Nate, taking some comfort in knowing that people were nearby who cared for her and would protect her.

"What could that man want with me?" she asked herself.

She thought back to her first encounter with him. She'd seen him working for the Highlander in the market. She gasped as the epiphany struck her. It was the seed. Her ability, her birthmark, being followed; everything started changing for her after she'd purchased the seed necklace from the Highlander.

"He knows! He knows something," she thought. "I have to find him."

As they at last stepped through the courtyard gate to the quiet and empty area beyond the wall, she began looking around eagerly to find him. She ran to the corner of the courtyard where he had jumped down but there was no one. He'd disappeared. Disappointed, she walked back toward the gate where Nate stood with his hands in his pockets, watching her curiously.

At his raised eyebrows, she shrugged sheepishly and said, "I thought I saw something."

At that moment, the handsome stranger came bursting through the gate, crashing into Elora. They both stumbled, but while he managed to regain his footing, Elora's skirts became tangled around her legs and she began to fall. With surprisingly quick reflexes, he reached out to catch her arm and pulled her up against him. She had no time to react, slamming into his chest with a yelp. He held her shoulders for a moment to steady her as she caught her breath and regained her balance. Startled by the sudden impact, and then flustered by his close proximity, Elora couldn't seem to remember how to speak. But before she could find her voice, he released her and took off around the corner of the courtyard.

"He must have seen the same thing," Nate mused aloud. "Are you okay?"

"Yeah, just a little stunned," Elora said with a forced chuckle, looking in the direction where the man had disappeared.

She was so confused. She had so many questions about what was happening and who those two men were.

Something strange was going on and she was clearly a part of it, but she had no idea why or how. It was both frightening and annoying. She pursed her lips in frustration.

"So, what is supposed to happen now?" Nate asked, peeking back into the courtyard at the crowd milling around inside.

Elora shook her head to mentally clear away the distractions and refocus on the celebration at hand. She took a deep breath and turned her attention to Nate.

"Trig didn't tell you anything, did he?" she said with a laugh.

"He told me what time to show up!" Nate replied in mock defense of his brother.

"Well, I suppose that was the singularly most important detail," she admitted with a laugh. "The reception comes next and it's supposed to be inside the church. I wonder why people aren't making their way in there yet."

"Oh, I know why," Nate replied bluntly. "It's amazing in there. Did you see all those flowers?" he said, looking back through the gate appreciatively. "I can't say I blame them for sticking around to get a closer look at everything."

Elora looked down to hide her blush, grateful that Nate wasn't aware that she was responsible for cultivating the courtyard.

"Alysa said there will be all kinds of delicious treats to eat," she said, changing topics as quickly as possible.

"Yes, my wife has been baking all week for this," he said, nodding as he leaned back against the courtyard wall.

"I am so happy to hear that!" Elora said as she rubbed her hands together excitedly. "Amber makes the most delicious cookies."

"Her baking skills were definitely one of my top reasons for proposing to her," he said, with a grin. "I want to thank you, by the way, for catching our little munchkin in there before she made a spectacle of herself and embarrassed her mother."

"Don't mention it. She's adorable," Elora gushed.

"Yeah. She takes after Amber in that," he said with a fond smile. "So, when do we get to go inside? I'm hungry and like you said, my wife's cookies are in there."

"We're supposed to wait until everyone is inside and has a chance to get a cup of wine. Then we announce the newly bound couple, they make a grand entrance, and everyone raises their drink in celebration," Elora said, holding up a pretend cup of wine in a mock toast. "Hey, speaking of the newly bound couple..." she said looking around.

"They are taking advantage of a quiet moment and a large bush," Nate said with a grin, nodding his head toward the part of the courtyard wall that adjoined the church.

Elora moved closer to the wall to see beyond the thick brush that obscured her view. A fleeting glance revealed that Trig had Alysa pressed against the wall and the two were kissing passionately.

Elora giggled and quickly looked away.

"Good for them," she laughed.

"No use wasting time," Nate chuckled.

His expression suddenly turned serious and he straightened from his position against the wall.

"Wait, so what you're telling me is that all these people have to go inside before we can eat?" he asked incredulously. At Elora's nod, he cried "Do they know that?"

"I don't know. Did Preacher Woodward make an announcement before the ceremony?" Elora asked.

"I don't remember. And apparently, nobody else does either," he said indignantly. "I'm going to fix that."

"You do that!" she encouraged. "Your wife's cookies await!" she said, laughing.

Nate pulled his hands out of his pockets and marched back through the gate and up the aisle to make his announcement. Elora took a step closer and peered down the aisle in amusement. She watched as Nate approached the front of the courtyard, stopping to scoop up his daughter and kiss his wife along the way. Elora couldn't help but smile at the happy little family.

"So, do the good people of Windom have a problem with bees?" said a deep voice from behind her.

CHAPTER 9

Elora jumped and spun around to find the handsome stranger standing a few feet away, a teasing smile on his face. She hadn't heard him approach and, as seemed to be the case whenever he was nearby, she was struck momentarily dumb.

He stood casually relaxed, his hands tucked in the pockets of his pants, his shirt sleeves rolled up to reveal his muscular forearms. He was lean, but muscular, and the fabric of his shirt draped across his broad shoulders in a way that made her heart race. She closed her eyes briefly, utterly intimidated by how beautiful he was, before working up the courage to make eye contact. Because he was a good head taller than she was, she had to look up to meet his gaze. When she finally raised her eyes to his, she found him watching her expectantly, awaiting an answer. She had no choice but to pull herself together. She shook her head in an attempt to regain her wits and took a composing breath, smiling bashfully.

"A few years ago this courtyard was the site of a traumatizing bee experience," she said, turning to look into the courtyard. "I wasn't there to witness it," she shrugged, "but clearly it left an impression on people."

"Clearly," he said, chuckling. "I thought they were all going to stampede."

He had an accent she couldn't place, which meant he must have traveled quite a ways to reach Windom. Impossibly, this somehow made him even more attractive.

"I think they probably would have if you'd actually seen one," she said, smiling as she cautioned another look at his face.

"It's a good thing I saw a wasp, then," he said gently, holding her gaze.

He was giving her an opening. Should she acknowledge the real reason behind his outburst during the ceremony? Elora stared into his eyes, unmoving for a moment as she considered her next words. This man was a stranger to her. He seemed to be aware of what was happening to her, of her birthmark, of her ability, even of the man who had been following her. She was desperate for the answers that he might have. But was she so desperate that she would reveal her secrets to a stranger? Whatever he may know, she couldn't trust him. Not yet anyway.

"I'm glad it didn't sting you," she said softly, her eyes still locked with his, her expression serious.

He watched her silently for a few seconds, perhaps a bit disappointed. But then his face relaxed into a smile and he chuckled.

"Me too," he replied.

Just then Nate's booming voice echoed through the courtyard.

"Attention good people," he said enthusiastically. "Please make your way inside the church where we will celebrate the newly bound couple with food and drink."

Guests were shockingly quick to comply. Elora looked up and found herself suddenly in the path of a swiftly moving crowd. Surprised, she couldn't move out of the way fast enough. Thankfully, the handsome stranger grabbed her hand and tugged her towards him just in time to avoid the rush of people. The movement was so abrupt that Elora lost her balance for a moment and instinctively placed a hand against his chest to steady herself. Embarrassed and awkward, she quickly removed her hand, laughing as she put some space between them.

"Thank you. You've caught me twice today and I still don't even know your name," she said, smiling shyly up at him.

"Well, the first time was entirely my fault, so don't thank me for that. I'm sorry for barreling into you like that," he said wincing.

"It's alright. I seem to have a habit of blocking the gate," she replied sheepishly.

"True," he agreed teasingly.

She laughed, enjoying the easy banter between them.

"My name is Asher, by the way."

"It's very nice to meet you Asher," she said smiling up at him. "My name is ..." she began but was interrupted.

"Mr. Weatherby? Is that you?" called out Douglas Redding, the head of the stable facilities.

A momentary look of annoyance danced across Asher's face as he tore his eyes from Elora.

"Yes?" Asher replied.

"I almost didn't recognize you! I see you spent some time with a razor," the burly middle-aged man said as he chuckled nervously. "I need to give you an update on your sorrel mare."

"Is everything alright?" he asked, immediately concerned.

"Yes, yes," Mr. Redding said, nodding reassuringly. "She's fine, but there was an incident earlier this morning. Someone attempted to take her from the upper paddock."

Elora's mouth fell open in shock. Things like that just didn't happen in Windom. She looked wide-eyed up at Asher to see his reaction to such disturbing information. His jaw was clenched, but his features remained neutral. He seemed angry but not surprised. Elora watched him curiously, as he crossed his arms and took a deep breath.

"Did you happen to catch the thief?" he asked calmly.

"One of my stable hands saw the guy closing the gate after he'd already taken your horse from the pasture. My man shouted and your mare shied and took off toward the barn, thank goodness. The thief ran in the other direction," Douglas explained.

Asher nodded as he listened.

"Did your man get a good look at him?" he asked.

"Dan didn't recognize him, which means he must not be from Windom because Dan knows just about everyone. He said the guy looked young. All he could see from that distance was that the man had light colored hair and was trim," Douglas replied.

Elora sucked in a breath at the description which accurately matched her stalker. She looked up at Asher and discovered that he had been watching her reaction. Their eyes locked but instead of finding a question there, she saw understanding. It was as though he knew what she had been thinking. Her head cocked to the side, puzzled. He held her gaze a moment more before turning back to Douglas.

"Have you already reported this to the Guard?" he asked.

"Yes. They are aware and have a Guardsman posted at the stable. We've moved your horse down to the lower pasture, closer to the barn so we can keep an eye on her. I'm sorry that this happened, Mr. Weatherby," he said apologetically.

"It's certainly not your fault, Mr. Redding," Asher replied graciously. "Thank you for your efforts. I'll be by later to check on her."

Douglas nodded gratefully before turning to join the few remaining people still making their way into the reception.

After he had walked away, Elora turned to Asher with a quizzical expression on her face.

"Pardon me for saying so, but you seemed oddly unsurprised by that," she said with eyebrows raised.

"No, I wasn't surprised," he answered. "I knew trouble would find me here at some point."

Elora took a step backward and gave him a sideways glance.

"Why would trouble be following you?" she asked warily.

He chuckled, tucking his hands into his pockets and shrugging his shoulders nonchalantly.

"Oh, trouble isn't following me," he said. "The problem is that trouble and I are looking for the same thing."

Elora tilted her head curiously and opened her mouth to ask another question, but stopped when Asher took a step closer to her and leaned down to look solemnly into her eyes.

"What did surprise me though, Elora, is that trouble seems to have found you first," he said lowly.

Elora stared back at him, her breath caught in her throat and a chill running up her spine. What was that supposed to mean? And how did he know her name?

"Tell your parents that I'm looking forward to supper," he said, as he backed away from her slowly.

Elora's brows furrowed in frustration as she realized that he was leaving. She lifted her hand and opened her mouth to protest.

"Wait!" she called.

But he only smiled before turning and walking quickly away.

"I told you that guy liked you!" came Trig's teasing voice from behind her.

Elora jumped and then sighed, suddenly understanding Asher's hasty retreat. She turned to find that Alysa and Trig had emerged from their brushy hiding spot and were watching her with excited smiles on their faces.

"Elora! Who was that?" Alysa nearly squealed as she rushed over to take Elora by the hands.

"His name is Asher," Elora said, laughing at Alysa's enthusiasm.

"Well, where is Asher going?" Trig asked, bemused. "What kind of man walks away from a lovely girl and good food?"

"The kind of man who just found out that someone tried to steal his horse." Elora replied with a shrug.

"Seriously?" gasped Alysa, covering her mouth with her hand.

"Ah yes, I heard about that" Trig said, nodding his head. "Will Holmestead was supposed to be at our ceremony but your dad sent him to secure the stables instead."

"That's too bad," Alysa said, shaking her head. "I'm glad he didn't try to send you," she laughed, reaching up to adjust their binding cord which Trig had draped victoriously behind his neck.

"The day isn't over yet, love," he said with a sardonic smirk.

"He wouldn't!" Alysa cried.

"You do remember that we're talking about your father, right? Michael Scott? Head Guardsman?" he asked, his eyebrows raised.

Alysa sighed in resignation.

"Well, let's just hope he doesn't," she said, pursing her lips.

"Here's hoping," Trig replied with a wink, draping his arm around her shoulders. He turned his attention back to Elora, asking "So, is his horse alright?"

"Mr. Redding said she wasn't harmed, but I'm guessing Asher's gone to check on her anyway," Elora said, watching as he turned to glance at her once more from a distance before breaking into a jog.

"What a pity," Alysa said, shaking her head. "You two seemed to be hitting it off."

"Yeah. Nice job keeping the drool in check," Trig teased, nudging Elora with his elbow.

Elora let out a gasp of mock outrage as she swatted his arm.

At that moment, Nate walked up and declared, "Alright! Everyone's in there. Let's get to it before the cookies are all gone!"

Elora shook her head and laughed as the four of them turned to walk to the church entrance. She couldn't resist searching out Asher's figure once more as he disappeared around a bend in the road. Excitement and fear swirled around in her stomach as she replayed their conversation in her mind. She had so many questions! In just a little while she would hopefully have answers. Her heart swelled at the thought of seeing him again. These next few hours were going to last an eternity.

As they neared the entrance, Alysa's mother pushed through the doors carrying two glasses of wine and handed one to Elora and Nate. She smiled excitedly at Alysa before withdrawing back into the church. Through the crack in the door, Elora could see nearly the entirety of Windom milling around and her stomach churned as she realized that she would be their center of attention shortly, even if only for a moment. Hopefully Nate would make the introduction. He didn't seem to mind the limelight.

"Are you ready?" Nate asked, looking around at everyone. They all nodded and he turned to Elora. "I'll be loud and get everyone's attention and then you can take it from there. My gift is volume, not eloquence."

Elora's mouth fell open in protest. This is not at all what she had expected to happen! But before she could get a word out, he placed her hand in the crook of his elbow and marched inside.

"Attention everyone! Attention please!" Nate bellowed jovially.

As the crowd quieted and all eyes were on them, he turned and looked at her expectantly.

Her eyes widened and she could feel the blush rising into her cheeks. Her mouth opened and for a terrifying moment she forgot what she should say. She laughed nervously and took a calming breath.

"It was our honor to stand beside them as they vowed to walk through life together. It is our pleasure to celebrate with you the first steps of their journey. Please raise your glass as I introduce for the first time..."

Elora looked over at Nate, silently asking for help as she moved towards the doors. He smiled and nodded. They both moved to grasp the handles of the church doors and began to pull them open to reveal the newly bound couple.

"Trig and Alysa Davenport!" Elora finished.

Happy cheers rang out as Trig and Alysa stepped forward.

Nate stepped forward and lifted his glass, shouting above the din, "To Trig and Alysa!"

The crowd echoed back in unison, "To Trig and Alysa!"

The joy in the room was palpable and as Elora caught sight of Alysa, her breath caught in her throat. Elora had never seen her sweet friend so happy. Alysa reached out and grasped Elora's hand for a brief moment before the couple was swept into the midst of the congratulatory crowd.

Elora lifted her glass, laughter on her lips and happy tears running down her face. This moment was perfection and she let herself be lost in it. Whatever was to come, whatever strange turns her life was about to take, for this one moment everything made sense, everything was right, everything was good. It is rare to recognize the moments that make life worth living when they're happening, but Elora recognized this one and she was going to savor every second.

CHAPTER 10

"It would appear, Ms. Kerrick, that God heard you even from the back row. It is quite miraculous what you have done with the courtyard," Preacher Woodward said, placing an affectionate hand on Elora's shoulder. "Well done, my girl."

Elora laughed nervously and took a drink from her cup. She'd been hearing similar compliments from nearly everyone for the past hour. They all seemed amazed and excited at the transformation of the courtyard, but she kept waiting for a suspicious or curious comment.

"Well, it's amazing what nature can do when you create the right circumstances," she rambled.

"I've already had another couple request to move their ceremony to the Courtyard. I know you toiled for the sake of your friend, but it's a gift we all appreciate. Thank you, Elora," he continued to gush.

“Oh, well, you’re welcome Preacher,” Elora replied, blushing and looking around for an excuse to end the conversation.

She saw her mother alone at the buffet table and jumped at the opportunity.

“I think my mother is motioning to me. Please excuse me, Preacher Woodward,” she said, smiling and rushing away before he could object.

She walked up to her mother hesitantly, scared of how she would react in light of all that had happened. Elora could tell that she was obviously upset, as her posture was tense and she was standing apart from the celebration. She reached out and gently touched her mother’s arm. Winnifred turned, and upon seeing Elora, let out a shuddering breath. She wrapped her arms around her, pulling Elora in for a close and lingering hug.

“Oh Elora,” her mother said, sighing into her hair. “I suppose there’s no point in denying it anymore”.

Elora could feel the tension ease from her mother’s body with the admission and Elora exhaled the breath she hadn’t realized she’d been holding. The pretense was gone. The curtain of secrecy had fallen. She sank deeper into the hug, tucking her face into the crook of her mother’s neck, savoring the closeness that had been absent for the past week.

“That courtyard, Elora!“ she whispered. “You certainly didn’t hold back,” she said chuckling softly.

“No,” laughed Elora. “I didn’t.”

Enjoying the moment of levity before pulling back from her embrace and looking somberly into her mother's eyes.

"But you did," she said soberly.

Winnifred nodded and closed her eyes for a moment. "No more. I hope you'll forgive us and understand why eventually," she said. "I promise, everything will be explained to you tonight. But not here, my love."

"Okay," Elora said quietly, a rushing sense of relief washing over her as the wall she'd built between her and her parents began to crumble. She pulled her mother in for another hug, whispering, "I've missed you."

"Me too," her mother whispered in reply.

When they stepped back from their embrace, both women had tears in their eyes. They looked at one another and laughed at one another's watery expressions.

"The courtyard is magnificent, sweetheart," her mother effused. "I'm just amazed."

Elora beamed with pride, for the first time able to celebrate her ability with another person.

"The entire time I was working in there I felt guilty and scared of potentially revealing myself to everyone," she admitted. "But I just couldn't seem to help myself."

"If I could do the things that you can, I'm not sure I would have been able to resist either. But it will be alright," her mother said soothingly. "In my experience, people will find a way to believe the unbelievable in order to make it fit their understanding of the world. They may know in their hearts that what you did in that courtyard was magical, but they will convince themselves that you simple have a *very* green thumb," she laughed.

"I hope so," Elora said, joining in with the laughter.

"I'm sure of it," her mother said reassuringly. "Perhaps you should be a little more subtle in the future though."

"Yes," Elora agreed. "Actually, working in the courtyard was really helpful in practicing how to control it."

"Will you show me later?" her mother whispered, her voice crackling with anticipation.

Elora nodded, giggling with excitement. She truly couldn't wait to share her gift.

"Your father and Asher are desperate to see what you can do. Your father could hardly speak this morning after we walked into the courtyard," she said, beaming.

"Speaking of Asher..." Elora said, her eyebrows raised. "Who is he?"

"Considering the way he went running out of the ceremony after you, I thought for sure he would have at least introduced himself," she said, baffled.

"He started to but we were interrupted," Elora admitted.

"I'm surprised I haven't seen him in here actually," her mother said, lifting her head to look around the room.

"He's not here. He left to go check on his horse. Someone tried to take it earlier this morning," Elora explained.

Winnifred immediately stiffened and turned to Elora, her eyes wide with alarm. She remained frozen that way for a few moments, staring at Elora with a fearful expression. Elora looked back at her with an increasing sense of panic.

"Mom?" she said at last, reaching out to touch her arm.

That seemed to jolt her mother into action. She began looking around frantically.

"We need to find your father," she whispered feverishly.

"What's wrong, mom? Why are you so scared?" Elora asked, anxiety making her voice sound small and childish to her own ears.

Her mother had Elora by the hand and was dragging her around the crowded church in search of her father. Winnifred was so focused on finding him that she didn't even hear her daughter, nor was she aware that she had begun to make a scene. People began to quietly make way for them as they wound through the aisles, watching with curious expressions.

At last her father appeared before them, the commotion of their search having caught his attention. He looked at Winnifred sternly, placing a hand on her shoulder.

"What are you doing?" he hissed. "Everyone is watching."

Winnifred snapped out of her panicked state and looked around nervously before turning back to Jonas. Upon seeing her fearful expression, his eyes widened. He took her hand and lead them to a quiet corner of the church.

"What is it, love," he asked, his voice gentle.

"They've found us," she whispered. "Someone tried to steal Asher's horse from the stable this morning."

He stared down at her in shock for a moment before pulling her to him and wrapping his arms around her. Elora stood as still as a statue behind her mother, watching them. He spoke quietly to her for a moment before lifting his eyes to Elora. She caught her breath at the raw emotion she saw there. Determination and anger were etched into the hard lines of his jaw and deep furrows of his brow. But the love that poured from his eyes was what truly frightened her the most. She could see that he was preparing to fight. And she had a terrible feeling that he would be fighting for her.

"Elora, you need to say goodbye to Alysa," he told her in a tone that brooked no resistance. "We will wait for you out front."

Elora was so alarmed by the way her parents were behaving that she merely nodded and turned to do as she was told. Quietly walking towards the place where she'd last seen Alysa, she formulated a reasonable excuse for her early exit. The celebration was nearly over and her duties as Witness were finished, so her presence was no longer required. But Alysa could read Elora like a book and would know something was very wrong. She was resolved not to diminish Alysa and Trig's happiness with whatever troubling circumstances were unfolding for her in this moment.

As she approached Alysa, she coached her features into what she hoped was a joyful but tired expression. Upon seeing her, Alysa turned and wrapped her in a jubilant embrace. She was relaxed and content and so incredibly happy. It soothed Elora just being near her.

Alysa stepped back from the hug, took one look at Elora's face and asked, "What's wrong?"

Elora sighed in resignation at her utter failure to fool her dearest friend.

"I'm just tired," Elora lied.

Alysa raised her brows suspiciously.

"And my mom is acting strange."

"I did notice that," Alysa admitted, nodding.

Elora winced.

"Yes. Well, I want to go home with my parents and make sure everything is alright," she stammered.

"I can understand that," Alysa said, smiling. "Thank you for everything you did today. It was perfect. Every moment of it," she gushed, pulling Elora in for one last hug.

"I love you, friend," Elora whispered, a lump rising in her throat.

Everything had very suddenly become so complicated and frightening. She held tightly to Alysa, finding solace in the familiar and unchanging bond between them. She had a terrible premonition that nothing would be the same once she walked through the door of the church, and she wanted to savor this moment. She released Alysa and stepped back, blinking the tears from her eyes to clear her vision. She stared at Alysa for a moment, intentionally committing the details of her face into memory.

"What is it?" she asked, laughing a bit self-consciously.

"I just want to remember you like this," Elora said, smiling as she tried to hide the sadness that had crept into her voice. "I need to go. They are waiting for me," she said, motioning toward the door where her parents were doubtless becoming impatient.

"Okay," Alysa said, frowning in disappointment.

But as Elora turned, she reached out and took hold of her hand to stop her. Elora turned and looked into her face.

"I love you too, friend," she said, smiling as she squeezed her hand affectionately.

Elora gave her one last smile before walking swiftly toward the exit. It felt as if there were a weight pushing on her chest, smothering her. Her stomach churned nervously. Her world had suddenly fallen into shadow, as though an ominous storm cloud had drifted in and blocked the joyful sunshine of what had been the loveliest of days.

As she neared the door, her parents came into view and a chill ran up her spine as she took in their expressions. She watched the way they looked around nervously and held tightly to one another's hand. She had looked to her parents for reassurance and protection her entire life. But it appeared, for the first time, that they were powerless to offer those securities. They were scared. They knew the entire story, were familiar with whatever mysterious danger was lurking, and they were well and truly terrified. She wasn't sure, in this moment, if her ignorance was a burden or a gift.

They visibly relaxed a degree as she approached. Her father moved to open the door as her mother reached out and took her hand. She squeezed it gently, trying to offer her daughter some small token of comfort despite her own obvious fear.

"Follow me," her father said quietly, taking hold of her mother's hand and leading her back into the courtyard instead of toward home as Elora had expected. There was a handful of people wandering around, admiring the flowers and enjoying the fragrant air. Her father smiled halfheartedly at a few friends who waved at them as they made their way quickly toward the desert willow growing near the rear wall. He stopped briefly beside the trellis as though to admire the purple wisteria blooms growing there.

"Dad? What are you doing?" Elora whispered, confused.

"I repaired this courtyard wall a few years ago," he whispered, as he watched for an unobserved opportunity.

Finally comfortable that they weren't being watched, he walked over to the tree and pulled a thick, low-hanging branch aside and slipped behind it. Elora furrowed her brows in confusion, looking around furtively to see if anyone had seen her father's suspicious behavior. There were a few minutes of rustling behind the tree, followed by a high-pitched squeaking noise and then a dull thud. Suddenly a beam of light pierced through from behind the branches of the tree. Her father pushed aside the branch and motion for them to join him behind the tree. Elora took the branch from his hand, holding it back for her mother to pass. To her surprise, her parents seemed to disappear. She quickly slipped behind the tree, releasing the branch and turning to find where they had gone. Suddenly, her father's hand reached out from the wall, grabbing hold of her wrist. She gasped and instinctively pulled back.

"It's alright, love," her father breathed, sticking his head back through a narrowly opened door that had long been obscured by weeds and vines.

Someone must have planted the willow too close to the door years ago and as it grew, it eventually made the door inaccessible. Her father would have found it when he was making repairs. Sneaking out this door, no one would know they had left the church. Her blood chilled in her veins as she realized that her parents felt the need to be so secretive, to hide as though someone were watching.

She took a calming breath before squeezing through the cracked opening. Once through the wall and free of the courtyard, they traveled quickly through a series of alleys and cut across a few small fields until they met up the with the road Elora usually took to the interior gardens. Walking along the edge of the road in the tall grasses, they briskly made their way home.

"Do you think anyone saw us?" Winnifred asked, nervously.

"I have no idea if we are even being watched at all, my love," he said soothingly. "But I don't want to make things easy if we are."

Elora walked quietly beside them, trying to control the panic that threatened to overtake her. She wanted to scream, force them to stop and tell her everything. But she held her tongue and focused on keeping from falling on the uneven ground beneath her feet.

The sound of wagon wheels broke the quiet rhythmic rustling of their feet in the grass. They all lurched further off the road, ducking down to avoid being seen. Though it appeared to merely be one of the field hands driving a wagon full of goods to the market, they stayed hidden and remained motionless long after he had passed.

"Dad?" Elora said quietly.

Her father made eye contact and waited for her to continue.

"Perhaps we shouldn't go home if the danger is so great," she whispered.

"Perhaps," he agreed, nodding. "But we must go home, nonetheless. Some things we need are in the house."

Elora dropped her head, sighing in frustration.

Her mother reached out to take her hand. "We will explain everything. I promise."

At that, her father rose and pulled the two women up to their feet. They made quick work of the remaining distance. As their house came into view around a bend in the road, they could see a young man sitting casually on their stone fence. Elora tensed at the sight of him, but her father seemed to become calmer with every step that brought them closer.

The man rose and began walking to meet them and called out, "It's alright, Jonas. They aren't here yet."

Her mother cried out a joyful release, and her shoulders drooped in exhaustion as the tension drained from her body.

Elora froze mid-step as she recognized the man.

"Asher?" she asked, looking to her father. This young man clearly played a significant role in whatever was happening. Her curiosity was on the verge of driving her mad. Jonas just smiled, too relieved and weary to explain anything quite yet.

Finally within arm's reach, her mother threw her arms around Asher, exclaiming, "Thank God. I was so frightened."

He returned her embrace, patting her back soothingly. "Everything is alright. But we do need to hurry a bit," he said gently.

Asher lifted his head, locking eyes with Elora for a long moment before turning to escort her mother to the house. He had a protective arm wrapped around her shoulders and she had looped her arm around his waist in a way that intimated familiarity and deep affection. Elora stood still, watching them walk away. Her father paused alongside her, waiting for her to move to the relative safety of the house.

"How does she know him?" she asked him quietly.

He looked at Asher and Winnifred walking into the house ahead of them and smiled. "She was like a mother to him once. Even helped bring him into the world, actually," he said, his eyes misty with nostalgia.

Elora stared after them, suddenly feeling like an outsider in her own family. A wave of jealousy washed over her as she realized that this man, who had appeared out of nowhere only a few hours ago, knew her parents better than she did. She shifted her gaze to her father, regarding him with new eyes. He had lived an entirely different life she knew nothing about. He had kept it from her, hidden it from her. He was like a stranger to her. And yet, he was the same father who had tucked her in every night, tended her scraped knees, and taught her the ways of the world. He loved her more than anyone. She would forgive him for this, she knew. But she was done waiting. It was time she knew everything.

Her father must have seen the hurt and anger in her eyes because he took her hand and clasped it tightly. Sadness, and perhaps even fear, flashed across his face as he gently lifted her chin with his hand and beseeched her with his eyes.

"Please Elora. Please remember, no matter what you find out or how it might seem, that everything we ever did, was to protect you," he said, his voice husky with emotion.

Elora stared up at him as she tried to make sense of the feelings swirling around within her.

"Please," he whispered, holding her gaze.

She gave him a faint nod to appease him and then turned away, breaking free of his grasp and quickly moving towards the house.

Asher stood watching their interaction, holding the door open for them to enter. Elora could feel his eyes on her as she made her way through the gate and up the walkway. Whatever her parents had kept from her, he knew it all and she resented him for it. She was jealous. She was frustrated. She was angry at her parents, at the situation, and whether it was fair or not, she was angry at him too.

"Elora," Asher said, reaching out to touch her arm as she passed.

She stopped, keeping her face downturned.

"If whatever you imagine is happening here has made you angry at your parents, then you are wrong," he said quietly.

She closed her eyes and took a shaky breath. That was it. That was officially more than she could take. Her hands trembled as the emotions that she had barely been keeping in check finally boiled over in the wake of his chastisement.

"Anger seems a very appropriate response, actually," Elora replied icily, looking up and locking him with a blistering glare. "I have been deceived, apparently for my entire life, by the people I trusted the most. Don't you tell me how to feel! You don't understand," she said angrily lashing out at him.

"You're the one who doesn't understand," he whispered harshly, closing the space between them.

"That's exactly right!" she exclaimed. "I don't understand anything! But you! Somehow you understand everything!" she cried, shoving him away from her. "It's like I'm a stranger in my own life! I feel like I don't even belong here anymore."

Elora stood panting, her eyes closed as she tried to regain her composure. She knew the anger she felt towards Asher was misdirected and she immediately regretted having spoken to him that way. She waited until her breathing had calmed before opening her eyes. She searched out her parents, finding her mother staring at her with a startled expression and her father frowning in concern. She finally hazarded a glance at Asher, who stood a few feet away quietly watching her.

Seeing that she had recovered from her outburst, he stepped towards her. He ducked his head to lock eyes with her.

"Actually Elora, you *don't* belong here," he said gently.

His close proximity made her heart race and the intensity of his gaze brought a blush to her cheeks. It took a moment for what he'd said to sink in but when it did, her brows furrowed in confusion. However, at his next words her eyes flared and her breath caught in her throat.

"I'm here to take you home."

CHAPTER 11

Elora backed away from him, looking in bewilderment between Asher and her parents. When her father subtly nodded in affirmation, she felt a sudden resurgence of the anger she'd only just managed to supress. This was so much bigger than she'd thought. They expected her to leave everything behind; her home, her friends, her life! It was too much.

She dropped her eyes to the ground, trying to wrap her head around the idea that her parents had been keeping a secret from her, hiding it from her, sheltering her from the truth for nineteen years. Perhaps that had been justifiable when she was younger, but she was a grown woman now and had been for quite some time. She wasn't going to follow blindly and trustingly like a child any more. She deserved to know. She deserved a say.

"This is my home," she said defensively.

"You're right, Elora," her mother said reassuringly, stepping forward to take her hand. "But Windom is not where we belong."

Elora pulled her hand away and turned, moving to put some space between her and the people threatening to destroy her life as she knew it. She took hold of a kitchen chair, needing something stable and concrete to bolster her.

"Where do we belong, then?" she asked, her voice rising in frustration.

"The Woodlands," her father replied gently.

Elora's eyes darted to his and her brows furrowed in confusion.

"What?" she whispered.

"You were born beneath the branches of the Ever Tree in the forest of Clarendon," Winnifred answered softly.

Her mother's voice trembled with quiet reverence as she spoke, her tongue rolling around the words with a soft lilt in an accent much like Asher's. A smile brushed across her lips as she, at long last, revealed the secret that had been tucked inside her heart for so long.

Elora had always known that she'd been born outside of Windom. It had been a defining characteristic of hers as a child. She could remember how townspeople would discuss the way her parents had wandered into their small town, weary and worn, with Elora no more than a few months old, tucked against her mother's chest. Despite their best efforts, no one had ever been able to pry the details of their past from her parents and after a few years, people had stopped asking. And after nearly two decades, their mysterious arrival seemed to have been forgotten altogether.

Forgotten by everyone except Elora. The secret of their past, of her origin, had nagged at her for her entire life. At long last she would have answers.

"Clarendon," she whispered, savoring the sound of the word, the name of her birthplace.

She felt a subtle shift, a gentle thud, as though she were finally landing on firm ground; as though she had at long last been planted and her roots were taking hold. Her fascination with the Woodlands and her dreams of the forest suddenly made sense. She had been born among the trees.

The weight of what was happening to her and the significance of what she'd just learned pressed heavily on her shoulders. Elora moved to sit in the chair, her legs suddenly weary.

"But the Woodlands are so far! How did we get here?" she asked, looking up at her father.

"The better question is why," interjected Asher, moving to sit in the chair beside her and resting his elbows on the table.

Her parents took seats across from them, trading worried glances with one another. Her father took hold of her mother's hand in a show of unity and to offer comfort as they finally lay bare the truth before their daughter.

"I'm not sure where to start," her mother faltered, her lilting accent growing more pronounced with each word. "There's so much."

It was strange, hearing the voice she'd known her entire life suddenly dancing around words with such a different inflection. Her mother suddenly seemed so foreign to her and yet it seemed right. Elora realized that for the first time ever her mother was revealing herself, the true authentic version of herself. A version that she'd been hiding for so terribly long.

"We don't have time to tell her everything, right now," Asher interrupted, looking meaningfully at her father across the table.

Elora glared at him. She didn't want him here to witness as she finally got the answers she'd waited a lifetime to hear. And she certainly didn't want him to get in the way of those answers.

"There will be time along our journey to fill in the gaps," Asher said, avoiding her gaze.

"I haven't decided to go on any journey," Elora stated firmly.

Asher turned his head and locked eyes with Elora. She returned his gaze coolly.

"The decision at this point isn't whether you're going on a journey, Elora," he replied bluntly. "The decision is who you're going with. It will either be with me and your parents, or with the Liana."

His response sent a chill down Elora's spine. She looked across the table with wide, startled eyes at her parents. The stricken look on their faces was confirmation enough for Elora that Asher was telling the truth.

"Who are the Liana?" she asked, a hint of fear in her voice.

"Once upon a time, they were heroic and righteous protectors, much like the Guard here in Windom," Asher began. "They defended the people of Clarendon and the Ever Tree from any who would seek to harm them. But their purpose was warped and twisted until the Liana became less a means of security than a force used to control the people."

"The Liana are the reason we fled Clarendon, Elora," her father said, his own accent beginning to emerge. "They rule with impunity."

"And cruelty," her mother added quietly.

"They are ruthless," Asher said grimly. "You need to choose me, Elora."

"I'm so sorry, Elora," her mother cried tearfully. "We should have told you everything sooner but we never imagined they would find us here. I honestly thought they had given up searching after nearly two decades. But they've found us somehow and now it's just too late to leave by choice."

"How much time do you think we have, Asher?" Jonas asked soberly.

"It depends," he replied. "How long has the blonde man been following you?" he asked, fixing his eyes on Elora.

Elora's mouth fell open as she realized that the man truly had been following her as she had feared. But even more terrifying was the fact that this proved Asher was telling the truth. The Liana really was in pursuit of her and apparently had been for a while. As she took in the wide-eyed expressions of her parents, a sense of panic started to take hold.

"You were being followed and didn't tell me?" her father asked incredulously.

"I thought I was being ridiculous!" she replied, throwing up her hands. "Bizarre things were happening all around me and I didn't feel like I could talk to you anymore!"

"How long?" Asher interrupted, repeating his question more forcefully.

"About two weeks," she said quietly.

Asher took a deep breath and sat back in his chair, clearly disturbed by her revelation.

"We don't have long then," he said. "I left the Liana a week ago and rode hard straight here. They would only be a day or so behind me, I expect, if what she says is true."

"How can you be sure?" Jonas asked anxiously.

"The Liana has been searching for you for the past two years," he said looking to Elora. "When my father learned that a search was underway, he feared for you and your parents and asked me to try to find you before they did. But it had been 19 years since the three of you disappeared and every track had long gone cold. I had no idea where to look, so I just stayed close to the Liana and watched. I thought there was little chance that I could find you on my own, but I could at least try to help you when they found you. They have searched nearly the entire continent by now. Each time they would move to a new region, they would send out pairs of scouts to all the towns in the area to hunt for you. The man following you is a scout. I actually know him. His name is Colin Hudson. He was a childhood friend," Asher said, grimacing.

"Trace Hudson's son is a member of the Liana?" Jonas asked, dismayed. "I can't believe that!"

"Clarendon is very different from the place you left," Asher replied, shaking his head. "Colin's partner must have left to relay your location to the rest of the Liana. They had a camp outside of Warren, about a week's ride from here. When I left a little over a week ago they were still clueless, which means the scout hadn't returned yet. But if they found you two weeks ago, then there's a good chance he made it back soon after I left. And they wouldn't waste any time coming for you, Elora. They are desperate to find you."

"Oh, Jonas," her mother whispered, lifting her hand to her mouth as she looked with terrified eyes to her husband.

After a moment of thought, Asher turned to Elora and asked, "How do you think he recognized you?"

"I have no idea," she replied bewildered. "The first time I saw him was in the market with one of the travelling merchants. I never spoke to him, or really even paid much attention to him. But I bought a necklace from his merchant."

"What necklace?" her mother asked. "I haven't noticed you wearing anything new."

"I paid more than I should have and I didn't want to own up to it," she admitted. "I kept it tucked beneath my tunic."

"Can I see it?" Asher asked.

Elora quietly rose from the table and walked down the hall to her bedroom. She could feel his eyes following her as she moved. In spite of the fear and anger and confusion that clouded her perception of him, there was an undeniable attraction.

She quickly retrieved the handkerchief from her dresser and carried it back to the kitchen. Taking her seat, she gingerly peeled away the folds of cloth until her necklace was revealed. She lifted it, letting the seed dangle in front of her eyes before gently lowering it onto the center of the table.

"The merchant told me it came from the Woodlands and I just couldn't resist it," she said. "I guess now I know why," she murmured to herself.

They examined the necklace as it lay on the table for a moment before her mother let out a little gasp. She reached out and lifted the necklace, holding it reverently as she brought it closer to her.

"You can see it?" Elora asked, her eyebrows lifted in surprise.

"Is this a seed from the Ever Tree?" she asked softly.

"It can't be," her father scoffed. "Who would dare to desecrate it like that? Piercing it and stringing it on a chain like a mere bauble."

He took it from Winnifred's hands and held it up for a better view. The sunlight through the window glinted on the few strands of silver lining the intricate grooves along its surface.

"No!" he whispered in horror. "It is! But why would someone do this?" he said angrily, laying the seed back down carefully in the center of the table. "No one but a Claren would even be able to see it."

"I guess that explains how he recognized Elora then," Asher sighed, leaning back in his chair.

"But what has happened to it?" her mother asked, looking from Asher to Elora. "It is so different. I hardly recognized it."

"Wait! What is a Claren? What is the Ever Tree?" Elora interrupted, utterly confused. "Can someone please start explaining," she exclaimed, her frustration bubbling to the surface again. "I've been more than patient."

Elora looked back and forth between her parents, her eyes glaring with indignation. Her mother reached out and gripped her hand in conciliation.

"You have," her mother said, nodding.

"There isn't time," Asher began.

"There is time for this," Winnifred interrupted, holding Elora's gaze.

Elora felt her spirit lighten as she looked into her mother's eyes, recognizing that she at last had an ally.

She felt acknowledge and respected. It was a salve to her wounded pride. Her heart swelled with love for her mother, who saw in her not a child, but a woman who deserved to know the truth.

Winnifred picked up the seed from the center of the table, rubbing it between her fingers tenderly. She raised her eyes back to Elora and took a deep breath.

"The Ever Tree is the heart of Clarendon," her mother began. "It is bigger and taller than anything you could ever imagine. It would take your breath away, Elora. There is no other tree like it," she said wistfully. "But the Ever Tree is so much more than a just tree to our kind."

"What do you mean 'our kind'?" Elora asked, confused.

"Elora, this will seem unbelievable after growing up in Windom all these years. But I hope that after discovering your own powers, perhaps you are open to the idea that this world is not as you had always thought. And perhaps you will be willing to accepting that what I'm going to tell you is the truth," said Winnifred, looking to her husband for an encouraging nod before continuing. "Clarendon, our home, is the dwelling of the Claren. You come from an ancient people whose connection to the forest, to the trees, goes beyond the ordinary. The Claren have the ability to plant and nurture a rare but essential plant species," she said.

"The Elysian tree," Jonas whispered reverently.

"The Elysian tree,' her mother repeated, nodding. "This species of tree has the special ability to change the soil, altering its composition in such a way that allows for the growth of a multitude of other tree species. There are actually very few trees that can survive without the benefit of an Elysian Tree nearby. A forest will appear and flourish wherever an Elysian tree is planted. And likewise, once it dies, the forest around it slowly withers as well."

"Unless a Claren comes along to plant another," her father said. "You see, there is only one Elysian tree capable of reproducing. All the others are descendants of this one magnificent tree. Every forest in the land began with a seed from the Ever Tree," he explained. "A seed just like this one," he said, taking the necklace from her mother and staring at the seed as it settled in his palm.

"The Woodlands would not exist without the Elysian Trees," her mother emphasized. "And the trees wouldn't be there if not for the Claren."

"So, I'm a Claren?" Elora asked, tilting her head as she tried to make sense of everything.

"We all are," answered Asher.

"So, if you were to go outside and plant this seed," she said, taking the necklace from her father and holding it up to Asher, "an Elysian Tree would grow?"

"No," he said shaking his head. "Only Claren with the Mark of the Ever Tree can do that."

"The Mark of the Ever Tree?" she asked, raising her eyebrows in question.

"The relationship between the Claren and the Ever Tree is complicated, almost symbiotic I suppose," he started. "I think your parents are better equipped to explain it since I haven't experienced it myself," he said, nodding towards her father.

"Every year, after the seeds of the Ever Tree have fallen, the Claren celebrate something called The Gathering," her father explained. "The community meets beneath the branches of the Ever Tree to search for that season's harvest of seeds. All Claren above the age of twenty take part. The seeds typically are much more vibrant," he said, pointing toward the necklace. "They are nearly silver in color and practically glimmer in the sunlight. Finding one twinkling from beneath the fallen leaves is always thrilling, no matter how many Gatherings you've attended," he said, smiling with nostalgia.

"Yes, it really is magical," agreed her mother. "But the truly significant part of the Gathering is that every year, a few young Claren will find their soulmates under that tree. You see, the seeds of the Ever Tree are charmed."

Elora cocked her head to the side and raised her eyebrows, doubtful.

"I realize it's hard to believe, love. But the Ever Tree brought your father and me together," her mother said, chuckling softly. "And someday it will show you the man who is meant for you."

"How?" Elora asked, curious.

"During the Gathering, if the time is right for you to find your soulmate, as you hold a seed it will begin to glow," her father said. "It begins softly at first but grows brighter and brighter with every moment until it's nearly blinding. In that final moment, as you close your eyes against the light, you receive a vision of your soulmate. And wherever that person may be, he will have a vision of you."

Elora couldn't help the gasp that escaped her lips. Her visions of the man in the forest came rushing to the forefront of her mind.

"Visions?" she repeated in a high-pitched voice before clearing her throat self-consciously.

She could see Asher watching her closely out of the corner of her eye.

"Yes, visions," her mother continued. "And then, that night, after the Gathering, there is a ceremony called the Pairing. It is something similar to the Binding Ceremony you have seen here in Windom."

"That seems really fast!" Elora cried, alarmed. "What if they don't even know one another?"

"In all honesty, I don't recall ever witnessing a Pairing where the couple wasn't already deeply in love, Elora. The vision you receive from the Ever Tree isn't just with your eyes, it's with your heart. You don't just see your match, you *see* him, you know him, and you recognize that he is meant for you. It's almost impossible to explain," her mother said, sharing a knowing smile with her father.

Elora listened, immediately comparing the description to her own visions. Her reaction to the man in her vision perhaps wasn't as strong immediately, but her feelings had very quickly deepened and strengthened for him in a way that didn't make sense. She'd never even seen his face. And yet she felt she knew him. Somehow, she perhaps even loved him. She found herself nodding subconsciously.

Asher cleared his throat and she jolted out of her reverie to find him watching her intensely. She tilted her head to the side in question. He looked away quickly, focusing on her mother across the table.

"You were telling her about the Mark of the Ever Tree," Asher reminded her.

"Yes, well, the Pairing is like the Binding Ceremony except instead of the cord, the couple holds the seed that brought them together within their clasped hands," her mother said, taking her father's hand and pressing their palms together. "The seed is still shining, though not nearly as brightly by now. As the ceremony is completed, there is a brilliant flash of light from between their hands. When they release their grasp, it is revealed that the seed has lost its glow and the couple are left with a darkened imprint on their palms."

"That imprint is the Mark of the Ever Tree," her father said. "It signifies that their hearts are claimed by one another and their hands are empowered with the ability to cultivate the Elysian trees."

"But you don't have the Mark of the Ever Tree." she said, looking between her parents, confused.

"The further we traveled from Clarendon and the Ever Tree, the lighter the Mark became. By the time we arrived in Windom, it had disappeared entirely," she replied, looking down at her palm, sadly rubbing the place where her mark had been.

"Has your mark faded too?" she asked, looking over to Asher.

"No. I have not been paired," he said, locking eyes with her. "There were no seeds on the year of my first Gathering," he said. "Or any year since."

"What?" her mother exclaimed, dismayed.

"That is one of the last seeds ever shed by the Ever Tree," he said, staring sadly at the seed in Elora's hand.

"What do you mean?" Jonas asked, his body rigid with concern.

"The Ever Tree is dead," Asher said gently.

Her parents were struck dumb with shock. They stared at Asher in disbelief.

"How?" Winnifred whispered.

"After Elora was born, after you left, the seeds began to fade. They became less and less powerful with every season. Eventually the seeds that fell were like this one, dull and seemingly lifeless. But there was still magic in them because the Pairings continued. But that changed three years ago. The Gathering that autumn yielded no Pairings and even worse, the seeds produced no trees," Asher said, his eyes waxy as he recalled the memory. "That was the last year the Ever Tree shed any seeds and by the following spring, it was dead."

"Oh, God," her father whispered in horror, grasping Winnifred's hand. "It was all true."

Elora looked with wide eyes at her parents before turning to find Asher watching her. He didn't look away, holding her gaze unflinchingly as though expecting a response. What could she have to say? He surely couldn't blame her for any of this.

"Why are you staring at me?" she whispered nervously. "This has nothing to do with me."

"This has everything to do with you, Elora," he replied, ducking his head to look at her more directly.

"What do you mean?" she asked uncomfortably. "Do you think this happened because we left?"

"No, this happened because you were born," he answered.

"What?" she cried, indignantly. "The Ever Tree died because I was born?"

"No. Let me clarify. You were born because the Ever Tree was dying," he explained.

"That didn't clarify anything!" Elora exclaimed, throwing her hands up in frustration.

"You aren't explaining this very well, son," Jonas interjected.

Asher sighed, shifting in his seat to face Elora.

"You were born to make this right, Elora," he said. "You are going to bring the Ever Tree back to life. It's your destiny."

"My destiny," she repeated, her voice incredulous.

"Three centuries ago," Asher began, "there was a Claren with the gift of foresight. She prophesied that one day the Ever Tree would fall, and that without it, the great forests of the Woodlands would vanish. But there was a chance for salvation and it would come in the form of a person she called the Renascent."

Elora looked with wide eyes back and forth between her parents. Did they really believe this? Was what he said true? Her heart was racing.

"You think I am the Renascent?" Elora whispered, terrified.

"You are," he stated confidently.

Her whole body sagged, weighted down by the overwhelming burden that had just fallen onto her small shoulders.

"How can you be sure?" she asked in a small voice.

"The prophesy states that this person will bear the Mark of the Ever Tree, not by Pairing, but by birth," he said, holding her gaze as though willing her to accept and embrace his words.

"The Prophesy is common knowledge among the Claren," interjected her father. "But it had been dismissed as a fairytale after 300 years passed without any of it coming true.

My parents told it to me as a bedtime story when I was a child. I never dreamed it could be real. But then you came along," he said gently, looking across the table at Elora.

"My best friend, Miriam Weatherby, Asher's mother, delivered you," Winnifred recalled, nodding to Asher. "She very nearly dropped you when she noticed the mark on your back, Elora. It was unmistakably, undeniably the Mark of the Ever Tree."

"We didn't know what to do. We were afraid that people would panic if they knew that the prophesy was real and that it was coming to pass. And even worse, we were sure that you would be taken from us once the Liana discovered that you were the Renascent," her father explained. "We tried to keep the Mark hidden, but one night, when you were nearly three months old we made a mistake."

"Every year at the peak of summer, there is something called the Celebration of Light," her mother continued. "The entire community gathers beneath the Ever Tree at night after the sun has set. Every light is extinguished and the forest is plunged into black. The darkness is overwhelming. But then suddenly, spots of light begin to flash and the forest comes alive with the dazzling display of a million fireflies. You can't see the stars through the forest canopy, but oh my, the fireflies are a magnificent substitute," she smiled, momentarily lost in her nostalgia. "It had always been my favorite night of the year, but you were too small and already sleeping so we weren't going to go. At the last minute, a friend of mine offered to sit with you so that I could attend with your father. And we couldn't resist. You were already sound asleep. I thought she wouldn't even have to touch you," Winnifred explained, an anguished look on her face.

"I could tell the minute we returned, just from the look in her eyes, that she had seen your birthmark," her father said. "We knew it would only be a matter of time before she spoke of it. And once word reached the Commander of the Liana, he would have stopped at nothing to get a hold of you. We would have been powerless against them. Our only choice was to run as far away as we could and hide you for as long as possible; until you were old enough to fulfill your destiny and strong enough to defend yourself against those who would attempt to control you." he finished.

"You are so much more than the Renascent, my love," her mother said, reaching across the table to take Elora's hand. "The prophesy doesn't dictate who you are, it merely says what you will do. We wanted more for you than a life enslaved to the prophesy."

"Perhaps we shouldn't have taken you away from Clarendon," her father said, his face creased with distress. "But we did it to protect you. And we always intended to take you back. I hope the Claren will be able to forgive us for that," he said, closing his eyes and dropping his head in shame.

Elora watched her parents, agonized that they had been forced to make such a choice, such a sacrifice because of her. Knowing what she did now, everything about her parents made so much more sense. She had a newfound understanding of why they had chosen to live so privately, so secretly. And more than anything, she found she could no longer be angry for the way they had lied to her all these years. They had put her first, always; above themselves, above their people, above everything.

Elora grasped her mother's hand, squeezing it tightly. "Thank you," she whispered.

Winnifred looked up at her and exhaled, some of the anxiety easing from her features.

Elora reached out to clasp her father's hand as well.

"I never should have doubted you," she said, apologetic and ashamed.

He smiled in return, relieved. They sat there, quietly holding hands, enjoying the feelings of comfort and completeness their reunion provided. But after a moment, an expression of profound sadness washed over her mother's face.

"Do they hate us?" she asked quietly, looking over to Asher.

"Not at first," Asher replied gently. "I think most people probably understood why you ran away. They were concerned of course. Nothing much changed after you left though, so people just sort of moved on. But when the seeds started fading, so did their compassion for you. And then when the Ever Tree died and there was no Renascent to save us, your leaving and taking Elora away was seen as a betrayal. The Claren are hurting and the forests are beginning to die. They need someone to blame. And the Commander has been very clear about who that should be," he stated grimly.

Elora watched as her mother's chin began to quiver. Her father lifted his hands to cover his face, distraught. Elora struggled to take a breath as the weight of her parents' grief pressed down on her. What would happen to them when they returned to Clarendon with her? What price would they pay for protecting her?

"Please don't," Elora said, her own voice trembling as she begged her mother not to cry, squeezing her hand comfortingly.

"We should have returned sooner," her father said, rubbing his forehead and sighing loudly.

Elora looked between her parents, tortured by the fact that they were facing such condemnation because of what they'd done to protect her. She wouldn't let them face it alone.

"I will make this right," Elora said, looking into her father's eyes, determined.

"You're the only one who can," Asher replied quietly beside her.

She looked over at him, biting her lip nervously.

"I hope you're right," she said. "I'm trying very hard to believe you."

"You don't have to believe me," he replied turning towards her. "Believe this," he said softly as he reached out to gently brush his fingers across the satin covering the birthmark on her back.

Her breath caught in her throat and she stared into his eyes, both startled and thrilled at his touch. Her skin tingled as though it had come alive beneath his fingers. He gazed back at her unwaveringly. Everything else seemed to blur and disappear besides the intoxicating blue-green of his eyes. She had no idea how long they sat transfixed before her father cleared his throat.

Elora jerked her gaze to her parents, trying to quell the self-conscious blush that threatened to warm her cheeks. They were looking back and forth between Elora and Asher, a surprised and somewhat alarmed expression on their faces. She cautioned a look back towards Asher to find that he was still watching her intently. She turned away, acutely aware of him and confused by the familiar and almost possessive way that he interacted with her.

"Elora," her father said, attempting to reclaim her attention.

"Yes?" she asked, trying to focus on him.

"May we see the Mark?" he asked hesitantly, shifting his eyes and nodding his head towards her back.

Elora's mouth fell open for a moment, caught off-guard by his request. But sensing their curiosity and enthusiasm, she couldn't deny them. She stood slowly, pushing her chair back from the table. Careful to avoid looking at Asher, she turned away from them, unwrapping the scrap of satin from her elbow and letting it fall to the side. At the sound of her mother's gasp, she dropped her gaze to the floor and tried to suppress her mortification. She let them look for a few moments until she self-consciously couldn't stand it one second more.

"Amazing," whispered her father, as she turned and sat back down.

Her cheeks were pink with embarrassment at their scrutiny. She cautioned a brief glance at Asher. His eyes nearly sparkled with excitement as he stared at her, awestruck. She looked away, uncomfortable but also exhilarated by his reaction.

"When did it start to change, Elora?" her mother asked, her voice breathy with wonder.

"About the same time that I gained my ability," she remarked, studying the table to avoid their fascinated stares.

"Can we see that too?" her father asked, struggling to contain his eagerness.

"I'll try. It might be hard to focus with all of you watching," she said hesitantly.

"Here," her mother said, beginning to stand. "I have some young strawberry plants that I just transplanted into a few pots out back. Let me grab one."

"I'll get it," Asher said, rising quickly and practically running to fetch the plant

Elora looked back and forth between her parents, trying not to let their keen expressions terrify her. She'd never performed under such pressure. What would she focus on? Would she even be able to focus?

Asher returned a minute later carrying a pot with a small cluster of green leaves. He placed it carefully in front of Elora. She looked up at him, nervous, and he smiled back encouragingly.

Elora reached out, grasping the pot with both hands and pulled it towards her. She stretched out her finger to gently brush one of the lush green leaves. Looking around briefly, she took in the rapt countenances of everyone at the table.

"Just try, sweetheart. I know this is a lot of pressure," her mother soothed.

Elora took a deep breath and closed her eyes, trying to block out everyone and everything. She let her thoughts drift to the forest. A calm came over her as she imagined the feel of the cool moist air on her skin and the rushing sound of leaves blowing in the wind. She lost herself in the memory of her favorite vision, only this time her feelings were heightened. Because this time she knew the truth of who she was. Because this time she knew her visions were real, that he was real, and that he was meant for her. She heard the familiar sound of a twig snapping and her heart began to beat faster.

"Elora," he had said.

Her breath hitched as she remembered the feel of his rough hand brushing against her cheek.

"Wait for me, Elora," he had whispered.

Her heart felt as though it would burst. She could hear the longing and the devotion in his words, in his voice, for her. She felt cherished. She felt wanted. It was nearly overwhelming, the anticipation of finally seeing him and finally sharing the same space that he did.

A note of desperation suddenly tinged her thoughts. She was supposed to wait for him. He was coming for her. How could she leave? But then, how could she stay? Either way she would lose. Her heart pounded and her chest heaved as panic took hold. He was too late. Willingly or not, she would be gone. An anguished tear slipped from beneath her eyelid.

Engrossed in her thoughts, she couldn't hear the concerned voices of her parents calling out her name. It was only the weight of Asher's hand pressing against her arm that broke her trance. Her eyes flew open and she looked around, startled and disoriented for a moment.

"It's alright," he said softly, reaching up to gently wipe away her tears.

She locked eyes with him briefly before looking away, embarrassed that he had seen her in such a vulnerable state. Her gaze shifted downward to the table and came to rest upon the strawberry plant. The small cluster of leaves now overflowed from the flower pot and dozens of luscious red berries dangled down the sides. She lifted her brows, as always surprised by her own ability.

The room remained silent for a few minutes, as everyone stared in awe at Elora and the plant now brimming with strawberries. They were speechless, trying to comprehend the miracle they had just witnessed. There was a big difference between knowing about her ability and seeing it.

"That was incredible, Elora," her father whispered reverently.

"But do you get this upset every time you use your ability?" her mother asked, frowning.

"No," Elora said. "I get emotional, but it doesn't always have to be negative. It just requires focus and intensity. I think it has more to do with the way my body reacts to the emotions than the emotions themselves. So incredibly happy thoughts can also awaken my ability."

"What were you thinking of?" Asher asked, curious.

"Something nice," she said, turning the plant in front of her to admire the juicy berries that were cascading like a waterfall over the lip of the pot.

"It didn't seem like a particularly nice thought," he muttered.

"It started out very nice," she said quietly, smiling to herself as she reached out to touch the largest berry.

She stared vacantly for a moment, recalling the terrible realization that her vision would never come true. Closing her eyes and taking a shaky breath, she resigned herself to the fact that she truly had no other option. She would have to go. If not for herself, then for her parents. She doubted they would leave without her and who knows what would happen to them at the hands of the Liana. Having made her choice, she knew she would have to leave now, before her heartbreak weakened her resolve. Turning to Asher, she lifted her gaze to lock eyes with him.

"When do we leave?" she asked.

His eyes widened in surprise. As the shock of her statement dissipated, there was a collective sigh of relief around the table as everyone realized that Elora was now a willing participant in her own rescue. Asher shared a knowing look with her father before answering.

"Tonight," he replied.

Elora returned her gaze to the plant on the table before her, nodding in acceptance, a look of determination on her face. Grasping a berry in her fingers, she gave it a sharp tug and held out the plucked fruit to him.

"Strawberry?"

CHAPTER 12

"Leaving Windom unfortunately won't be as easy as walking out the gates at this point," Asher said, sitting back in his chair twirling the strawberry stem between his fingers worriedly. "Colin has been following you for quite a while and is probably very familiar with the area by now. He knows all the places you go and the people you associate with. And unfortunately, he also knows that I'm here too, considering that he tried to steal my horse this morning. I guess I shouldn't have gone to the barber," he said smiling sardonically. "He wouldn't have recognized me otherwise. I had grown a pretty good disguise."

"You certainly had," Winnifred acknowledged, nodding. "I nearly shut the door in your face last night!"

Elora's mouth fell open as she recalled the man with long hair and a thick beard whom she'd encountered in the road. She turned to study Asher with wide eyes.

"That was *you*?" she asked, incredulous.

"Yes," he said smiling. "I thought I'd draw too much attention attending the ceremony looking like some backwoods ruffian so I had a long visit with the barber this morning. Unfortunately, I did a good job of drawing attention even without the scraggly beard," he said grimacing.

Elora nodded, sympathetically. "That darn wasp."

Asher's shoulders began to shake as he quietly chuckled at her teasing. A wide smile spread across her face as she watched him. He turned towards her and she couldn't help but notice the way laughter made his blue eyes even brighter. He was so strikingly handsome she couldn't bring herself to look away.

"The fact that you can tease me right now makes me worry that you might not understand the gravity of this situation," Asher said, his chuckle fading to a sly grin.

"Maybe it just means I'm brave," she replied quietly, shrugging her shoulders.

"I hope so," he replied, the smile fading from his lips. "You'll have to be."

She nodded solemnly, the moment of humor past.

"So what are we going to do?" her father asked, his voice somber.

"You mentioned last night that you had bought some horses from a farm a few miles outside of town," Asher said, nodding to her parents.

"That's what you were doing on Sunday?" Elora asked, her brows lifted in surprise. "Buying horses?"

"We had already decided to take you home, Elora," her father replied. "The minute we saw that rosebush, we knew it was time. We bought three horses from a rancher outside the walls and paid him to board them while we made preparations for the journey."

"What other preparations have you made?" Asher asked.

"There are three saddlebags in our closet packed with canteens and bedrolls, but that's all so far," her mother replied, shrugging her shoulders. "We hadn't intended to leave quite this soon."

Asher nodded in understanding.

"We will make do," he said. "The horses and canteens are enough. I have my knife and bow. Elora will be able to grow food for us obviously," he said, motioning to the strawberry plant. "The rest we can figure out as we go."

"I will need seeds, though," Elora interrupted.

He looked at her, and nodded in acknowledgment.

"The problem at this point is how to get out of here undetected," he said, rubbing his chin as he considered their situation. "Colin is going to be expecting us to run. He may not try to stop us from leaving, but he will surely track us and turn us in to the Liana at the first opportunity."

"So we wait until dark?" her mother asked.

Asher nodded his agreement.

"How many gates are there in the wall?" he asked.

"There are four, but only the North Gate is regularly used. The other three remain locked unless there is a need for the town to evacuate," Jonas replied.

"So leaving through the gate is out of the question," Asher said, sighing. "How secure is the wall?" he asked.

"It is thick and well-guarded," Jonas said. "It would be incredibly difficult to go over the wall. And even if we could, getting down the other side would be treacherous."

"I can get us over the wall," Elora interrupted quietly.

Everyone turned to look at her, surprise in their eyes.

"Trig will get us out," she said solemnly, her heart squeezing painfully at the idea of asking her friend to break the rules and put himself in danger.

"Are you sure?" Asher asked firmly.

"I'm sure," she answered, exhaling deeply as guilt and regret settled onto her chest. "If I ask him, he will."

"Alright," Asher said. "So, we'll go over the wall after dark, retrieve your horses and go from there."

"What about your horse though?" Elora asked, frowning. "Isn't she in the stable?"

"After I left you this morning, I moved her out beyond the wall," Asher replied. "With Colin here, she wasn't safe. She's in a cow pasture out past the wheat fields."

"I haven't climbed anything besides the ladder in the storage shed for twenty years," Winnifred mused, smiling. "I hope I can make it over the wall."

"Climbing is second nature to us, my love," her husband soothed, nudging her with his shoulder. "We spent half our lives up in the trees. I'm sure it will all come back to us quickly."

"Clarens do a lot of climbing?" Elora asked, thinking back to how easily she had scaled the wall a few weeks past.

"You could say that," Asher muttered, smiling. "That reminds me," he said, turning to her parents. "Do you still have your Elysic cloaks?"

"Yes. We couldn't bear to get rid of them. They were all that we had left of Clarendon," her mother said, smiling.

"They may prove useful tonight," he remarked.

"I'll get them," she said, rising from the table and disappearing into the master bedroom.

"So what now?" Jonas asked, anxiously.

"I need to talk to Trig," Elora reminded him.

"I'll go with you," Asher said in a voice that brooked no disagreement. "Now that Colin knows I'm here, he might do something brash. You shouldn't be alone."

"That's fine. I don't want to be alone," Elora replied, shaking her head.

The very thought of being alone now that she knew she was being watched and pursued sent a chill throughout her body.

"You and Winnifred should see about gathering some seeds for Elora," Asher said, looking across the table at Jonas.

"These will come in handy for that!" Winnifred exclaimed, returning with two long cloaks made of thin, drab brown fabric.

The cloaks slid from her hands like water, flowing onto the table into a puddle of silky cloth.

"I've never seen anything like this," Elora said, reaching out to rub the material between her fingers.

"It's woven from the silk of caterpillars who feed on the Elysian trees and then stained with dye made from the bark," she explained, running her hand over the smooth fabric. "It's beautiful, but more importantly, like every other part of the Elysian Tree, it's invisible to everyone but the Claren."

Elora froze. "The trees are invisible?"

Winnifred nodded, smiling. "Except to us."

"So are the seeds," Asher said, watching as her expression shifted from surprise to understanding.

"That's why no one else could see the seed on my necklace," she remarked, shaking her head in amazement. "I thought I was going crazy."

"I'm sure you did," her mother replied sympathetically, reaching across the table to grasp her hand.

"That's how the scouts knew you were a Claren," Asher said softly. "This is how they recognized you, Elora," Asher noted, motioning to the necklace laying on the table between them.

Elora looked down at the seed, a mixture of emotions playing across her face. She had brought this threat upon them. She had unwittingly revealed their location to the enemy. She pushed the necklace away from her, suddenly disgusted.

"I wish I had known," she whispered.

"I wish we had told you," agreed her father, guilt and regret darkening his features.

Asher looked down at the necklace that was now resting in front of him. Suddenly his head tilted and he squinted his eyes. He picked up the seed, studying it closely.

"The last seeds of the Ever Tree were brown. This one has veins of silver scattered over the surface," he noted, his voice tinged with excitement. "Is this how it looked when you first purchased the necklace?" he asked.

Elora looked up, quirking her brows in curiosity at his tone. Her gaze shifted from Asher to the seed that he was holding with now trembling fingers.

"Actually no. It has changed color a bit. Those silver strands started appearing soon after I got it," she admitted.

Asher's face broke out into a euphoric smile and he laughed quietly in amazement.

"What?" she asked, confused. "What is it?"

"You're bringing it back to life, Elora," he whispered, looking at her in awe. "You truly are the Renascent."

She glanced over at her parents to see that they too were staring at her in wonder. It was all there in their eyes, the pride, the expectation, the reverence, the hope. It was too much! Elora began to twist her hands nervously in her lap. Her heart began to beat faster and her cheeks warmed as the weight of their belief pressed down on her.

She cautioned another glimpse at Asher and found him watching her, his expression a mixture of relief and admiration. Suddenly she couldn't catch her breath. She looked away quickly but Asher must have seen the fear in her eyes. His brows furrowed in concern and he reached out to quiet her anxious hands, covering them with one of his. She jerked in surprise at his touch, turning to lock eyes with him. He returned her gaze for a moment before something caught his attention and he diverted his eyes. She turned just in time to see a flower burst into bloom on the plant before her and ripen into a bright red berry. She tore her hand out from beneath his and pushed the plant away from her.

"Stop it! Don't look at me like that!" she cried, glancing around the room at all of them.

Her parents recoiled in shock at her outburst.

"It's alright, love," her mother said soothingly, the awe-struck expression washed from her face.

"No, it's not! I can't be the Renascent," she said, her chin quivering as she fought back tears.

"But sweetheart, you are," affirmed her father, nodding.

Elora covered her face with her hands in frustration as her mother gave him a look of reprimand.

"Two weeks ago I was nothing but an ordinary farmer," she lamented, her voice muffled behind her hands. "And now I'm supposed to save the Ever Tree, the Claren, and the entire Woodlands," she said letting her hands fall to her lap as her shoulders slumped.

"This is exactly why we brought you here," her mother said, shaking her head sadly.

"So that you could suddenly surprise me with this crushing burden after a life of utter normalcy?" Elora asked bitterly.

"No!" her father exclaimed. "We brought you here so that you wouldn't be crushed! So that you would be strong enough to carry this burden when it did come to rest upon your shoulders."

Elora hung her head, shamed by his words. Hot tears fell onto her hands as feelings of guilt and despair overwhelmed her.

"And you are," her father continued gently.

Elora shook her head in denial, closing her eyes in an attempt to stem the flow of tears that were now streaming down her face.

"Look at me, sweetheart," he urged her.

Elora took a shuddering breath and brushed her hands roughly over her cheeks before lifting her eyes.

"You are," he repeated, holding her gaze. "You are strong enough, Elora."

"You think I'm strong enough to be the Renascent?" she asked in a small voice.

"Yes, but more than that, I think you're strong enough to be Elora Kerrick; to stay true to yourself despite the Mark on your back," he affirmed.

Elora nodded, taking another deep breath as she tried to regain her composure.

"What can we do to help you sweetheart?" her mother asked, desperate to somehow make things easier for her.

Thinking for a moment, Elora looked back and forth between her parents.

"I need you to remember that I'm still just me," she answered. "To the rest of the Claren I'm going to be the Renascent. But to you, can I just be your daughter?"

"Of course," her mother replied, nodding as she looked to Jonas for agreement.

"We will do our best to treat you as we always have, sweetheart," he said.

Elora nodded her gratitude. She lifted her gaze to stare solemnly out the window behind them, blinking to clear the tears from her eyes. As she looked out at the same view she'd seen her whole life, her heart sank. Fresh tears slipped down her cheeks as she thought about leaving Windom, the only home she'd ever known. She quietly mourned the loss of her life here and the only future she'd ever imagined.

"Things have changed so quickly," she said quietly. "I thought I would never leave Windom," she admitted. "It was a wonderful place to grow up," she said, smiling sadly at her parents.

"Yes, it was," her mother agreed. "You were safe here, and for that we will always be grateful to this place."

"Safe and normal," Elora sighed. "Everything was so much simpler an hour ago. All I wanted in life was to find someone to love and to make things grow."

"That's all I want too," Asher uttered quietly from where he sat beside her, drawing her attention.

"And that's why you're here," Elora asserted, nodding her head in understanding.

"When I set out to find you, my motives were not nearly so selfish," Asher replied, staring down at the seed in his hand, gently rubbing his thumb across it's intricate surface. "I wanted to save our way of life and preserve the Woodlands. But now that I'm here with you, I must admit that my cause feels more personal."

"You want to find your soulmate and realize your purpose," she stated. "And you can't have those things without the Renascent."

He lifted his eyes, fixing her with a heartfelt gaze.

"True," he acknowledged. "I can't have those things without you."

"But what if I fail," she whispered, biting her lip nervously as she gave voice to her greatest fear.

"You won't," he said earnestly. "This should give you confidence, Elora," he said, holding up the seed. "You did this without even trying. The silver in this seed is proof that you are powerful. That you are destined," he reasoned.

Elora shifted her eyes down to the seed he held grasped between his fingers. He was right. The seed had changed. She didn't understand how, but something she had done was bringing the seed back to life.

He leaned toward her, capturing her attention and holding her gaze. Her breath caught at the intensity in his eyes.

"You won't fail," he repeated with quiet conviction.

Elora couldn't look away. His belief in her was absolute. It was equal parts terrifying and exhilarating. She had no choice but to trust him. Hopefully he had enough faith for the both of them. At last she found the strength to look away, exhaling deeply the breath she hadn't been aware of holding.

"Let's put this back where it belongs," Asher said, pushing his chair away from the table.

A moment later, Elora jumped as the necklace came to rest on her chest. The skin on the back of her neck tingled where his fingers gently brushed against her as he fastened the clasp. She lifted her hand to grasp the seed that was now cradled in the hollow of her throat.

The sound of her father clearing his throat caught everyone's attention.

"I know you have more questions and you deserve answers to them all, but I fear we are running out of time, love," he reminded them, with an apologetic grimace.

Elora nodded and moved to stand. From his place behind her, Asher pulled her chair back as she rose.

"How long do you think it will take you to retrieve the seeds?" he asked her parents.

Winnifred was standing, draping her Elysic cloak around her shoulders.

"Perhaps a little more than half an hour," her mother replied.

"Why are you wearing that?" Elora asked, curious.

"I'd rather not have to stop and explain what I'm doing out there on my day off," her mother explained.

"And someone might protest if they catch me walking out of the storage shed with a bag full of seeds," she said as she fastened the cloak at the base of her throat.

It hung nearly to the floor and moved like water as she walked, flowing and swirling around her ankles.

"You look like a Claren," Jonas said, smiling fondly at her mother.

"I feel like one," Winnifred replied, laughing.

Jonas stepped towards her and lifted her chin to kiss her sweetly before pulling up the hood of her cloak.

"Take care of my daughter," Jonas said, looking pointedly at Asher who nodded in reply.

"We love you both," her mother said, smiling at Asher and Elora before turning and walking through the door.

"Yes, we do," her father said, making eye contact with each of them. "See you again soon" Jonas called walking out behind her.

Elora stood staring out the open door after her parents, watching her father jog to catch up to her mother's brown figure as she walked down the road toward the gardens.

"No one can see her?" she asked, her tone doubtful.

Asher moved to stand beside her, his arm brushing against hers as he leaned forward to catch sight of them before they walked out of view.

"No one can see her," he confirmed, chuckling at her bemusement. "Shall we?" he asked, motioning towards the open door.

"Let me grab a satchel first. My clothes and boots from this morning are at Alysa's house. I'm going to need them," Elora said, feeling slightly awkward and uncomfortable, and perhaps a bit excited to be alone with Asher.

She retreated to her bedroom, returning a moment later with a leather bag. She looped the strap across her body and the bag came to rest on her hip.

"What do you plan on telling him?" Asher asked.

"The truth," Elora replied bluntly, fixing him with a glare that dared him to suggest otherwise. "Hopefully he'll believe me."

"Well then we should take this," Asher said, lifting the remaining Elysic cloak from the table. "In case he needs proof."

"Or in case you need to quickly disappear once Trig finds out you intend to steal me away," Elora replied.

"Or that," Asher muttered, holding out the cloak for her to take.

She avoided his eyes as she took the cloak from his hands and gently stuffed it into her bag.

"I hope you won't hold all of this against me," he said quietly, his voice gruff.

"I'm trying not to," Elora answered, standing before him, staring at the ground.

"In another world we would have grown up knowing one another, climbing trees, causing trouble, playing beneath the branches of the Ever Tree as Claren children do," he said softly, his accent intoxicating.

"That sounds nice," Elora replied, her voice tinged with longing.

"We would have been friends," he said confidently.

"I don't know about that," Elora protested. "I never caused trouble as a child. I don't think I would have befriended a trouble-maker," she teased, trying to hide the smile threatening to lift the corners of her mouth.

"You should befriend this one," he bantered back, "because Elora Kerrick, you're about to cause a whole bunch of trouble and you're going to need my expertise."

She couldn't help the laugh that escaped.

"Alright then. It's nice to meet you Asher Weatherby and I suppose we can be friends," she said extending her hand to shake his as he chuckled. "Though it would have been a whole lot nicer if we had met beneath the Ever Tree," she said smiling up at him.

The laughter faded from his smile as he held her gaze.

"Perhaps someday we will," he replied quietly.

Elora could feel the heat of a blush climbing up her cheeks at his words. She quickly looked away, clearing her throat as she released his hand.

"Are you ready to go?" he asked her, bringing them back to task.

"Yep," she answered quickly.

Asher walked over to the door, unlatching it and holding it open for her to pass.

Elora walked to the doorway but froze before crossing the threshold.

"Colin is out there," Elora said, suddenly frightened at the thought of him following her, watching her.

"I'm right here," Asher said encouragingly.

He placed his hand on her lower back to nudge her forward but immediately jerked back as he realized that he had come in contact with her bare skin. He had accidently touched the Mark of the Ever Tree. His eyes grew wide and he stammered an apology.

"It's alright. It won't burn you, I don't think," Elora teased, enjoying the blush that colored his cheeks.

"Maybe it did!" he replied, indignant.

"Did it?" Elora asked, her brows knitted in concern.

"No," he answered, smiling bashfully as he motioned toward the door, encouraging her to move.

Elora rolled her eyes and nervously walked out of the house.

CHAPTER 13

They walked in silence for a few minutes, each watching vigilantly for any sign of Colin. Elora's body was stiff with apprehension and her eyes darted back and forth furtively. She jumped at every sound, gasped at every unexpected movement. Sensing her fear, Asher took hold of her hand and tucked it into the crook of his elbow.

"I won't let anything happen to you Elora," he reassured her.

She looked up at him with frightened eyes, nodding unconvincingly.

"You don't believe me?" he asked, affronted.

"I don't really know you," she asserted. "My only experience of your prowess is when you nearly tackled me this morning."

"I caught you though," he said, defensively.

"That's true," she conceded, nodding distractedly as she continued watching for Colin.

"Elora, I have been searching for you for two years. There is nowhere I haven't gone and there isn't much I haven't seen by now," he asserted.

Elora looked up at him, making eye contact as she considered his words. She hadn't really thought about all he had done to find her or what he might have gone through in that time. In light of that, she appraised him with different eyes. He was still attractive of course, but more than that now, he was impressive. She did feel calmer, knowing how capable he must be to have survived. However, her newfound appreciation for him came with a healthy dose of guilt. What he must have sacrificed for her. She was indebted to him. How could she ever deserve what he had done?

"Thank you," Elora said uncomfortably, fixing her eyes forward as they walked. "I know you must have given up a lot to find me."

"Not as much as you might think," he said, trying to put her at ease.

She nodded, casting her eyes down at the ground.

"Elora, without the Ever Tree, there wasn't much left for me to give up," he stated sadly.

"I'm not sure whether I should feel better or worse because of that," Elora replied sighing.

"None of this is your fault," Asher assured her. "I don't blame you for the way things are."

"I would understand if you did," she said softly, cautiously peaking up at him.

"Well, I don't," he said firmly. "Honestly Elora, searching for you gave me something productive to do and I was grateful for it," he admitted.

"Don't you miss your home?" she asked, imagining how it would feel when she had to leave Windom in just a few hours.

"I miss my family, but no, I don't miss Clarendon," he replied, shaking his head. "I felt relieved the day I walked away from my home. Clarendon is a sad place without the Ever Tree," he said, frowning. "So much of our culture and our purpose depended on it. Since the seeds stopped falling, there have been no trees to plant and the Claren are left to helplessly wait, knowing that it is only a matter of time before the Woodlands start to disappear. It was depressing to be there."

"How long before that will begin to happen?" she asked, guilt tugging at her heart.

"It already has," Asher answered. "The Claren have been cultivating the forests of the Woodlands for centuries, continuously planting new Elysian trees to replace the ones that are nearing the end of their lifespan. But it's been three years now. The oldest trees are already beginning to die and there are no seedlings to fill their void. The forests are already beginning to thin."

"That's awful," Elora whispered, weighted down by a new sense of urgency.

"It is," Asher agreed, nodding. "But because the Woodlands are so vast, it may not be apparent for decades. Hopefully it won't come to that," he said, looking at her meaningfully.

She nodded, swallowing nervously.

They walked in silence for a few moments, both lost in thought as they kept watch for Colin. Asher suddenly let out a deep sigh, drawing Elora's attention.

"I have to admit, selfish as it may seem, that the worst part of losing the Ever Tree isn't what is happening to the Woodlands," he said, self-consciously shoving his hand into his pocket. "It is far more personal for me and all of the younger Claren who were not yet paired when the Ever Tree died. We were left with no way to find our soulmates."

"But can't Claren just fall in love like the rest of the world?" Elora asked, confused.

"Yes. And that's what's started happening now that three years have passed without any pairings," he said, nodding. "But the Claren are scared."

"Falling in love is scary for everyone, you know," Elora said quietly.

"I guess so," Asher admitted. "But we have always relied on the seeds to guide us to our soulmates. It's the only way to earn the Mark of the Ever Tree."

"Does it matter though, how they find one another?" Elora asked. "The tree doesn't make two people soulmates. They are soulmates because of who they are and the choices they've made. The Claren have a way to find their soulmates, Asher," she said. "They just have to be brave and trust their own hearts to recognize them."

"But what if they choose the wrong person?" he asked, looking down at her earnestly. "One day the seeds may start falling again. And when they do, what if all those Claren discover that they actually belong with someone else? Then the pairings they have made and the families they have started would be torn apart."

"But why? Does the seed steal their free will? Would they really forsake the people they have chosen?" she asked, aghast.

"I actually don't know the answer to that," Asher admitted. "To earn the Mark of the Ever Tree, to be able to plant the Elysian Trees, you have to be paired to your soulmate."

"But when you choose a person, they *become* your soulmate," Elora argued. "And you choose to continue loving that person even if there are times when you think you chose wrong," she said with conviction. "If you win someone's heart, you deserve to keep it."

"Even if that person is meant for someone else?" Asher asked.

"If that person has chosen you, she cannot be meant for anyone else," Elora stated decisively.

"Elora, you haven't seen what it's like," Asher said, shaking his head. "I grew up watching soulmates find one another beneath the Ever Tree. Destiny is real."

"Maybe it is," she conceded, looking up at him. "But I watched my friends fall in love. I stood beside them as they chose one another. Their love wasn't ruled by some sense of destiny. It was a choice. And you cannot tell me that they aren't soulmates."

"Perhaps they are," Asher said. "But they aren't Claren, Elora. They can't know their destiny. Not the way we can. Or could, rather, when the Ever Tree was alive."

"But maybe it's better that way," Elora said softly.

"What do you mean?" Asher asked, surprised.

"I can see how there is safety and security in a love that is destined," she said. "But there is strength and bravery and intention in a love that is chosen. Maybe in some ways, it's better to be chosen."

Asher looked down at her, his expression unreadable as he considered what she had said. They walked in uncomfortable silence for a few minutes as Asher surveyed their surroundings for anyone trying to follow them.

"Have you chosen someone, Elora?" he asked quietly.

She jerked her eyes up to his, surprised by the unexpected question. Her mouth fell open slightly as she took in his wary expression. He seemed more than just merely curious. She thought for a moment how to answer, unsure of what to say. Had she chosen someone? Did it even matter since she couldn't have him?

"Kind of," she began noncommittally. "Not really." She hesitated before settling on, "Not anymore," with a shake of her head.

"Not anymore." he repeated. "But there was someone once," he stated flatly, looking for confirmation.

She nodded her head, staring off down the road as she considered her visions and her deep connection to the man in them.

"What happened?" Asher asked.

"It's complicated," she said, trying to avoid giving an explanation.

Her vague answer did nothing to quell his interest, rather intensifying his curiosity. He moved in front of her, forcing her to stop. She looked up at him in surprise.

"Your parents never mentioned anyone," Asher asserted, his brows furrowed in concern.

"Well, they didn't know about him," she admitted.

"Was he at the ceremony this morning?" Asher asked.

"No," she answered curtly, beginning to find his prying irritating.

Asher stood quietly watching her a moment before he asked a question so insightful that it made her gasp.

"Were you thinking of him when you grew the strawberries?" he asked carefully.

"Enough, Asher!" she cried. "Why do you even need to know? I've already agreed to go with you!"

She dodged around him and tried to start walking down the road towards Alysa's house but Asher quickly grabbed hold of her elbow. She stopped, staring down at the ground as she tried to control her annoyance.

"Is he why you were crying?" Asher asked softly, his eyes quickly scanning the roadside around them before settling back on her face.

"Yes," she finally admitted. "I was upset because I'm going to leave tonight and I'll never even get to see him," she confessed. "Asher, I really don't want to talk about it with you."

"I don't understand," he continued undeterred. "You've never seen him?" he asked.

Defeated, Elora sighed from deep down in her soul before lifting her eyes to his.

"I have visions of him," she confessed quietly.

Asher froze, his eyes widening a bit.

"I know it sounds crazy and ridiculous," she stammered, embarrassed.

"You've had visions?" Asher asked haltingly.

She looked up at him expecting to see judgement and ridicule, but instead saw only surprise and curiosity in his eyes. She exhaled a sigh of relief.

"Yes," Elora answered. "Well, visions might not be exactly the right word since I can't actually see anything in them," she said shrugging as she looked up at him. "I've had them for as long as I can remember."

"Do your parents know about this?" he asked, astounded.

"No," she said, shaking her head. "I thought they were just daydreams for the longest time. Until he started showing up in them and I recognized that they were something more."

"What happens in your visions?" he asked.

"Sometimes when I close my eyes, I'm transported to what I imagine is a huge forest," she explained. "There's the rustling sound of leaves blowing and branches creaking in the wind. The air is cool and moist on my skin and it smells sweet and musty."

"That sounds about right," Asher said nodding, a hint of a smile on his lips as he remembered what it felt like to be deep in the forests of Clarendon.

"About two weeks ago, I was experiencing a vision when I discovered, for the first time, that I wasn't alone. There was a man there calling for me, searching. And when he finally found me, he reached out and I felt him touch my hand. All it took was that brief moment, that small touch. I felt instantly connected to him," she said, shrugging her shoulders in bewilderment. "Right from the start I had these completely irrational, unexpected feelings for him."

She smiled as she lost herself in the memory of that moment. Her skin began to tingle as she recalled the feel of his hand on hers. She looked up to find Asher watching her with an unsettling intensity. She cleared her throat and shifted her gaze downward to study her fingers as they fidgeted with the strap of her satchel.

"He's come to me a few more times since then," she continued. "I've still never seen him and I know literally nothing about him, not even his name, but I believe in my soul that he's a real person. And just being near him elicits these intense emotions," Elora said, smiling quietly to herself. "It feels like I'm meant to be with him somehow." Her face fell. "And that's why I was crying earlier. Because it can never happen."

"What?" Asher asked, his voice a mixture of surprise and disappointment. "Why?"

"He's only ever really spoken to me once in my visions. And when he did, it was to ask me to wait for him," she answered.

"I don't understand the problem," Asher said, quirking his brow.

"We have to leave Windom tonight," she explained.

"Yes we definitely do, but why does that matter?" Asher asked, his expression skeptical.

"Once I leave, I just can't imagine he would ever be able to find me again," she replied, her voice small.

Elora turned and began walking again and Asher silently matched her stride. She could feel him glancing at her when he wasn't keeping watch for Colin.

"*I* found you," he said after a few moments.

Elora looked up at him in surprise. Her heart squeezed as a glimmer of hope took hold.

"Yes, you did," she admitted. "Wait," she said, furrowing her brows. "How *did* you find me?" she asked.

Asher continued talking as though he hadn't heard her question.

"Besides, perhaps he didn't mean wait for him here," he said, lifting his arm to indicate Windom. "Maybe he meant wait for him here," he said, thumping his hand over his heart.

She walked a few steps, staring down at the ground beneath her feet as she considered what he'd said. A slow smile tugged the corners of her mouth upwards and she looked up at him, her face a mixture of hope and relief.

"Perhaps he did," she mused.

"You know, I'm pretty surprised that you were willing to just give him up like that," Asher said, shaking his head in disappointment. "Your feelings must not have been that intense."

"Well, I didn't want to," Elora said defensively. "And anyway, no matter how strongly I feel, I tend to lead with my head more than my heart. And my head says that I would be a fool to let these crazy visions affect the choices I make in reality."

"But what does your heart say?" he asked.

"That I love him," she admitted quietly.

Elora looked up at Asher who was watching her intently and she was suddenly overcome by a wave of embarrassment. She covered her face with her hands, mortified.

"I can't even believe I'm saying these things out loud," she mumbled through her fingers. "It all sounds so ridiculous."

"It doesn't sound ridiculous," he replied softly.

"Yes, it does," she said, dropping her hands from her face.

"No, it doesn't," he reiterated more forcefully. "You said he began appearing to you two weeks ago?" he asked.

Elora nodded.

"Right around the time your seed appeared in Clarendon," he noted.

Elora's hand flew to the seed hanging around her neck and she looked up at him with wide eyes.

"It doesn't sound ridiculous, Elora," he said. "It sounds like you've been Paired."

Elora inhaled sharply as he gave voice to her own suspicions.

"He's your soulmate," Asher continued.

Elora jerked her eyes up to him, startled. He was looking down at her, his expression serious. She shook her head in denial.

"He's your soulmate, Elora," Asher asserted again. "I know you feel it. You admitted that you love him just a moment ago."

"But it doesn't make sense!" she cried.

"Is love always supposed to make sense?" he asked carefully.

"But how can I trust it? It's a love built on nothing," she agonized. "I don't even know him."

"It's not enough to know that you're destined?" Asher asked hesitantly.

"Is it?" she asked.

"I always believed that it would be," he answered raising his eyebrows, surprised at her reluctance. "That's how it's worked in Clarendon for centuries."

"I guess I just always expected that I'd give my heart to the man who earned it, who deserved it; not to someone I've never even met," she said, frowning. "I thought I would get to choose."

Asher looked away from her and busied himself scanning the fields around them. They fell into an uncomfortable silence. Elora couldn't help but feel that she had said something wrong.

"Have I insulted you somehow?" she asked hesitantly.

"No," he answered, forcing a smile. "I was just wondering if you might end up resenting him because he wasn't your choice."

"I don't know," she said, looking off into the distance as she considered his question. "Maybe it won't even matter in the end whether I fell in love with him by choice or by destiny, as long as I love him."

He nodded but his posture remained rigid.

"Do you think you'll know him when he finally finds you?" he asked holding her gaze.

"I hope so," she smiled. "But I don't know. All I have to go on is his voice and I've only really heard that once. I guess I'll just have to trust my heart to recognize him," she laughed. "So I'm in no better shape than all the rest of the Claren after all."

"I suppose that's true," he replied smiling.

"At least I know he's out there somewhere looking for me," she said wistfully.

"I'm sure he is," Asher said, tucking his hands into his pockets as he walked.

"I hope it doesn't take *him* two years to find me," she said, nudging Asher with her shoulder in jest.

"You should probably just hope he's not ugly," Asher replied, laughing.

Elora shook her head, amused. They walked a fair distance in amiable silence, enjoying a new level of comfort and the beginning of what looked like a friendship.

Nearing Alysa's house, the air between them took on a different tone. Elora began to recognize the finality of what she was about to do and her stomach began to churn with nerves and dread. Her face turned pale and her mouth settled into a grim line. Telling Trig and Alysa about all of this and asking them to help her escape would make it all real in a way it hadn't been before. She was leaving.

A dull, smothering pain settled around her heart as she looked up the front steps at the house she'd considered a second home for most of her life. She took a shuddering breath and tried to fortify herself against the tears beginning to pool in her eyes. She bit her lip to stop its trembling. Blinking hard to clear her vision, she quickly wiped away the tears that were caught in her eyelashes.

Asher watched her silently as she struggled to compose herself. He reached out a comforting hand to rub her shoulder.

"Please don't be nice to me right now," she said, attempting to smile up at him. "I'm trying to be tough."

He nodded his understanding and stepped back to give her space.

At that moment, the door opened and the newly bound couple emerged from the house, laughing and chattering excitedly.

"Elora!" Alysa cried with enthusiasm. "I'm so glad you caught us!" she exclaimed, running down the stairs to wrap her in a hug.

"Yes. You have impeccable timing Elora," Trig teased. "Who would have thought it would be this difficult to get some time alone with my bride," he said, looking to Asher for sympathy.

"We were just leaving to go home! To our very own house!" Alysa gushed.

"When did you get a house?" Elora exclaimed.

"Apparently Trig was keeping some secrets from me," Alysa said, with a besotted grin at her husband.

Elora smiled, shaking her head.

"Well done, my friend," she said, smiling at Trig.

"Well, we certainly weren't going to spend our first night together in there. With them," Trig, said, motioning behind him at Alysa's parents' house with a look of horror on his face.

"No, of course not," she chuckled. "It was foolish of me to come looking for you here now that you say it like that."

"You were looking for me?" Alysa asked, surprised. "I thought you were just coming to get your things."

"Well, that too," Elora said, shrugging.

"I'll be right back," Alysa said, holding up a finger as she turned and ran back up the stairs and into the house.

"Is everything alright?" Trig asked, eyeing Asher suspiciously.

Elora smiled uncomfortably in reply. He furrowed his brows in concern and walked down the steps towards her but was intercepted by Alysa who returned with lightning speed.

"I knew you would be needing these," she said smiling as she handed over the work boots and clothes that Elora had worn earlier that morning.

Elora took the boots and neatly folded pants and tunic from her and stared down at them, marveling at how different her life had been when she had been wearing these only hours ago. She suddenly became acutely aware of three pairs of eyes watching her with curiosity and growing alarm. She quickly busied herself stuffing the clothing into her satchel.

"Why were you looking for me?" Alysa asked carefully, reaching out to grasp Elora's forearm.

"Both of you actually," Elora replied, making eye contact with Trig.

"It would be better to speak inside," Asher interrupted, stepping forward. "Privately."

"And you are?" Trig demanded, moving to put himself between Asher and the women.

Asher took a step back to diffuse the situation but crossed his arms and steadily returned Trig's stare, making it clear that he was not intimidated.

"It's okay Trig," Elora interrupted. "This is Asher. He's a friend," she said, locking eyes with Asher for a moment.

"You don't seem very happy considering you've made a new friend, Elora," Trig noted warily, but he eased off, moving to stand beside Alysa.

"You're not from here," Alysa said, looking at Asher curiously. "I don't recognize your accent."

"No," Asher said, shaking his head. "I'm not from here."

"What brings you to Windom?" she asked, ever friendly.

"I came to see the Kerricks," he replied, smiling politely and shifting to briefly make eye contact with Elora.

"Can we go inside to talk?" Elora asked.

"We aren't going back in there," Trig said, shaking his head. "It was hard enough getting out of there the first time. I'm not going through that again."

"Let's go to our house then," Alysa suggested. "We'll have privacy there," she said, slipping her hand through the crook of Trig's arm.

"Not the kind of privacy I was hoping for," he muttered, turning to escort her down the road to their new home.

"I love the sound of that," Alysa declared smiling, ignoring Trig. "Our house," she repeated happily. "I can't wait for you to see it, Elora!" she gushed.

Elora fell into step beside them, attempting to set aside her despair for a few moments more. She laughed, enjoying the teasing and flirty banter that flowed easily between Trig and Alysa. She looked back to see Asher following slightly behind, quietly listening to their playful back and forth, chuckling quietly. He made eye contact, giving her a sad, sympathetic smile. She turned away from him, the reality of what was about to happen settling around her. She knew that once she began talking, the joy of this day would be gone forever. Feelings of sorrow and guilt dropped like a weight onto her chest, taking her breath away.

"Here we are!" Alysa exclaimed as they arrived in front of a small but cute little house.

There was a beautiful little basket full of flowers hanging beside the door and a lantern waiting to be lit above the entryway. Alysa pushed open the door to reveal a small sitting room with a sofa and two chairs. There was a small kitchen off to the right with a small potted lavender plant in the middle. Elora recognized it as the one she had given her earlier that spring to match the little lavender plant that used to live beside her own bed.

"Your handiwork," Alysa said, pulling a bloom from the basket and smiling at Elora as she led them through the doorway. "My mom picked a few from the Courtyard earlier to make it pretty in here," she explained, lifting the bloom to her nose and drinking in the fragrant scent. "It was enchanting, Elora," she said, reaching over to touch her arm. "Absolutely breathtaking. I'll never know how you managed it."

This was it. This was her opening. Elora looked up, locking eyes with Asher as he stepped through the threshold. He nodded his encouragement and moved to stand beside her.

"That's actually what I'm here to talk about," Elora said, her voice unsteady.

"You're here to talk about the flowers?" Trig asked curiously as he latched the door closed.

"Not exactly," Elora said hesitantly, "but that's probably the best place to start."

"Maybe we should sit," Alysa said, her brows furrowed in concern.

Alysa and Trig led the way to the small sitting area and nestled comfortably together on the sofa. Elora was slow to follow, dreading the conversation that was about to happen. Asher waited patiently for her to pass, before taking the chair next to hers.

As she moved to sit, Elora realized that she still held her work boots in one hand. She seized on the opportunity to procrastinate just a few seconds more.

"Oh here, let me give these back before I forget," she said as she slipped her feet from the shoes Alysa had loaned her for the ceremony.

She leaned over and quickly tugged on her boots and tied the laces. Rising, she handed the slippers back to Alysa.

"Oh Elora," Alysa chuckled. "Work boots and a ball gown. It is probably the most fitting combination you could ever wear," she teased. "It sums you up perfectly."

Elora laughed in reply, nodding in acknowledgement of the truth. She swept her hands beneath her to arrange the skirt of dress as she sat. Smoothing the fabric over her knees, she gingerly touched the intricate vines her friend had embroidered. She looked up to Alysa, her eyes watery with deep affection.

"Do you remember what you said to me the day that I tried this on for the first time?" Elora asked, smiling.

Alysa shook her head. A frown pulled at the corners of her mouth as she exchanged a worried glance with Trig.

Elora reached up to her throat brushing past the seed necklace to touch the flower pendant that Alysa had fastened there this morning. Lifting the chain, she followed it with her fingers to find the clasp behind her neck and unhooked it. She gently laid it on her lap, and lifted her eyes to Alysa.

"You put this pendant around my neck and then you admired how perfectly this ensemble suited me because," Elora paused, trying to summon the courage to say the next words.

"Because you make the flowers grow," Alysa finished for her.

"Because I make the flowers grow," she repeated quietly, touching the pendant in her lap.

There was only one way they were going to believe her. She would have to show them. Rising, she held the pendant out to Alysa who took it, her face a mixture of surprise and confusion. Elora walked into the kitchen and returned to her seat a moment later with the small lavender plant. She wrapped her hands around the small clay pot and took a deep breath as she closed her eyes.

This time the tingling sensation in her hands was nearly immediate as she tapped into the emotions bubbling just beneath the surface. She allowed herself to imagine, just for a moment, what it would be like to tell her dearest friend goodbye. A hot tear seeped from beneath her eyelashes, rolling down her cheek and dripping onto her hand. She gasped and opened her eyes, breaking free of the terrible thought.

Her gaze fell to her lap and as expected, the small pot was now overflowing with lavender. She slowly lifted her eyes to see the reactions of her friends.

Alysa was staring wide-eyed at the plant, her hand covering her mouth. Trig had risen from his seat and was standing as still as a statue, frozen in shock. They remained that way for a few moments before Asher cleared his throat, breaking their trance. Alysa finally dropped her hand from her mouth and took a deep breath. She locked eyes with Elora and her lips spread into a smile.

"You make the flowers grow," she whispered.

CHAPTER 14

"That was unbelievable!" Trig exclaimed, smacking his hand to his forehead as he plopped back down onto the sofa.

"It was incredible!" Alysa amended. "You're incredible, Elora," she gushed.

Elora chuckled self-consciously, keeping her eyes fixed on the lavender plant in her hands.

"This certainly explains the Courtyard, doesn't it," Alysa said, giggling as she reached out to touch the lavender blooms. "How wonderful," she sighed.

Leaning over, she took Elora's hand and gave it an affectionate squeeze. The simple, familiar touch brought tears to Elora's eyes. Oh, how she would miss her. It was almost more than she could bear. She kept her face downcast to hide her emotions, but Alysa was too astute, quietly waiting until Elora could no longer avoid her. She lifted her face and Alysa caught sight of her watery eyes.

"Elora!" she gasped, moving to kneel beside her. "What's wrong?"

Elora couldn't speak past the lump in her throat. She blinked, letting loose a tear that left a cool trail down her hot cheek. Alysa looked up to Trig, her face worried and scared. Elora wasn't one to cry.

"Oh Elora," she whispered, lifting her hand to caress her cheek, wiping away the wayward tear with her thumb.

"Is this your fault?" Trig asked, jumping to his feet as he angrily glared at Asher.

Asher looked up at him briefly before returning his attention to Elora. The lines of his face were furrowed in worry and he was gripping the arms of his chair. He was clearly disturbed by seeing Elora so upset.

She looked over, locking eyes with him for a moment. He lifted his eyebrows, a simple question, looking for reassurance that she was alright.

Trig had obviously taken Asher's dismissive behavior as affirmation of his guilt. He had begun moving towards him, ready for a fight. Elora finally found enough composure to speak.

"No!" she shouted just as Trig grabbed a fistful of Asher's shirt and pulled him up from his chair.

She quickly handed the lavender plant to Alysa before jumping up to separate the two men. She put a calming hand on Trig, silently asking him to release Asher. Trig looked at her dubiously but reluctantly loosed his grip and took a step back.

"None of this is his fault," she asserted, reaching up to smooth the wrinkles Trig had left in Asher's shirt. "You could probably say he's actually come to my rescue," she said, looking up to lock eyes with him for only a moment before averting her gaze nervously.

"Rescue from what?" Trig demanded.

"Because I have this gift," Elora explained, motioning toward the lavender plant, "I am valuable to some very determined, very powerful people who would seek to exploit me. Asher came to warn me and to help me avoid being taken by them."

"How will he do that?" Alysa asked hesitantly as she placed the potted plant on the ground and rose to her feet.

"You don't trust the Guard to protect you?" Trig asked, affronted.

"You cannot protect her from them," Asher stated firmly, drawing all eyes to him.

"Yes, we can," Trig argued emphatically.

"I don't mean to insult you," Asher placated. "But you don't understand what you're up against. There are many of them and they have a distinct advantage."

"How will you protect her?" Alysa asked again, more forcefully.

Asher's eyes darted to her for a moment, but before he could acknowledge her question, Trig drew his attention back again.

"There are more than two hundred Guardsmen in Windom, all well trained and intimately familiar with the terrain," Trig stated, crossing his arms and widening his stance.

Asher sighed, annoyed by Trig's bravado. He shifted, mirroring Trig's aggressive posture.

"It would not matter if there were twice that many," Asher replied, shrugging his shoulders.

Trig shook his head, clenching his jaw angrily.

"The Guard has taken an oath to protect all citizens of Windom with our lives, if necessary. She doesn't need you," he said.

"If your Guard gets between the Liana and Elora, their death would be a certainty," Asher said with quiet intensity. "And it would be a waste."

"You underestimate us," Trig said, smirking.

Asher remained quiet for a moment, holding unflinching eye contact with Trig. He took a deep breath before shifting his gaze downward and locked eyes with Elora. He slowly leaned over, bringing his face close to Elora's. Her breath caught in her throat. Her heart pounded as she was held captive, powerless to pull her eyes away from his.

"Excuse me," he whispered as he looked down and reached his hand into the satchel at her hip.

Finally comprehending his intentions, she released the breath she'd been holding in a rush.

She moved to help him, holding the satchel open as he took hold of the Elysic cloak hidden within. His hand brushed against hers as he pulled the fabric free, leaving a warm tingling sensation in its wake. Her eyes jolted upwards and locked with his again briefly before she pulled her hands away and stepped back. He shook the cloak out in front of him, sorting out the top from the bottom.

Elora watched the faces of her friends as they tried to figure out what he was doing. She could tell by their confused expressions that they truly could not see the cloak. Asher draped the fabric over his shoulders and quickly pulled the hood up over his head.

Both Alysa and Trig gasped in shock and jumped backwards.

"Where did he go?" Alysa exclaimed, her voice strangled.

"He's still right here," Elora said, gesturing to Asher who was standing beside her in what appeared to them as empty space.

"You can't fight an enemy you can't see," Asher said as he pulled back his hood and unfastened the cloak, revealing himself to them once again.

Trig sat down hard on the sofa behind him, his face a mixture of fear and anger.

Alysa leaned over to Elora, asking in a whisper, "You could still see him?"

Elora nodded, soberly.

Alysa fell into her seat beside Trig and reached out to grasp his hand, looking for the reassurance of something familiar and tangible.

"How?" she asked, looking up at Elora.

"I don't even know how to start explaining it to you," Elora said, sighing.

"These Liana, they can disappear like that?" Trig asked.

Asher was carefully tucking the cloak into a tight roll but briefly lifted his eyes to Trig and nodded.

"Fifty or so of them," he said solemnly.

"That many?" Elora asked, turning to Asher in surprise.

She suddenly realized how little she truly knew about what she was up against and a new fear gripped her. She turned frightened eyes to Alysa, who quickly rose to her feet and put a supportive arm around her shoulders.

"How will you protect her, Asher?" Alysa asked in a tone that demanded his attention. "Fifty against one is impossible odds."

"You can't fight that many by yourself," Trig said, leaning forward and resting his elbows on his knees as he considered the situation.

"No," Asher acknowledged. "But I understand how they work, how they think. I can keep her safe," Asher answered.

"You won't be able to avoid them for long in a small town like Windom," Trig said, shaking his head.

"No, not for more than a day at the most," Asher agreed.

"You have to leave," Alysa said quietly.

Elora suddenly found it difficult to breath. Heat rushed to her face and her heart pounded against her chest. This was the moment she had been dreading more than any other and it was finally here. She couldn't think, couldn't speak. All she could do was feel. Her emotions were overwhelming and she closed her eyes against them, against the grief of her dearest friend, against the end of the beautiful life she had loved. The tears began flowing in earnest and Elora did nothing to stop them.

Alysa turned and took hold of both of Elora's shoulders.

"I don't want you to go," she said, her voice thick with emotion and her chin trembling as tears flooding her eyes.

Elora nodded and stepped forward to bury her head in Alysa's neck as a sob broke free. Alysa's arms wrapped tightly around her. The room was quiet save their quiet weeping.

After a few moments, Trig walked over to offer comfort and share in their heart ache. He placed an arm around each girl and rested his chin on the top of Alysa's head. Closing his eyes, he struggled to fight back tears of his own.

"Why do you trust him Elora?" Trig whispered to Elora once her crying had subsided. "How do you know he's telling you the truth?"

"Because my parents trust him," she answered. "Because they know him, and have known him his entire life. And they are truly terrified of the Liana."

"Are they going with you?" Alysa asked.

Elora nodded.

"I think they are probably in even more danger than I am, actually," she said, her voice quivering.

"When are you leaving?" Trig asked, looking over his shoulder at Asher.

He was still standing quietly on the other side of the room, his hands in his pockets and a somber expression on his face. He had respectfully given the three friends a moment of privacy to mourn, but having been invited back into the conversation he moved closer.

"Tonight," Asher replied, eliciting a gasp from Alysa.

"The threat is that close?" Trig asked, raising his eyebrows in surprise.

"One of them is already here and has been following Elora for a couple of weeks," Asher explained. "More will follow and likely soon."

"Oh my God, Elora!" Alysa exclaimed, pulling her in close.

"What can we do to help?" Trig asked.

"That's actually why we're here," Elora answered. "We need you to get us over the wall."

"All of you?" Trig asked.

"The two of us and my parents," Elora nodded.

"Can your parents climb like you?" Trig asked.

"They can climb," Asher answered positively.

"Well, it will be difficult, but I can get you all up and over the wall," Trig said, nodding. "Getting down the other side, however, will be awful," he muttered with a grimace. "The surface of the exterior side of the wall is jagged and spiked. I can't imagine anyone getting down without injury, particularly in the dark."

Elora's eyes widened with fear and her stomach sank. She exhaled deeply and began twisting her hands nervously, staring at the ground. This would be so much more difficult than she had anticipated. Was it worth it? Was it really so important to return to Clarendon on her own terms? Was it worth risking her life and the lives of her parents? She looked up and locked eyes with Asher who was watching her with a look of concern.

"No, Elora," he said firmly.

Her mouth dropped open in surprise and her hands stilled.

"I know what you're thinking and the answer is no. I won't let you," he said, crossing his arms defiantly.

"What if something happens to them because of me?" Elora asked. "If I just go with the Liana then no one has to get hurt."

"You think they won't hurt you?" Asher asked, his voice low.

"I think they need me," she answered, her voice shaking.

"Elora, as much as they need you, they also fear you. You are a threat to their power over the Claren," he said solemnly. "They will break you. You will end up a pawn of the Liana. And your parents will suffer all the same."

"But what does it matter how I get there? Won't they just capture me once I reach Clarendon anyway?" she asked despondently.

"It matters," said Asher, stepping closer to her. "The Claren need to see their Renascent return with dignity. They need to witness your strength. They need to know your goodness. They need to see that you are willingly fulfilling the prophesy. They need to love you."

Elora averted her eyes as he spoke. It became harder and harder for her to breathe as the pressure and responsibility pressing down upon her shoulders increased with every word from his lips. She closed her eyes, shaking her head against the incredible burden.

Asher closed the distance between them and reached out to gently grasp her upper arms. He waited for her to finally look up at him before continuing.

"And they will. They won't be able to help themselves," he said quietly. "The Liana would not dare touch you after that."

He held her gaze unwaveringly. He wasn't afraid. He wasn't doubtful. He believed in the truth of what he had said. It was comforting. It was thrilling. She couldn't bring herself to look away.

"You're coming with me," he said in a soft, firm voice.

She nodded slowly and finally found the strength to close her eyes, cutting loose from the intensity of their connection. She took a step back from him and inhaled deeply.

"What about the wall? What about the spikes and the jagged rocks?" she asked timidly.

"You're a Claren," he replied bluntly.

"What is that supposed to mean?" Trig interrupted.

"It means she can climb anything," Asher answered, keeping his focus on Elora. "We just need you to get us over the wall. Can you do that?" Asher asked, turning to look at Trig.

"Yes," Trig answered resolutely.

"Good," Asher nodded.

"Are you planning to travel by foot after that?" Trig asked, his eyebrows raised in concern.

"I have a horse pastured near the wheat fields," Asher answered. "And the Kerricks have horses boarded a few miles outside of the settlement."

"Okay," Trig nodded, thinking. "Remember the place where you first told me to propose to Alysa?" he asked Elora.

Elora nodded, managing a small smile as she locked eyes with Alysa.

"I think that would be the best place to make this happen," he said. "It's far away from town so it gets pretty dark, and the wheat fields are just on the other side of the wall there."

"Sounds good," Asher agreed.

"There's a cow pasture not far from there with a lean-to built on one end. Do you know it?" Trig asked.

"Yeah, that's Danny Jenkin's property. He has a milk cow," Elora said, nodding.

"I'll meet you there after dark," he said.

"Alysa should come too," Asher interrupted.

"No. I don't want her anywhere near any of this," Trig replied, putting a protective arm around his bride.

"I can understand that," Asher nodded. "But because Elora has been followed for the past two weeks, I am concerned that Alysa may be at risk. Colin would be aware of their close relationship and might seek to use her to get to Elora," he said.

Elora looked stricken and fresh tears sprang to her eyes. She pulled away from Alysa, stepping backwards and lifting a shaking hand to cover her mouth. He was right. She'd spent countless hours with Alysa these past two weeks. She'd unknowingly put her friend in danger and the guilt burned like an ember in the pit of her stomach. She locked eyes with Alysa and the fear she saw there took her breath away.

"I'm so sorry," Elora whispered.

Alysa gave a slight nod, bestowing forgiveness despite the terror that had taken her heart into its vicious grip.

"You don't leave my side," Trig said, pulling Alysa to him.

She nodded in reply as she stared up at him with frightened eyes.

"How do I keep her safe once you're gone?" Trig asked, his voice hoarse with fear.

"I hope that the danger will leave with us," Asher replied.

Trig nodded but obviously found no comfort in Asher's answer.

"So, we will see the both of you in a few hours," Asher confirmed.

"Right," Trig answered, nodding.

Elora stood still, staring at her two dear friends as guilt and grief vied for control of her heart. She hated to leave them, hated to involve them, hated that friendship with her had put them at such risk. They looked utterly shell-shocked. No one said a word or shifted a muscle for a few moments.

"We should be getting back, Elora," Asher said gently, finally breaking the silence.

Neither Alysa nor Trig acknowledged their leaving, so distracted and overwhelmed by what they had learned and what had been asked of them. Elora nodded and slowly moved to follow him to the door. Before stepping through the threshold, she turned to take one last look.

"Thank you," she said. "For everything."

Taking hold of the handle, she pulled the door shut behind her. Closing her eyes and resting her forehead against the rough wooden panels of the door, she took a moment to calm her emotions.

"That was horrible," she whispered.

"Actually, it went much better than I had expected," Asher said, shrugging.

Elora stepped away from the door and began walking back towards her home as Asher fell into stride beside her.

"I know that must have been very hard," he said, keeping his eyes on the road before them as though to give her privacy.

"The hardest thing I've ever done," Elora admitted, her voice small.

"So far," Asher replied quietly.

CHAPTER 15

It was nearing dusk as Asher and Elora headed home to meet up with her parents. They walked in melancholy silence for quite a while, Elora playing distractedly with the seed on her necklace. The guilt of involving her dear friends in this unbelievable and dangerous situation gnawed at her. If something happened to Trig because he helped them, how would she ever be able to live with herself? And if Alysa fell victim to the Liana, she wouldn't want to live at all.

"You have good friends," Asher remarked beside her, breaking the silence.

"I do," she replied, smiling in spite of her sadness.

"You can tell a lot about a person by their friends," he nodded thoughtfully. "It speaks highly of you, their eagerness to help."

"I don't know that I will ever deserve what they are risking for me tonight," she said quietly.

"You're wrong about that," he said comfortingly. "But if that's how you feel, then let it inspire you. Make it worthwhile."

"How do I do that?" she asked. "I just barely understand what is going on! And I'm not completely sure I even believe it."

"How can you say that when you have so much proof already?" he asked, incredulous. "The Mark of the Ever Tree on your back, your ability, and that seed you wear around your neck all prove that this is real."

She walked quietly beside him for a few steps deep in thought. Reaching out, she placed a hand on his forearm, pulling him to a stop. She looked up to find his eyes, stone colored in the waning light, focused intently on her. Her heart thudded in her chest as she was temporarily overwhelmed by her attraction to him. She couldn't bring herself to break eye contact and couldn't manage to have a coherent thought while lost in his eyes. He returned her gaze, unfaltering, and she wondered if perhaps he was as affected as she was. A warm breeze blew a strand of hair that had come loose from her updo across her cheek. Asher lifted his hand to carefully tuck it behind her ear. Her breath caught in her throat at the surprisingly intimate gesture. The brush of his fingertips against her skin startled her out of her trance. She looked away, trying to remember what she had been trying to say only a moment ago.

"Why do you believe that I can fix the Ever Tree?" she asked earnestly. "How can you be so sure?"

"I trust the prophesy," he said confidently. "I have faith that you will be everything that we need you to be."

"Are you sure it's faith and not just desperation?" she asked quietly.

"Let's call it hope," he replied, with a small smile as he put his hand on the small of her back, urging her to continue walking.

After taking a few more steps, Elora looked up to see something unsettling. There was a figure approaching in the distance. Elora froze and her heart seemed to stop for a moment.

"Colin," she whispered.

Except it wasn't only Colin. He wasn't alone. He was flanked by 5 other men, all wearing Elysic cloaks. Though they were walking briskly towards Elora and Asher, the men thankfully hadn't spotted them yet.

"They're here," Asher said, unable to hide the alarm in his voice.

He quickly grabbed hold of Elora's elbow and pulled her off of the road and onto the porch of a nearby house.

"What do we do?" she asked, panicked.

Asher tried opening the door to the house, but it was locked. While trying to remain inconspicuous, he began looking around for a means of escape or somewhere to hide, but there was nothing.

Elora pressed her back against the building, wishing she could simply disappear. Asher moved closer to shield Elora from view, placing his forearm on the wall near her shoulder.

She looked up at him desperately, hoping he would know what to do. Her life up until now had been full of gentleness and simple goodness. She felt wholly unequipped to handle something like this.

His eyes locked with hers and she could see that he was afraid. But more than afraid, he was angry.

"We should have left yesterday," he said, castigating himself.

"I wouldn't have gone with you yesterday," Elora said, shaking her head.

"I should have made you leave," he said, his voice gruff.

"I'm glad you didn't try," she said softly.

"You won't be in a few minutes," he replied.

"What should we do?" Elora asked, peering under Asher's arm at the approaching men.

"I won't be able to stop them, but I can slow them down," he whispered.

She jerked her eyes back up to his in shock.

"No," she whispered, horrified.

"You'll have to run. Faster than you've ever run, Elora. Find your parents and hide. Stick with our plan," he said harshly. "I'll find you after I get away."

"Asher, no!" she exclaimed quietly.

"Yes," he replied firmly.

"What if you don't get away?" she asked, her voice shaking.

"Don't think about that," he said, lifting his head to see how close the men were.

"I can't let you sacrifice yourself for some prophesy!" she cried.

Asher studied her for a moment, taking in every detail. Elora searched his eyes, confused at the depth of emotion she saw there.

The scuffing sounds of boots on cobblestones became audible as the Liana approached. The men were nearly upon them.

Asher took a deep breath in preparation for what he was about to do.

"Please Asher, don't!" she begged him.

"I'm not doing it for the Prophesy," he whispered, giving her one last meaningful look. "Run, Elora!"

He started to push himself away from the wall but Elora grabbed hold of his shirt with both hands and forcefully pulled him down to her. She lifted onto her toes, catching his lips with hers in a clumsy, frantic kiss. She closed her eyes, terrified to see what would happen next. She silently begged him to accept the intimacy she was offering in place of the violence he'd been expecting.

Startled, Asher's hands flew to grip her upper arms and for a brief moment it seemed as though he would push her away. His lips were unyielding, his posture rigid as he struggled to abandon his original plan. Elora's heart ached and her stomach fell, believing that she had lost, that he was determined to carry on as he had intended. Her fingers began to loosen their grip on his shirt and she slowly sank down from her perch on her toes.

Suddenly Asher's lips turned soft and warm. His mouth opened and he began returning her kiss in earnest. His hands drifted up from her arms to gingerly cup her jaw, his fingertips sinking into the hair at the nape of her neck. He leaned into her, pressing her against the building, hiding her body behind his. With a gentle nudge of his thumb he tilted her head slightly and deepened the kiss. His lips moved over hers, tender but passionate. She had never felt this way before, never experienced the thrilling sensations coursing through her body.

Though timid at first, Elora quickly lost herself in the kiss. She lowered down off her toes and leaned her head back as he ducked to better reach her upturned face. She gripped his shirt for dear life, surprised by the onslaught of emotions that the kiss had awakened.

A few whistles and laughter from the road revealed that they had indeed been noticed by the passing soldiers, but no attack came. The men continued on as Elora remained hidden, disguised within Asher's ardent embrace.

Overwhelmed by the way he was holding her, kissing her, it took Elora a moment to realize that she could no longer hear footsteps. Asher seemed to recognize that the danger had passed at nearly the same time. He pulled back slightly, breaking the kiss. Her heart pounding, she opened her eyes to find him watching her. He held her gaze for a long moment before shifting his attention back to her lips. To her surprise, he slowly leaned down and softly, briefly kissed her once more.

She couldn't seem to remember how to breathe. If he hadn't been pressing her against the wall, her knees would have buckled. Unsure of what to think, what to do, she stared back at him. While their kisses had been thrilling and passionate before, that last unnecessary and unexpected caress was something else entirely. It had meant something. But what? She finally managed to tear her eyes away from his, but found that they merely travelled downward of their own accord to focus on his lips instead. She wished he would kiss her again. Self-conscious, she closed her eyes in an attempt to hide her desire.

Rubbing his thumb gently across her cheek, Asher finally broke the silence, whispering, "Your idea was much better than mine."

Elora's eyes flew open as she laughed in surprise. Asher chuckled, stepping back to put some space between them. Unprepared for the sudden loss of his support, she sagged against him. His hands moved to her shoulders to steady her. The enormity of what had nearly just happened seemed to hit her all at once and she let out a shuddering exhale. Overcome with relief, she dropped her forehead against his chest and loosened her grip on his shirt which was still bunched in her fingers. She felt his chin drop to rest on the top of her head and his arms wrapped around her. She felt utterly safe and protected, if only for this moment, and she savored it.

Finally recovered, she released his shirt and they separated. She quirked her eyebrows curiously as he began examining their surroundings.

"What is it?" she asked.

"Just checking to see if anything started growing," he said, smiling at her wryly. "Your heart was beating pretty fast."

"I have to be focused on something for that to happen," she said, blushing.

"Are you saying you weren't able to think straight?" he asked, grinning.

"You know, your heart was beating pretty fast, too!" she cried, laughing.

"Yes, it was," he replied, smiling fondly at her.

She smiled back, utterly bewildered and confused by him. They had only met this morning and yet the familiar way he interacted with her, the way he spoke to her, the way he looked at her, the passionate way he'd kissed her belied a much deeper connection. It was both comfortable and thrilling. She didn't understand it. It didn't make sense. And yet it felt right.

Shaking her head in amusement, Elora moved to leave the porch. Asher took hold of her arm, stopping her.

"Where are you going?" he asked, all teasing gone from his voice.

"Home," she replied. "We can cut across that field there to avoid the road," she said, motioning to a pasture a short distance down the lane.

"The Liana are here now, Elora. You can't go home," he said, shaking his head.

"But my parents," she started, letting the words fall off her tongue as fear set in.

Asher lifted his head, looking up and down the road before taking hold of her hand and pulling her across the pavement and down a dark alleyway. They sidled along, hiding in the shadows of the buildings that lined the narrow road until they reached an overgrown field full of tall grasses at the other end. He charged into the waist-high vegetation dragging her along behind him.

Her dress made running through the field difficult, dragging against the grass and tripping her feet. Despite her best efforts to pull the dress out of the way, she kept stumbling and knew it was only a matter of time before she would fall. Her frustration finally boiling over, she tore her hand out of Asher's grasp. But she hadn't realized just how much he had been bracing her. She tried frantically to untangle her skirt from her legs before she lost her balance, but her momentum got the better of her and with an involuntary yelp, she tumbled forward. Fortunately, Asher had turned to see why she had wrested her hand free and was able to catch her before she dove face first into the ground.

"Can we stop please?" she asked, breathless with panic and exertion as she righted herself, tugging the wayward skirt out from beneath her feet.

He nodded, looking around cautiously before sinking down onto his knees beneath the grass. Elora did the same.

"I'm sorry," he relented in a hushed voice. "We needed get away from there."

Elora nodded her understanding as she ran her wrist across her brow to catch the sweat before it could drip down into her eyes.

Lifting her fearful eyes to his, she quietly asked again, "What about my parents?"

"Let's hope they didn't make it home yet," Asher replied.

"I'm not leaving without them," Elora said, her voice trembling.

"I know," Asher nodded. "Surely they noticed the Liana like we did and stayed away from the house. They aren't exactly being covert, brazenly walking around like that," he said, his brows furrowed in confusion and concern. "Colin wasn't even wearing a cloak," he added quietly.

"They did seem strangely relaxed," Elora said, twisting her hands nervously.

"They seemed confident," Asher amended.

"It's as if they expect to just walk in here and take me, like there were fetching a sack of grain," Elora whispered.

"That's exactly what they expect to do," Asher said soberly.

Elora eyes were suddenly ablaze with indignation. Her hands balled up into angry fists and she pressed them into her lap.

"Well, that's not how it's going to work," she seethed.

"Good," Asher said nodding his head approvingly. "It's better to be angry than scared."

"Oh no," Elora corrected. "I'm really, really scared too. I'm just trying to be brave about it," she said, her voice defiant but shaky.

Asher smiled before quietly admitting, "Me too."

Elora looked at him quizzically.

"You don't seem scared," she said.

"I am," he replied, holding her gaze.

"This conversation isn't making me feel any better," she whispered.

"I'd have to be an idiot not to be terrified when it comes to the Liana," he said. "It's not important that we're scared. It only matters that we're brave. It only matters that we win."

Elora nodded solemnly before quirking her eyebrows in question.

"What will winning look like?" Elora asked, quietly.

"Freedom," he said.

"You mean keeping me free from the Liana," she clarified.

"Not just that," he said. "I mean setting us all free."

"But you're already free," Elora said, her eyebrows lifting in confusion.

"As long as the Liana controls Clarendon, none of us are free, Elora," he replied solemnly. "Not really."

"I don't understand. What does that have to do with me?" Elora asked, confused. "I'm not liberating anyone. I'm going to Clarendon to save the Ever Tree," Elora said.

"You're going to Clarendon to fulfill the Prophesy," Asher clarified.

Elora furrowed her brows, perplexed.

"Isn't that what I said?" she asked.

"Not exactly," he replied.

CHAPTER 16

"The Prophesy was written centuries ago, Elora," Asher explained. "It had become the stuff of fairy-tales even before our parents were born. The details had been watered down with each generation until only a shadow of truth remained. Most Claren believed it to be nothing more than a bedtime story, as your father said, passed down through the generations as little more than entertainment. All anyone remembered of the Prophesy was that the Ever Tree would fall and that a savior would appear, born with the Ever Mark and gifted with the power to restore the Tree."

Elora nodded. That was her understanding of the Prophesy as well.

"But when my mother helped bring you into the world and saw the Mark on your back, she recognized that the Prophesy was real and was coming true," Asher said, locking eyes with Elora for a moment before continuing. "At that time Peter, my father, was working in the Registry as a Chronicle, a record keeper. The Registry is a giant cavern that descends deep underground. It holds all the records of Clarendon dating back thousands of years. There are shelves chiseled into the cavern walls from floor to ceiling, filled with books detailing the history of our people. Every birth, every death, every pairing is written in those books. Giant scrolls containing precise maps of the Woodlands are kept there, as well as ledgers tracking the age and location of every Elysian Tree. Every bit of knowledge that is vital to our people is stored in the Registry. I hope you'll get to see it someday," he said shaking his head in awe. "It is incredible to be there, surrounded by the histories of the people who came before us, who lived this calling and entrusted it to us to continue it. It makes you understand in a way nothing else can, that you are a part of something incredible." His eyes were distant as he pictured it in his mind. "It's humbling and inspiring all at once."

"It sounds amazing," Elora said, watching him intently.

At the sound of her voice, Asher's eyes darted to hers and it was as though he couldn't look away. A warmth crept across her skin and the air around them seemed to hum with electricity as he held her gaze. Her fingers began to tingle, the tell-tale sensation of her powers awakening. She quickly closed her eyes and shook her head, consciously trying to suppress the intensity of these unexpected feelings.

She heard Asher take a deep, shaky breath, and took comfort in the fact that he'd apparently been as affected as she had.

"So, everything is stored in the Registry," he reiterated, regaining his focus and continuing his explanation. "Including the Prophesy."

Elora nodded.

"Because the contents of the Registry are so valuable, only Chronicles are allowed to handle them. Claren place requests for information and Chronicles are responsible for researching and providing answers. When the Liana came into power they began monitoring the requests, controlling the flow of information, and people became much more cautious with their curiosity," Asher said, frowning angrily. Taking a deep breath, he continued. "All that to say, when my mother came home and told my father about you and her fears that the Prophesy was coming to pass, he decided to see for himself what exactly the Prophesy actually said. When he found an opportunity, he secretly sought out the Prophesy where it had been stored and long forgotten deep within the cavern. And luckily he wrote it down, because soon after your family disappeared and rumors of your Mark began circulating, the Prophesy disappeared."

Elora's eyes widened in surprise, and Asher nodded to further underscore the truth of his words.

"Do you think the Liana took it?" she asked, enthralled.

"It couldn't have been anyone else," he replied, shrugging. "Fortunately, because he was a Chronicle, my father was able access the Prophesy without alerting the Liana, or else he likely would have disappeared too," he said, raising his eyebrows contemptuously.

"But why are they so set on keeping the Prophesy a secret?" Elora asked, frowning.

"Because of what it says," he replied.

Elora's brows furrowed. "What do you mean?"

"I told you the Prophesy had been watered down over time," Asher said, holding her gaze. "Some important parts were lost in the retelling and eventually forgotten altogether. Someone wanted to keep it that way."

A chill ran down Elora's spine. She was a part of the Prophesy. If the Liana had destroyed a sacred script to keep a secret, they were capable of anything. Perhaps even capable of destroying the Renascent. But her parents were preparing to take her back to Clarendon. Surely they would never do that if they knew she was in such danger.

"Do my parents know what the Prophesy really says?" she asked softly.

"No," Asher said, shaking his head.

"Why not?" Elora asked, her voice raised in indignation. "They, more than anyone, had a right to know!"

"My father wanted to tell them, intended to tell them," Asher said, attempting to placate her. "And he tried to. But he couldn't," he continued. "My father looked at the Prophesy on a night when the Registry was empty. On a night when everyone else was gathered beneath the

Ever Tree. He did it during the Celebration of Light," he answered. "The night your Mark was discovered."

Elora sighed as the puzzle pieces fell into place.

"Your family was gone before he had the chance," he said.

"Your father has kept this secret for all these years?" she asked.

"It was far too dangerous to say anything," he answered.

"He didn't tell anyone?" she asked, astonished.

"He told my mother," Asher answered. "And me."

"You know the Prophesy?" she asked quietly.

Elora held his gaze for a long moment, torn between curiosity and fear. She needed to know, but was terrified to hear with certainty what her future would hold, the miracle she was expected to perform. Did she want to hear it?

Asher didn't wait for her to ask. He began to speak in a measured, even cadence, the words rolling off his tongue like a familiar song.

The Claren betrayed.
Their secret defended.
Sovereignty surrendered,
The Sentry ascended.

A pairing denied,
The Promise decayed,
The Great Tree withers,
The Woodlands fade.

Ever Renascent,
Marked from birth,
Sees truth in the darkness,
Draws life from the earth.

A grief relived,
The truth revealed,
An evil righted,
A people healed.

Gifted savior,
Chosen one,
The cord is woven,
The rift undone.

The seed alights
With mated soul,
Ever awakens,
The Covenant whole.

Elora stared at the ground, quietly thinking, trying to absorb the significance and decipher the meaning of the mysterious verses. It was much more ambiguous than she had expected. The only part she understood with certainty was that the Renascent would be marked from birth.

"It's beautiful, but so vague," she said, frowning.

"It is perhaps less vague to someone who has been living as a Claren," Asher suggested.

“Do you know what it means?” she asked, lifting her eyes to his.

“I’ve had a long time to think about it and there are still a few points that I can’t figure out, but for the most part, I believe I do know what it means,” he replied. “The Prophesy describes the rise of the Liana and the subjugation of our people,” Asher said, pulling a blade of grass and twisting it between his fingers. “It then tells of a terrible betrayal which creates a rift between the Claren and the Ever Tree,” he continued, looking up to lock eyes with Elora. “But then you come along, born with the Mark and destined to heal the Tree. And in the course of saving the Tree, you will save all of us.”

“I save the Claren? From what?” she asked, her brows furrowed.

“The Liana,” he said, holding her gaze.

“What?” she whispered, her eyes wide in shock.

“You’re going to bring down the Liana,” he repeated, his face earnest and his eyes unwavering.

“That’s impossible,” she said, shaking her head in disbelief.

“I wouldn’t think you’d be so quick to say something like that anymore,” he said, his face somber.

She stared back at him a moment, unable to deny the truth of his reply. Shifting her gaze upward, she exhaled deeply and tried to absorb the gravity of what had just been revealed to her.

“So I’m their enemy, but also their savior,” she said quietly.

Asher watched her, his lips pressed into a hard line as he nodded his head.

"So what do you think they plan to do with me?" she asked.

"Control you," he said softly.

"Do you think they mean to kill me?" she asked in a small voice.

"No," he said, shaking his head. "They need you to heal the Tree," he replied. "The Liana are Claren, after all. The death of the Ever Tree devastated them too. Their orders are simply to bring you home, by any means necessary. But their 'means' are ruthless, Elora," he said bluntly.

Elora bit her lip nervously, this new bit of information both comforting and unsettling.

"How do you think they mean to control me?" she asked timidly.

"They certainly are not above violence and imprisonment," he said bitterly. "But I think they are more likely to manipulate you using the people you love."

Elora looked up, her eyes wide with fear as she realized that the threat the Liana posed was not to her alone.

"My parents!" she gasped, horrified. "Do you think the Liana would kill them?" she asked, her lip trembling.

"No," he soothed. "The foot soldiers of the Liana aren't evil, they are just terribly misguided. Their tactics are abhorrent, but they truly believe that they are doing good. Beyond that though, Claren do not kill one another. It's our most sacred law. Not even the Liana would dare to break it."

"Why not?" Elora asked, somewhat mollified by that answer but still uneasy.

"Because of the Covenant," he answered.

"The one from the Prophesy?" she asked.

He nodded briefly before lifting his head above the grass for a moment to survey the surrounding area. Sinking back down, he returned his gaze to Elora and continued his explanation.

"The Covenant is between the Claren and the greater power who created the tree. Our unique relationship with the Ever Tree depends upon our faithfulness to that promise. The Claren believe that if someone intentionally kills another of our kind, the murderer will lose the Mark or any chance of ever receiving one," he said.

Elora nodded, trying to wrap her head around it all.

"But they have it wrong," Asher continued. "The murderer won't be the only Claren to bear the punishment. We all will pay the price for the broken Covenant. And the reason we lose the Mark," he finished, locking eyes with her, "is because we lose the Tree."

Elora held his gaze for a moment as the significance of his words sunk in. Her lips parted and she gasped as she put two and two together.

"Someone broke the covenant," she whispered.

"Someone broke the covenant," he repeated, nodding.

"Then what's protecting my parents?" Elora asked, the pitch of her voice rising. "Why would they honor the covenant when it's already been destroyed?"

"Because most of them don't know that," he replied. "I doubt most of the Liana even know that Covenant is a part of the Prophesy. They don't realize that it was murder that killed the Ever Tree. They don't understand that you were born because the Covenant was broken."

Elora exhaled deeply, staring at the ground as she tried to piece together the puzzle, filling in the holes of the story with all of this new information. She froze as an idea took shape, the epiphany sending a chill down her spine. She lifted her eyes to his.

"My destiny isn't just to heal the Tree. It's to renew the Covenant," Elora whispered.

"Yes," he replied, nodding somberly.

"How?" she asked.

"That's one of the parts I haven't been able to figure out," Asher admitted.

"Great," Elora said, covering her face with her hands in frustration. "That's great."

"Sorry," he said, sighing.

Elora stared at the ground, deep in thought about everything that Asher had just revealed to her. She was scared to be the Renascent. The responsibility seemed too great to bear. Even more so now. When her only task had been to heal the Ever Tree, she had thought there was at least a chance of success because of her ability. But now that she was supposed to somehow restore the Covenant too, she felt overwhelmed and completely inadequate.

"Elora, I don't know what will happen once we reach Clarendon," Asher said beseechingly, drawing her attention. "All I know is that the Liana can't get their hands on you. And we don't have much longer to get you out of here."

Elora nodded in understanding.

"We have to find my parents," she said, concern creasing her brow.

Asher looked at her with a guarded expression before dropping his eyes to the ground.

"Do you have any idea where they would go?" he asked, brushing dirt from his pants as he moved to stand.

"I can only think they would have returned to the storage shed," Elora replied. "It's about a quarter mile that way," she said, pointing.

"Can you get us there without using the main roads?" he asked.

Elora nodded.

"I'll need to get out of this dress though. It's too difficult to move quickly though the fields and over fences in this skirt," she said, looking up at him awkwardly. "I think the tall grass will give me enough privacy if you could just turn around for a few minutes," she suggested as she pulled the strap of her satchel over her head and kneeled to retrieve her clothing from inside.

"Of course," he said, spinning abruptly, his posture suddenly rigid.

Elora thought perhaps she'd even seen an embarrassed blush creep into his cheeks before he'd turned.

She made quick work of it, sliding into her pants before reaching behind her to unfasten the single button at the nape of her neck. She kept her eyes on his back, trusting that he was a gentlemen but leery all the same. Pulling her tunic over her head, she wrestled to pull her arms free of the dress before poking them though the sleeves. She tugged the dress down and stepped out of it, gently folding and rolling the fabric until it would fit into her satchel.

"You can turn back around now," she said softly as she carefully tucked the dress into her bag.

She looked up to find him watching her intently. She held his gaze for a moment before embarrassment drove her eyes downward. She self-consciously began tying the laces of her boots.

"Alyssa was right about that dress. It really does suit you," she heard him say.

Elora smiled, reaching out to brush her fingers over one of the vines that had been lovingly embroidered onto the skirt. She couldn't help the tears that pricked her eyes as she thought of her friend. Closing the flap of her satchel, she lifted the strap over her head and stood. Swiping her hand over her eyes, she turned and began walking toward the storage shed.

"She made it for me, you know" Elora said quietly, struggling to speak around the lump in her throat.

"She's very talented," Asher said, following closely behind her.

"She made it especially for me to wear for her Binding today," Elora continued. "But I think she really made it with my own Binding in mind," she said, smiling at the thoughtfulness of her friend. "Though I guess that won't be happening anymore," she said flatly, the smile falling from her lips.

Her foot suddenly became entangled in a particularly thick clump of grass and she began to trip. But before she could hit the ground, she felt Asher's strong fingers wrap around her elbow. With a quick tug he pulled her back onto her feet beside him. She clumsily bumped against him as she struggled to regain her balance. Startled and breathless, she looked up at him with wide eyes. As their eyes locked, she seemed to forget how to breathe altogether.

"You can wear it for your Pairing instead," he said softly, holding her gaze.

It took her a moment to regain her wits enough to look away and step free of his grasp. She turned and began walking across the field again, taking greater care to lift her feet as she made her way through the tall grass. She considered what he'd said for a few minutes.

"It's not the same," she said, keeping her eyes focused on the ground. "Binding and pairing. They aren't the same."

"Are they really so different?" Asher asked.

"Yes," she replied, convicted.

"But does it matter?" he countered. "Really?"

"Pairing is two people matched by destiny. Binding is two people choosing to tie themselves together," she answered. "It matters."

"There you go fixating on the idea of "choice" again, " he said, shaking his head with a chuckle.

"It's not funny," she said indignantly, stopping to glare back at him.

"No, I know it's not," he said, returning her gaze solemnly.

He stopped beside her, pausing to look around carefully before returning his eyes to her. He ducked his head to capture her full attention.

"I just hope you won't let that stand in the way of your own happiness," he said gently.

She stared back at him, distracted by his closeness and unsettled by his words. He lifted his head and continued walking across the pasture. She stood motionless for a moment, staring at his back, his long confident strides putting distance between them as she considered what he'd said.

"Does it matter?" she thought, doubting her own convictions. "Does it matter why someone falls in love or just that they do?"

Her parents had been paired and the love they felt for one another was undeniable and steadfast. It was no less real or worthy than a love that had developed through courtship or been earned through effort. Love is love. But is it? How can it be the same?

She shook her head, confused but still convinced. She felt it in her soul, she knew it in her heart. It mattered.

She looked up, realizing that she'd lingered too long, lost in her thoughts. Asher was standing a good distance away, looking back at her, he head tilted in question. She adjusted the satchel at her hip and made her way quickly toward him. She smiled sheepishly as she neared.

"Sorry," she said softly. "You distracted me."

"I get that a lot," he said, teasing. "I've heard I'm fairly good looking."

She laughed, grateful for the comic relief. He chuckled in return and she couldn't help the way her stomach flipped at the sound. She looked away shyly and continued to walk past him.

"I noticed you didn't argue," he said, trudging along behind her.

"What?" she asked, confused.

"You didn't contradict me, about my dashing good looks," he clarified. "I noticed."

Elora laughed and turned to look at him. She rolled her eyes at the satisfied smirk on his face.

"I was not distracted by your handsome face," she said. "I was thinking about what you said."

"So I'm handsome AND insightful," he said, puffing out his chest. "I'm really enjoying this conversation."

"Oh my gosh," she said, shaking her head in bemusement. "It must be exhausting carrying around that ego."

He laughed and she couldn't help the smile that stretched across her lips.

They walked in silence a while, a new lightness about them, the tension broken temporarily by the much needed moment of humor. Elora kept her eyes downturned, trying to keep her footing in the tall grass. Looking up, she caught Asher watching her. He looked away quickly and busied himself studying the horizon. She returned her gaze to the ground, self-conscious but also exhilarated by his attention.

"You're fairly distracting yourself, Elora Kerrick," he said quietly a moment later.

She jerked her eyes up to look at him in surprise. Her heart was thudding in her chest, thrilled that he found her appealing and startled by his boldness in saying so. He wasn't looking at her, seemingly avoiding her gaze by once more examining the horizon. She continued to stare at him wide-eyed, questioning whether she could have imagined what she'd heard. But then he turned and locked eyes with her, removing all doubt. His gaze was unflinching and earnest. He was attracted to her and obviously felt no need to hide it.

"Oh," Elora whispered, her lips lingering around the sound as her brain tried to work through the shock of this revelation.

Asher chuckled at her loss for words.

"Don't panic. It was only a compliment," he said, reaching out to touch her arm. "I'm not trying to court you."

She laughed, slightly relieved, though perhaps a bit disappointed. They walked on a few paces before a frown settled over her features.

"Not that I want you to, but why not?" she asked, trying not to be offended.

"Because we're Claren," he answered simply.

"Claren don't court one another?" she asked.

"No," he replied, shaking his head with a frown, his eyes searching the horizon.

"I suppose you just wait for the Ever Tree to do it for you." she said sardonically. "It makes sense. I mean, why put in the effort?"

"It's not because we're lazy," he replied, shaking his head in amusement.

"It seems lazy," she repeated, shrugging.

"It's because we respect one another," he explained.

"Courting is very respectful," Elora said indignantly.

"You're right. It's a very respectful way to choose a spouse," Asher admitted. "But for Claren, courting leads to broken hearts and hard feelings."

"I don't see how that's any different than courting for the rest of the world," Elora argued.

"It's different," Asher answered, shaking his head. "For the rest of the world, courting is the only way to find your soulmate, to choose your spouse. But Claren don't choose. We don't have to search. We only have to wait."

"So Claren see courting as disrespectful?" she asked.

"It is," he replied firmly. "It is wrong to create those memories and steal away pieces of someone's heart just because you're too impatient to wait for your soulmate."

"So no courting," she said, nodding in understanding.

They walked on in silence for a few minutes, lost in thought.

"That's kind of sad, actually," she blurted out suddenly.

"What?" he asked.

"It's sad that Claren don't work to earn one another's affections," she clarified. "That's a big part of why this whole Pairing thing bothers me so much. I was rather looking forward to being courted."

"Who says you won't?" he asked, grinning.

"You just did!" she exclaimed in a hushed cry, furrowing her brows in frustration.

"I intend to court my soulmate," he said shrugging his shoulders.

"But doesn't the Pairing ceremony happen right after two people are paired?" Elora asked, confused. "That's not a lot of time to court someone."

"Who says a courtship ends at the ceremony? I intend to court her for the rest of my life," he replied with a wink.

Elora couldn't help the blush that crept up her cheeks at the thought of spending a lifetime being romanced by Asher.

"Do I still seem lazy?" he asked, grinning.

Elora laughed, shaking her head.

"That sounds pretty wonderful actually," she said. "Do all Claren feel that way about courting?"

"Not all. But I would say most," he replied.

"Well, hopefully the man in my visions shares your views on courting," Elora said wistfully.

"You can hope for that," he agreed, nodding. "Or maybe you should just hope the man in your visions is me," Asher replied, nudging her shoulder jokingly.

She chuckled, though her heart skipped a beat at the suggestion.

Between the sound of her laugh and the rustle of the grass against their legs, she nearly missed the words he muttered next.

"I know I am."

He'd whispered them, as though he hadn't meant for her to hear. Her breath caught in her throat but she kept her face downturned, unsure of how to react. She allowed herself a brief glance upwards a few moments later, but found him busily studying their surroundings. Perhaps she had been mistaken. Perhaps she had imagined it. But what if she hadn't?

CHAPTER 17

Elora took the lead as they continued on in silence, each lost in thought. The air seemed to hum with a thrilling sort of tension between them. Suddenly they came upon a rough patch of terrain, where the ground lowered into a dry creek bed and wiry grass gave way to course and scrubby brush. The distractions of a moment ago faded away as they had to stay focused on keeping their footing. The rise up to the other side was steep and the ground sifted beneath their feet at they climbed out of the creek bed. Having reached the top, Asher turned to offer Elora a hand up which she gratefully accepted. Winded, they stopped for a moment, to catch their breath.

Though the hottest part of the day had passed, the sun was still punishing as it made its downward journey. Elora lifted her arm, wiping the sweat from her forehead with the sleeve of her tunic. She sighed and looked around, trying to get her bearings.

"The interior gardens are just on the other side of Tim Pryor's field," she said, motioning to a large fenced corral in which two horses lazily munched grass and swatted flies. "You can see the storage barn just there."

In the distance, the peaked roof of a faded and sun-baked wooden building was visible above the scrubby overgrowth.

"Do you think you can get us in without being seen?" he asked.

"I can get one of us in," she said. "With the Elysic cloak."

"It should be you," Asher said, grimacing. "You can get what we need and get out much more quickly than I could."

"I thought we were here to retrieve my parents," Elora said, confused. "What do we need?"

"You should get seeds," he said, holding her gaze.

"But my parents are getting the seeds," she replied quietly, her brows furrowed.

"You need to get some, Elora," he repeated solemnly. "Just in case."

"Just in case we have to leave without them, you mean," she finished, shaking her head emphatically. "I won't go without my parents," she said, turning and continuing on angrily in the direction of the barn.

Asher ran after her, catching her arm and pulling her to a stop. He grasped her shoulders and turned her to face him, waiting for her to look him in the eyes.

"I don't want to either," he said earnestly. "But the Liana can't have you Elora. You know that. And your parents know that too."

Elora stared at him, tears pricking her eyes as she realized that he was right.

"Maybe they will be there," she said in a small voice.

"I hope so," Asher said gently. "But you still need to get the seeds even if they aren't."

Elora nodded, shifting her eyes away from his face. Turning out of his grasp, she began walking away from him without a backwards glance. He fell into step behind her and they walked in uncomfortable silence.

They kept to the tall grasses, alert and cautious now that they were approaching a more populated area. The grazing horses lifted their heads and watched with interest as Elora and Asher walked along the outside of the split-rail fence of their paddock. The barn was moving steadily into view.

With each step, Elora's heart seemed to pound ever harder until it felt as if it would explode from her chest. She was trying desperately to remain optimistic but it was impossible to ignore the terrifying possibility that she might find the barn empty.

Suddenly the gritty sound of turning wagon wheels broke the peacefulness of the air. Elora and Asher quickly moved away from the fence and crouched down low in the dense vegetation. They watched as a horse drawn cart pulling a load of manure passed by the end of the corral.

"There's a road up ahead that separates this farm from the gardens," Elora said, speaking in a low voice as she nodded towards where the wagon had been.

"You should put the cloak on," Asher whispered.

Elora pulled the silky fabric from her bag and wrapped it around her shoulders. It flowed around her body like water. It was cool against her skin and the sensation sent thrilling shivers down her spine. She fastened it at her throat and turned towards Asher. He reached out, pulling the hood up over her head until her face was hidden within its shadow.

"How do I look?" Elora asked, glancing up at him.

"You look like a Claren," he whispered with a small smile.

She felt a pang in her stomach, both pleased by his words and heartsick as she remembered her father saying the very same thing to her mother only hours ago. Oh, how she hoped they were in that barn.

They rose and carefully crept closer. The air was silent save for the soft sounds of workers cultivating the soil and the sporadic chatter of gardeners finishing a hard day's labor. Everything seemed normal and calm. Elora and Asher stopped as they neared the edge of the road. Hiding behind a thicket, they watched the barn for a long while, looking for any sign of the Liana. Asher finally looked at her and raised his eyebrows in question. Elora nodded that she was ready.

"If it feels wrong, don't go in there," he said. "We can make it without the seeds."

"I'm going in there for my parents," she reminded him tersely.

"I know," he whispered, avoiding her angry stare.

She waited for him to lift his eyes so that she could have the satisfaction of seeing his regret at having forgotten about her parents. But she saw more than regret in his eyes. She saw sadness. She saw pain. Her annoyance was immediately replaced by a sickening sense of fear. He hadn't forgotten about them. He had given up on them. He didn't think they were there. Elora shook her head in denial.

"They are in there, Asher. They have to be," she said, her voice cracking.

Asher held her gaze, torn between inflicting the pain of honesty or giving in to the comfort of a lie. He finally nodded, unwilling to steal away the tiny bit of hope she was clinging to so desperately.

"I'll wait for you here," he said quietly. His jaw clenched and his lips were pressed thin as he struggled to hide his worry. He took hold of Elora's shoulders and ducked his head to look her directly in the eyes. "You move quickly. No matter what you find, Elora," he said squeezing her arms to emphasize his point. "You get your parents, you grab the seeds and you run back out here."

She nodded, struggling to suppress a sudden wave of nausea. Her wide eyes were darting back and forth between his as the danger of what she was about to do finally began to register.

"I mean it, Elora. If you're not back here in 5 minutes, I'm coming to get you. And I don't care who sees me," he said. "Hurry."

Elora nodded again, struggling to swallow past the lump of fear in her throat. She closed her eyes and took a deep breath, attempting to gain some composure.

Suddenly a cool, moist breeze wafted through her hair and the soothing roar of a thousand leaves rusting in the wind filled her ears. A deep sense of peace came over her. She was no longer hiding in the scrubby brush of Windom, she was standing beneath the forest canopy of Claredon. It was not Asher standing beside her, it was *him*.

"It's time to come home."

His voice was soft, barely above a whisper. She gasped as she felt the warm, rough skin of his hand brush across her cheek. Her heart swelled with affection and she couldn't help the smiled that crept across her lips. She sighed, soaking up the comfort of his presence and letting the stillness of the forest settle deep into her bones. Taking one last calming breath of deliciously sweet forest air, she opened her eyes.

Asher was watching her. The anxiety that had hardened his features only a few moments ago had been replaced by a look of fascination.

"You had a vision," he whispered.

She nodded, smiling.

A particularly loud shout caught their attention and they both jerked their heads to see what had happened.

Apparently Joe Callahan, one of the gardeners, had nearly stepped on a snake. This was her opportunity. Everyone was watching Joe. She stood and walked the remaining few paces to the edge of the road. But she paused to look back at Asher one last time.

"If I'm not back in 5 minutes, you come get me," she reminded him. She took a final calming breath before stepping out of the thicket.

Suddenly a warm pair of arms were wrapped around her, pushing her backwards into the thicket. She began to panic, thrashing against the person who was now carrying her deeper into the brush. It took a moment before she could register the words being whispered against her ear.

"Hush, darling. It's me. It's alright," came a familiar voice.

She immediately stopped fighting and calmed in his arms. Reaching up, she pushed the hood of the cloak off her head and looked into the loving face of her father.

"Dad!" she cried with a relieved sob and threw her arms around him.

"It's alright, honey," he said, holding her tightly.

"Jonas! Thank God!" Asher exclaimed. "Where's Winnie?"

Elora was smiling joyfully up at her father, overwhelmed by their sudden reunion. It took a moment for her to discern his anguished expression through her tear clouded vision.

"Dad?" she asked, suddenly frightened.

Stepping back and wiping her eyes, she began to look around nervously. Where was her mother? Her gaze came back to rest on her father only to find a sight that scared her more than anything ever had. He was crying.

"Dad? What's wrong?" she asked, her voice rising in panic. "Where's mom?"

"They have her," he replied and his shoulders sagged in defeat.

"What?" Elora cried. "How?"

Her father sighed deeply and roughly rubbed the tears from his face.

"We made it to the barn without seeing anything out of the ordinary," he explained. "So I waited a little ways down the road, pretending to do some work on the stone wall around Tim Fletcher's field, while your mother went on alone to retrieve the seeds. She was on her way back to me when they appeared out of nowhere. There were at least 10 of them, all in Elysic cloaks. They surrounded her," his voiced cracked and he paused before continuing. "I was able to duck behind the wall and stay out of sight. They took her bag, but tossed it into the brush when they found it was just full of seeds. I followed them back to our house. They are holding her there."

"She's there alone with them?" Elora struggled to get the words past her quivering lips.

Her father nodded, closing his eyes and struggling to swallow his emotions.

"I hid across the street, watching the house and praying that you weren't going to come home and walk into a trap. A little while later, a blond haired man and 5 cloaked Lianas left the house and headed towards town. I thought for sure your poor mother had been forced to tell them that you'd gone to talk to Alysa and Trig. I figured it was only a matter of time before they caught you. But they came back an hour later empty handed. You must have left the Scott house before they got there."

"We weren't at the Scott house. We were at Alysa and Trig's new home," explained Elora, glancing over at Asher. "Oh God, I hope the Scotts are alright," she groaned.

"They must have been coming back from looking for us there when we saw them," Asher said, locking eyes with Elora.

"You saw them?" her father exclaimed, his eyes wide.

"Yes. That's why we didn't go home," Elora explained.

"Thank God for that," her father sighed. "Well, when they couldn't find you, I guess they decided to split up and search. I followed three of them to the storage barn just now and was on my way back to the house when I spotted you," he said.

Elora's eyes grew wide and her knees went weak as she realize how close she had been to running directly into the hands of her enemy.

"We were looking for you," she said quietly.

Her father sighed, hugging her tightly against him. She closed her eyes and tried to gain control over the torrent of emotions swirling through her brain. Finally regaining some composure, she leaned back from his embrace.

"We have a way out," she said.

"No. Don't tell me," he interrupted. "I don't want to know anything."

"What? Why not?" she asked in surprise.

"I can't tell them what I don't know," he said, holding her gaze.

"What do you mean?" she asked, her body stiffening in apprehension as she stared into her father's sad eyes.

"I won't let her go through this alone, Elora," he said, gently caressing her face. "I'm not going to leave her here. I have to try and free her."

"They'll catch you, Noah," Asher said, the tone of his voice somber and sure.

"Maybe they won't," Elora cried, giving him an angry glare.

"It doesn't matter if they do. I have to be with her. I can't leave her behind, sweetheart," her father said, pleading with her to understand.

"But we can help you!" Elora cried, grabbing hold of his shirtfront.

"No. You can't," he said quietly. "Asher's right. They probably will catch me. But they cannot catch you, Elora."

"Dad..." Elora couldn't speak anymore as a sob broke free. She hid her face in his shirt and fell apart.

"If they capture you, all of this would have been for nothing," he said gently, wrapping his arms around her.

"But I can't do this without you," she said, struggling to get the words out.

"Yes you can," he said. "Asher will get you home. I trust him and so should you."

"But I need you," she said, whispering her final plea, knowing in her heart that he would not be moved.

He lifted her chin, looking steadily into her tear soaked eyes. He smiled sadly.

"I can't leave her, Elora. She's my soulmate," he said softly. "Someday you'll understand."

She nodded and took a shuddering breath.

"I love you, Dad," she said, holding him tightly and trying not to think that this may be the last time she ever would.

He stepped away from her after a moment and reached over to embrace Asher.

"Take care of her, son," he said quietly. Then turning to look at both of them, he said "Take care of each other."

Elora and Asher looked at one another, taking a moment of comfort in their shared grief at the way this was playing out.

"Here," her father said, walking quickly back towards the road and carefully retrieving something from the brush along the edge. He held out the bag of seeds her mother had collected from the storage barn.

"I grabbed it on my way back here. I couldn't just leave it there in the road. Not when getting these seeds cost your mother so dearly," he said sadly. "I'm glad you can use them. She will find solace in knowing that she helped you."

Elora took the bag from his hands and gently tucked it into the satchel on her hip.

"You two need to get away from here," her father said, locking eyes with her. He reached out to embrace her quickly one last time before he turned and without a glace backward, walked to the edge of the brush. He paused for a moment, checking to make sure it was clear before darting across the road and disappearing into the brush on the other side.

Elora stared after him, her eyes wide with shock and fear. This wasn't happening. She couldn't believe this was happening.

"We need to move now," Asher said, grasping her shoulders and forcing her to look away from the place where she'd last seen her father. "The Liana are everywhere. We need a place to hide. Where can we go?"

Elora gaped up at him, struggling to focus. How was she supposed to keep her wits about her when her heart was breaking, when her entire world was quaking. She couldn't do this without her parents. She didn't want to do this without them. She had no reason to do this if not for them.

"I was doing this for them," she whispered, bemused as she fixed her eyes on his. She laughed a joyless laugh. "And now they are gone. What's the point?"

"They aren't gone," Asher replied. "Winnie is captured and your father is going to rescue her."

"He's going to fail. You both said it. And then the Liana will have them both," Elora said, her lip quivering as she tried to suppress her tears.

"If they are captured, there's a chance you can save them Elora," Asher said, holding her gaze.

Elora took a shuddering breath and shook her head in disbelief.

"I'm a gardener from Windom," she said, gesturing dismissively to herself. "You think I can save them?" she asked, chuckling bitterly.

"A gardener from Windom probably can't," he admitted. " But the Renascent can.

Elora froze. She had forgotten. Before, she had merely been going along with Asher and complying with the desires of her parents. She had been scared into running away with them. She had been trying to understand this fantastical new reality that was supposedly her purpose, but she hadn't believed it. Not really. But not anymore. If it gave her the power to save the people she loved, she would no longer fight her calling. She would be the Renascent. She would embrace her gift and fulfill her destiny.

The look of desperation slid from her face and was replaced by one of determination. This was her fight now. She was the Renascent.

"I can save them," she whispered.

CHAPTER 18

"We have to move, Elora!"

The urgency of Asher's plea finally broke through the fog of distraction and jolted her back into the moment. She looked up at him and the panic in his eyes set her heart racing. Just then, she heard the soft sound of scuffling boots coming from the road.

It was too late to go anywhere.

Asher quickly lowered onto his stomach in the scrubby grass, pulling Elora down beside him. They each held their breath as they watched a pair of Liana charge into the brush across the road where her father had disappeared. She gasped, in shock and terror. They had seen him.

Asher and Elora lay immobile, barely breathing, staring at the place where the men had disappeared. She had no idea how long they stayed that way, too frightened to move and desperate to know if her father had evaded the Liana. But suddenly the grasses began to shift and the cloaked figures stepped back onto the road, her father walking reluctantly between them. He had been captured. His face was bloodied and he was limping. Her heart stopped at the sight of him.

Tears flooded Elora's eyes and left cool tracks as they rolled down her hot cheeks to drip onto the blades of grass beneath her face. This was her fault. He wouldn't have been on the road if he hadn't stopped to warn her. She bit her lip to hold in the sob that threatened to break free and give them away. She closed her eyes against the reality of what was happing.

Her fingertips began to tingle as her gift awakened, called forth by the overwhelming emotions swirling through her body. The blades of grass surrounding them began to lengthen, growing thicker and climbing higher until their prostrate bodies were completely shielded from view. She needed to stop. She needed to control it but she felt powerless against this torrent of sadness and fear. Until she felt Asher's fingers tenderly close around hers. She was not alone. The storm raging inside of her quieted. Her heartbeat slowed and the tingling in her hands subsided.

They remained still for a long while after the men had passed out of sight and the air around them became quiet and calm, marked only by the sounds of rustling grass and calling birds. At last, Asher rose slowly and nervously looked around. Elora lifted onto her knees and paused to rub the tears from her face. Asher's outstretched hand suddenly came into view and paused expectantly, waiting to pull her up. She looked up, locking eyes with him, and was startled by the depth of sadness she saw there. Slipping her hand into his, she accepted his help and rose to her feet only to be immediately pulled into his arms. As the momentary surprise of his embrace faded, she relaxed and sank into the welcome comfort he was offering. Though as the hug lingered, she began to wonder if perhaps it had not been for her benefit alone. He sighed and loosened his arms, stepping back and looking away.

"Your father is going to be a hard man to live up to," he said quietly.

Elora nodded, blinking away the tears summoned by his words. She watched him for a moment, seeing that he too was as shaken and moved by what had just happened. It was comforting in a small way, knowing that she was not alone in her emotions. Asher at last glanced her way and caught her staring at him. Too numb to be embarrassed, she didn't look away. Fresh tears tickled her chin as they dripped onto the Elysic cloak. Sighing, she lowered her eyes and realized that she was still wearing it. Having watched her father being abused by people wearing such a cloak, she couldn't stand to have it on one more second. She busied herself with untying the strings at her neck, stopping midway through to wipe her face with rough hands. It dropped from her shoulders and she tucked it carefully into her satchel, beside the small bag of seeds and her binding dress. When she had finished, she returned her gaze to Asher. He stood with his hands on his hips, looking up at the sky. He breathed a deep sigh before turning and fixing his eyes on her.

"I'm sorry," he whispered.

"Me too," she said, taking a shuddering breath. "You weren't lying," she said, her eyes welling up again. "They were ruthless. Horrible."

"They are," Asher agreed, nodding. "Now you know why you have to come with me."

Elora dropped her eyes to the ground, trying to control the tears that just kept coming.

"Will you still come with me?" he asked hesitantly, unnerved by her silence.

"I have to," she said, her face grim. "It's what my parents wanted. I owe them that."

Her voice broke, and she closed her eyes, looking upwards as she attempted to find some composure.

"And it's the only chance I have to save them," she whispered.

"We can't stay here anymore, Elora," Asher said gently.

"I know," she said, sighing. "I'm alright now. We can go."

"It's not safe to be wandering around anymore. The Liana could be anywhere, everywhere by now," he said. "We need to find somewhere to hide."

"The sun is already starting to set, so we only have a couple of hours before it's dark enough to attempt the wall," Elora said. "I think I know of a place we can go until then."

"Is it close?" Asher asked.

"It's not terribly far, but we will have to cross that road at some point," she said, gesturing to the road bordering the gardens.

"That road is crawling with Liana, Elora," Asher said, shaking his head.

"But we have to cross it anyway to get to the wall," she answered, sighing.

Asher rubbed his face, huffing in frustration.

"We can back track and cross further away from the barn at least," she said.

Asher nodded his reluctant agreement and they began walking back through the brush along-side the horse paddock.

"Where are we going," Asher asked as he waded through the tall grass.

"There's a small shed behind the school house where tools and things are stored," she replied. "No one would ever look for me there and it's not far from the spot where Trig told us to meet him."

"Sounds good," Asher said.

They fell into an anxious silence as they made their way around the paddock and behind Tim Pryor's farmhouse. Walking beside his chicken coop, they could hear the soft clucking of chickens settling down for the night, a sign that the sun was quickly heading toward the horizon. As they crept quietly along the border of his property, Tim's dog padded over, wagging his tail happily to see Elora. She kneeled down to ruffle his fur affectionately.

"We're friends," she said, looking up at Asher.

Suddenly, the dog's ears perked and he took off towards the road. Asher grabbed Elora's hand and pulled her hastily back to hide behind the chicken coop.

They could hear the dog barking incessantly at something. Tim Pryor appeared in the barn doorway, drawn by the sound, and began heading towards the road to see what had upset his dog.

"What is it Hal?" he called out as he walked. "What is it boy?"

He disappeared out of view and Elora exchanged a nervous look with Asher.

"Come on boy, there's nothing there," Tim called out a moment later.

Hal was undeterred and continued barking excitedly. Tim returned to his work, shaking his head.

"Crazy mutt," he grumbled as he faded into the shadows of the dark barn interior.

Hal's barking was suddenly interrupted by a sharp yelp. He came running back into the yard with his tail between his legs and crawled beneath the front steps of the farmhouse to hide.

Elora looked at Asher with alarm. She turned her gaze back towards the road, her throat suddenly dry with fear. She watched with bated breath, expecting a Liana to come walking up the drive at any second. When minutes passed and no one came, she let out a shuddering sigh of relief.

"So I guess the cloaks don't work on dogs," she whispered.

"No," Asher whispered in reply.

"They're everywhere," she said, lifting a trembling hand to tuck a loose strand of hair behind her ear.

She looked up to find Asher watching her with worried eyes, his brows furrowed with concern.

"This isn't going to work, Elora. We can't just keep sneaking around," Asher sighed. "We need a plan."

She nodded in agreement and they both fell silent as they considered their options.

"What do you think they are looking for?" Elora asked. "I mean, the only person who can really identify me is Colin," she said quietly.

"The other scout, the one who sold you the seed, knows what you look like too," Asher reminded her.

"But that's only two of them," she said. "I bet the rest wouldn't be able to recognize me if I walked right past them!"

"There's a framed sketch of you on the mantel in your house, Elora," Asher said, shaking his head. "And I'm sure Colin would be able to describe you well enough to make you identifiable to the others."

"I don't think so," she argued. "That sketch is old, and there are a lot of girls in Windom with brown hair and green eyes just like me."

"I doubt Colin's description of you was as simple as 'She has brown hair and green eyes,'" he said, scoffing. "But if came down to that, I'm sure they would gather up all the brown haired, green eyed girls in Windom to find you," he said.

Elora's eyes widened as she imagined the Liana terrorizing the young women of Windom in search of her.

"That won't be necessary though," Asher continued. "Because they will recognize you, Elora."

"You only think that because you know already who I am," she said, shaking her head.

"I knew you were the Renascent the minute I saw you," he said, holding her gaze. "I don't know exactly how, but I did. And so will they."

"Oh," she said, lowering her eyes to the ground, dejected. She thought back to the first time he'd seen her and the way he'd reacted. "Is that why you were staring at me this morning when we passed one another on the street? Because you recognized me?"

"No, I first recognized you last night when you were walking home in the dark," he replied. "I was staring at you this morning because you are beautiful."

Elora's eyes snapped up to his in surprise and her breath caught in her throat.

He looked back at her, his gaze unwavering and sincere.

"Which is probably how Colin described you as well," he continued. "So can you please drop this idea that you are going to be able to walk right past them unnoticed?"

Elora nodded, trying to convince her heart to beat at a normal rhythm.

"I think you're right though," he said. "Our best bet is to figure out a way to hide your identity. We might be able to get past them if they don't recognize who you are."

"What about you? Don't they know you?" she asked.

"Colin is the only one who really knows me," he said. "They won't be looking for a man anyway, since they already have your father. I think I can get by unnoticed."

Elora thought for a moment, distractedly playing with the strap of her satchel. Her breath suddenly caught in her throat as an idea struck her. She lifted the flap and reached into the bag, grabbing a handful of silky fabric. She watched the way the Elysic cloak flowed between her fingers like liquid, becoming even more confident as her plan took shape. The corners of her mouth quirked upwards.

"Are there women among the Liana?" she asked.

"Yes, a few," Asher replied.

She smiled at him, nearly laughing at the simplicity of the solution. He furrowed his brows, curious at her sudden change in demeanor. She pulled the cloak completely out of her satchel and wrapped it around her shoulders. Reaching behind her, she tugged the hood of the cloak forward over her head until her face was hidden in shadow.

"Well?" she asked expectantly.

Asher's eyes lit with excitement as he too broke into a smile.

"That could work," he said. "But you'll be out in the open. You can't act timid or scared. You'll have to be convincing. Can you do that?"

She pushed the hood back to look him in the eyes.

"I think I have to," she said, the smile sliding from her lips.

"We'll have to separate," he said, clearly uncomfortable with the idea. "But I'm not letting you out of my sight," he stated firmly. "I'll just follow a short distance behind you."

Elora nodded.

"What should I do if I run into a Liana?" she asked, suddenly nervous as she considered more deeply what she was preparing to do.

"Just keep walking and try to act calm. If he salutes you, salute him back like this," he said, touching his right hand to his left shoulder briefly. "But stay quiet."

Elora mimicked his salute and he nodded his approval.

"But what if he tries to talk to me?" she asked anxiously.

"Claren don't talk to one another while cloaked," Asher said, shaking his head. "At least not in the vicinity of a non-Claren. It would risk exposing our existence to the rest of the world," he explained.

"Are you're sure I won't have to talk to them?" she asked, warily.

"They won't talk to you if I'm nearby," he assured her. "Keeping our way of life a secret is one of our most sacred laws. Revealing the gifts of the Ever Tree is a crime punishable by exile. "

Elora paused and her eyes widened as a troubling realization took shape. Asher had used the cloak to convince Alysa and Trig to help them. Had he really risked expulsion from Clarendon to save her? Why would he do that?

"What?" Asher asked, seeing her worried expression. "What's wrong?"

"Nothing," she said, shaking her head. "I'm just nervous."

"It will be alright. I feel good about this," he said reassuringly. "And I'll be right behind you."

She nodded, studying him quietly for a moment. Watching their surroundings and deep in thought, he was unware of her scrutiny. Her heart thudded in her chest as she was struck once again by an unexpected pang of attraction. His short, dark blond hair was sweaty and tousled after hours spent hiking through the fields of Windom. A hint of stubble was becoming visible along his jaw as the day drew on. The way his shirt draped across his broad shoulders implied a strength that made her stomach flutter. He had rolled up his sleeves to reveal the sinewy muscles of his forearms, which were flexing repetitively as he anxiously clenched and unclenched his fists. He turned his head, suddenly fixing his sea-blue eyes on hers and she forgot how to breath entirely for a moment. He was truly striking; utterly noticeable.

"I think you need a disguise too," she said, swallowing self-consciously and trying not to blush.

"Ok," he said easily. He rubbed his hands on the dusty ground near his feet and brushed them across his sweaty face, marring his handsome features with dark streaks of dirt. He wiped his hands and dabbed at his face with his once white shirt.

"Better?" he asked, looking to her for approval.

"What disguise where you going for?" Elora asked, her eyebrows raised.

"Farmer, gardener, I don't know," he said, shrugging. "I don't have a lot to work with here."

"Ok," Elora said, chuckling. "I guess that works. Though if you had asked me first, I would have told you to get dirt from over there instead," she laughed, pointing a short distance away.

He looked to where she had pointed and furrowed his brows.

"Why?" he asked.

"Because I think you probably just smeared a good bit of chicken poop on your face," she said, nodding her head towards the coop they were crouched behind.

A fleeting look of disgust flashed across his face, but was immediately replaced by a smirk. He shrugged nonchalantly.

"I've heard chicken poop is good for your skin, actually," he said, with a surprising level of sincerity.

Elora nodded indulgently, trying to stifle her laugh.

"Here, have some," he said, brushing a finger across his cheek and reaching towards Elora's face.

She gasped, dodging his hand and reaching out to grab his arm.

"No?" he asked chuckling.

"No," she said, giggling. "You keep your chicken poop to yourself."

They smiled at each other, enjoying a light-hearted moment and forgetting for just a little while the danger they were about to face. But too soon, reality set back in, descending upon them like a heavy blanket, smothering their laughter.

"Are you ready?" he asked.

Elora nodded, reaching back with shaking hands to pull her hood forward over her head.

Asher reached out, taking hold of her trembling hands with his steady ones, trying to impart some calm.

"I'm going to go first to see if anyone is nearby. I'll give you a signal when the road is clear and then you just walk towards the schoolhouse. I'll follow," he said.

"We don't have to walk far down this road," she said. "There's an intersection about a quarter mile from here where we can get off this main road. The crossroad runs right past the schoolhouse."

"Alright, here I go," Asher said. "Be careful, Elora," he whispered, squeezing her hands gently one last time before releasing them.

He stood and looked around before quickly walking along the edge of the barnyard towards the road. Near the road, Tim Pryor had several bundles of firewood stacked and marked for sale. Asher paused for a moment, grabbing a smaller one and hefting it onto his shoulder, a further effort at disguise.

Elora watched carefully, waiting for his signal. He stepped into the road and looked in both directions before turning back and waving her forward. She took a deep breath, stood and stepped quickly towards the road. Pausing for only a moment to lock eyes with him, she walked boldly into the road and began making her way down the short but nerve wracking route to the schoolhouse.

She walked for a few minutes without seeing a soul. She could hear the comforting sound of Asher's boots scuffing occasionally in the dirt a distance behind her. Though the sun was beginning to set and the heat of the day was beginning to wane, it was still oppressively hot beneath the cloak. Elora could feel sweat trickling down her spine as she quickly moved down the road.

The crossroad was nearly in sight when a figure appeared on the horizon. Her mouth went dry and her breath caught in her throat as he came nearer and the shimmery brown fabric of his Elysic cloak came into view. It was a Liana.

"Don't panic. Don't panic. Don't panic," Elora whispered to herself over and over.

He was coming closer. Elora unconsciously slowed her pace, terrified of crossing paths with him. Suddenly she heard music coming from behind her. It was Asher. He was humming the tune to the Binding Hymn and he sounded much closer than he had been before. She took a calming breath, relieved and emboldened by his presence.

The Liana guard was approaching steadily on the opposite side of the road. He seemed unfazed by her presence as far as Elora could tell. Asher began singing in earnest, making his presence known and hopefully precluding any attempts at interaction between Elora and the Liana. She watched carefully as he came closer and could see that he was focused not on her, but Asher. Just as he was about to pass, the guard turned his face to her and casually lifted his arm in salute. Elora stiffly returned the gesture and continued walking.

It took everything she had to keep her body moving despite her paralyzing fear. She could barely breath. She listened but couldn't hear anything beyond Asher's somewhat clumsy rendition of the song she'd last heard just a few short hours ago at her friend's Binding, when her world had still been right and normal. She forced herself to take a deep breath and began taking larger steps, trying to get to the crossroad as quickly as she could.

The intersection at last came into view and she breathed a sigh of relief. As she rounded the corner, she cautioned a look backwards. Her blood ran cold in her veins and she faltered, nearly tripping. There, a short distance behind Asher, was the Liana. He was following her. The worried look on Asher's face told her that he was aware of their company. He subtly tilted his head, indicating that she should keep going before suddenly dropping his bundle of wood and kneeling, acting as though his boot lace had come untied. She regained her footing and tried to calm her nerves, trusting that Asher had a plan.

She had walked only a few paces down the road towards the schoolhouse when a dull "thunk" broke the silence. She froze, too scared to turn and see what had happened. Suddenly Asher was beside her, his face pale, his chest heaving.

"Asher!" she cried, pulling back her hood and throwing her arms around him in relief.

He returned her embrace briefly before pulling back.

"We have to hurry," he said.

"What happened?" she asked, peering over his shoulder but the road was empty.

"I knocked him out with a piece of firewood," he said as he grabbed her hand and began pulling her down the road.

She looked up at him, her eyes wide and her mouth agape.

"He'll be fine," he said, shaking his head.

"But where is he?" she asked, turning to look back once more.

"I dragged him into the grass on the roadside," he said. "He was out cold. But I don't know for how long. We really need to get out of here. Which direction is the school?" he asked, tugging her along.

"That way," Elora said, pointing off to the right side of the road.

Asher charged off the road and down into the ditch that ran alongside, dragging Elora with him. They pushed through a thicket and across a field, moving with careless speed and silent urgency. The roof of the schoolhouse finally came into view.

"The shed is around back," Elora said, panting from exertion.

As they neared the open area around the schoolhouse, Asher pulled her to a stop behind the cover of a scrubby cluster of bushes. They waited quietly, watching and listening for any sign that they were not alone.

"I'll follow you," he said finally, nodding for her to make a run for the shed.

Elora sprang out into the open, running as fast as she could past the front of the schoolhouse. She rounded the building and darted over to the decrepit old shed which was hiding in the shadow of a bushy crape myrtle which had long ago shed its last blooms. She tore open the door and rushed inside the cramped space, squeezing to the back of the shed to make room for Asher. She turned around just in time to see him step through the doorway.

He swung the door swiftly closed, careful not to let it bang. The small shed was dark, save for the slivers of fading sunlight that shone through the cracks between boards and danced among the floating particles of dust. Elora could only barely make out the features of his face, though he was only a foot or so away. Their rapid breathing was the only sound.

Elora closed her eyes, leaning her head back against the wall as she tried to calm her frantically beating heart. She lifted her hands to wipe at the sweat that was dripping down her face.

"It's so hot in here," she whispered, sighing.

"Here, this will help," Asher said, stepping closer to untie the cloak and pull it from her shoulders.

She took the cloak from his hands, her fingers brushing against his in the process. She looked up into his face, every fiber of her being acutely aware of his proximity.

"Are you alright?" she asked gently.

"Yes, are you?" he asked in reply.

"Yes," she said. "But I'm not the one who just clocked a guy and dragged him into the bushes," she said.

"No, but you were the one he was chasing," he whispered.

Elora swallowed, attempting to suppress the terror his words summoned.

"I'm surprised he even noticed me with you singing like that," she said with a forced chuckle.

"Pretty good, huh!" he joked.

"It was an interesting song choice," she teased.

"Well, I couldn't sing a Claren song or it would have given me away. And that Binding song was the only thing I could think of," he explained. "I really impressed myself considering I'd only heard it the one time this morning."

"Yes, you were wonderful," she said dismissively. "But why was he following me?" she asked, trying to get back on topic. "Did I make a mistake?"

"I honestly don't know. I didn't see any obvious reason for him to doubt your disguise," he replied. "Maybe he was just curious."

Elora nodded, despite feeling uneasy with his answer.

The light was fading quickly now as the sun was setting in earnest. She could hardly see more than a vague outline of his body.

"Thank you for stopping him," she said quietly.

"Of course," he replied gently.

"You keep doing that," she said, shaking her head.

"Doing what?" he asked.

"Making sacrifices for me," she whispered. "Taking risks. Breaking laws. I don't think I could live with myself if you were exiled from Clarendon because of me."

"Clarendon doesn't hold anything for me without you," he said, his deep voice the only sound in the darkening shed. "But you don't have to worry," he said, shaking his head. "I didn't kill him, Elora. I won't be exiled."

"No, but you showed the cloak to Trig and Alysa," she said.

Asher was silent for a moment.

"I know," he said solemnly.

"They won't tell anyone," she assured him.

"I believe that," he said, nodding. "But it doesn't really matter. It had to be done."

He continued to amaze her. He had given up years of his life to find her and continued to put himself in danger in order to protect her, all because of the Prophesy. She hoped, for his sake, that it was true.

"I know you're doing it all for the Prophesy, but I still feel indebted to you," she whispered, closing her eyes against the weight of the burden.

The air plunged into uncomfortable silence. She waited nervously for him to say something but he didn't make a sound. She began to worry that she had upset him.

"Asher?" she asked tentatively, reaching out to lay her hand on his forearm.

"You don't owe me anything," he said quietly.

She was startled by the hint of anger in his voice. Her hand dropped from his arm and she tried to place some distance between them, but her back was already against the wall in the small shed.

"I'm sorry, I didn't mean to..." she fumbled.

"You've done that twice now," he interrupted, his voice gentle but disappointed.

"Done what?" she asked.

"Claimed that I'm only helping you because you're the Renascent," he said.

"Aren't you?" she asked hesitantly.

"No," he replied earnestly. "At least not anymore."

Her brows furrowed in confusion. She wished it weren't so dark. It was hard to interpret what he really meant, what he was feeling without being able to see him.

"You are more than the Prophesy to me, Elora" he whispered. "This is personal to me now. We're in this together."

Her eyes widened in surprise at his admission. She took a shuddering breath. It was as though a weight had been lifted from her. A warm feeling spread throughout her chest as she discovered a connection, a friendship with him that had not been there before. She was still struggling to grasp the reality that her parents would no longer be with her on this journey. And until this moment, she had not realized how alone she had felt.

But why? She wanted to believe him, but how could she? They had only just met. They hardly knew one another. How she wished she could look into his eyes at this moment, to see the sincerity that she hoped were there. She desperately wanted to trust that he meant what he said. But his devotion to her just didn't make sense without the Prophesy.

"I don't understand" she said. "I thought you wanted me to be the Renascent?"

"You are the Renascent," he said gently. "What I want doesn't matter."

"Would you still be with me if I chose to ignore the Prophesy?" she asked.

"The Prophesy will haunt you, Elora. You won't be free of it until it is finished," he said gently. "You don't really have that choice."

"I don't believe that," she said, adamantly.

"I know you don't," he said, chuckling.

"But what if I refused to return to Clarendon?" she asked hesitantly. "Would you still help me evade the Liana then?"

"I would help you, even if you ran away from your destiny," he said. "But you must know that destiny cannot be prevented. It can only be delayed."

"Why would you help me then?" she asked, bewildered. "You clearly believe I should fulfill my duty as the Renascent."

"I do," he said. "And I know that someday you will."

"So then I'm not wrong in thinking that you're helping me because of the Prophesy," she argued.

"You're wrong," he reiterated. "That's not why."

"But if the end result is the same, does it even matter why?" she asked quietly.

"It matters," he said softly. "You are not a means to an end. I'm not helping you because you're the Renascent."

"Then why?" she asked

"Because I want you to be free," he replied.

"Yes, I know. So that I can fulfill the Prophesy," she said, remembering their earlier discussion.

"I want you to be free of the Prophesy, Elora," he corrected. "I will help you finish this because I want you to be free."

"You want me to be free," Elora repeated, still confused.

"I need you to be free," he stated resolutely.

"Why?" she whispered once more.

The shed fell silent. She could feel the answer to her question dancing in the air. Her skin hummed with awareness and her heartbeat quickened as she recognized the truth. He cared for her. But he would not give voice to it. He never would. Not until he held a glowing seed from the Ever Tree in his hand. He was saving those words for his soulmate.

CHAPTER 19

The sun had slipped below the horizon a while ago, though the heat of the day still radiated from the earth around them making the shed stuffy and uncomfortable. Elora sighed, shifting her weight from one foot to the other. Why hadn't she chosen a bigger place? Preferably one where they could have comfortably sat without fear of snakes and spiders. What a stupid hiding place. How she hated to feel foolish.

"This shed might not have been the best idea," she whispered apologetically.

"Well, no one has found us, so it wasn't a terrible idea either," he said reassuringly.

Surprisingly, he didn't seem as disappointed in her choice as she was. She exhaled, relieved that he wasn't standing across from her in the dark secretly seething with annoyance at her pitiful evasion skills.

"Do you think Trig is ready for us?" Asher asked. "It's been dark for nearly an hour now."

"Maybe," she said. "I guess there's only one way to find out."

She heard Asher slowly swing the door open, its rusty hinges squeaking in protest. The world was dark and quiet outside the shed. A full moon was rising in the night sky, casting pale beams of light that faintly illuminated the shed. Asher looked back at Elora and she was able to see him clearly for the first time in a while.

Though he was the same man who'd followed her into the shed a short time ago, she saw him differently now. There was a closeness, a comfort between them that hadn't been there before. And beneath that, there was the thrilling excitement of unspoken affection.

"I'll follow you," he said quietly, standing beside the entrance to let her pass.

Elora quickly walked past him, out of the stagnant atmosphere of the shed and into the fresh night air. Breathing deeply, she sighed in relief. A sudden cool gust of wind tugged at the loose strands of hair that had broken free from the updo that Alysa had so lovingly arranged that morning. She attempted to tuck them behind her ear as they swirled around her face. She heard Asher gently close the door behind them. As she turned to face him, the moonlight dimmed and he became hidden in darkness once more. Elora looked up to see storm clouds moving swiftly towards Windom, obscuring the moonlight, swirling across the night sky like leaves caught in a current. The gentle rumble of thunder sounded in the distance.

"It's going to storm," she said quietly, concern in her voice.

"Then we should hurry," Asher replied softly.

They carefully made their way towards the lean-to where Trig would hopefully be waiting, the moon sporadically lighting their way through fleeting gaps in the clouds. The wall quickly came into view, lit by large, evenly spaced torches stretching in either direction around the settlement. Guardsmen paced along the top of the wall, standing watch despite the coming weather.

"There it is," she said breathlessly, pausing to take it all in.

Elora's relief was tempered by dread as she considered the prospect of repelling down the jagged and treacherous exterior surface.

"You can do this," Asher said encouragingly, sensing her trepidation.

Elora began to turn towards the sound of his voice but was suddenly startled by a flash of light and a thunderous boom of thunder. As she looked beyond the wall at the impending the storm, another bolt of lightning illuminated the sky. She gasped and turned wide eyes towards Asher. He was frozen, staring towards the wall in shock. He had seen it too. Hidden in the shadows, cloaked Lianas were also patrolling the wall, standing guard, watching for her.

"What do we do?" Elora asked, her voice trembling.

"I don't know," Asher replied haltingly.

"Maybe we could hide in a wagon and sneak out of the gate instead," she suggested.

Asher shook his head adamantly.

"I have to think they are following wagons, searching them," he reasoned.

"So you think scaling the wall really is our only way out?" she asked anxiously.

She couldn't see his face in the darkness, but his silence was confirmation enough.

"But we can't get past them," she whispered, defeated. "There's just no way."

They stood quietly for a few minutes, overwhelmed and grasping for a solution. Elora was despondent, her panic growing with each flash of lightning, each fleeting glimpse of the hooded figures walking the wall.

"I should just surrender before anyone else gets hurt," she whispered at last.

"You are not going to surrender," Asher said, forcefully.

"But it's hopeless!" she cried. "I won't put those Guardsmen in danger like that. Or you, for that matter."

"Stop it, Elora," he hissed.

"No, Asher! Enough!" she exclaimed. "I'm not going to let you make any more sacrifices for me."

"That's not for you to decide," he replied.

"We can't beat them, Asher," she said, her voice small, her spirit broken. "I give up."

She began to walk away from him but he reached out and grabbed hold of her arm, pulling her back to face him.

"I won't let you," he growled.

“I’m not worth it, Asher,” she whispered.

“Yes, you are!” he said, grasping her shoulders roughly.

Elora stood before him, struggling to comprehend how she could ever bear the guilt and responsibility of knowing people might be injured, maybe even killed, because of her. There would be a cost for her freedom. But then, surrender would come at a heavy price too. There was no way for her to win.

“Asher ...“ she whispered, grappling for words.

“You are worth it,” he interrupted. “So are your parents. So are the Claren. So are the Woodlands,” he said gruffly, his accent thickening with emotion. “They are all worth fighting for.”

She couldn’t see his face clearly in the darkness but could hear his quickened breath, could feel the tension in his fingers as he struggled to control his frustration.

“And so am I,” he added quietly.

Elora inhaled sharply, closing her eyes against her warring emotions, torn between the two terrible choices before her.

“Don’t make me live the rest of my life without my soulmate,” Asher whispered.

Moonlight broke through a brief opening in the clouds to reveal his face. They locked eyes and Elora knew in that moment that her resistance was futile. His words and his voice were pleading. He wanted her to choose. But his eyes were determined. He had already made the choice for her.

"I won't let them have you, Elora," he said bluntly, holding her gaze.

He meant it. Whether she wanted him to or not, he would stand between her and the Liana. He would save her, even from herself.

"But we can't win," she whispered, her words nearly lost in the wind from the coming storm.

"We have to try," he replied softly. "Please."

His hands dropped from her shoulders but the intensity of his stare held her captive all the same. His gaze was unwavering and earnest. She couldn't seem to look away, confused and intoxicated by the expression in his eyes. The longer she remained spellbound to it, what had at first appeared to be fierce determination began to seem much more like devotion. His eyes dropped momentarily to her lips and her breath caught in her throat. They darted back to hers again before finally focusing on a windswept lock of hair clinging to her cheek. He lifted his hand, gently brushing back the hair and tucking it behind her ear. She swallowed nervously, overwhelmed by the intimate touch. He inhaled a shaky breath, seemingly as moved as she was and lifted his gaze to fixed his eyes on hers once more.

"Now, where's the lean-to?" Asher asked finally, putting the matter to rest.

She nodded in resignation and turned to lead him the short distance remaining to their destination.

They quickly came upon the worn and weathered split-rail fence of the cow pasture. Climbing over it, they could see the faint glow of a lantern coming from beneath a sturdy wooden three-sided structure in the far corner of the field. Asher took her hand, protectively tugging her behind him as they neared the back of the lean-to. Despite her efforts to move quietly, a twig snapped beneath her foot as she made her way through the scrubby field. A shadowy figure stepped to the edge of the light.

"Elora?" came Alysa's voice calling quietly.

Elora was about to reply when Asher's hand clamped quickly over her mouth. She stared up at him with wide, confused eyes. He motioned for her to crouch down and placed a finger over his lips, telling her to keep quiet. Moving with surprising agility, he silently made his way around the small building, staying in the shadows as he searched for any sign of a Liana in their midst. Satisfied that Trig and Alysa had not been followed, she watched as he finally stepped into the light. There was a cry of surprise from within the lean-to.

"Are you alone?" Asher asked, looking around carefully.

"We didn't see anyone," Trig answered, pointedly. "But apparently we wouldn't."

Asher nodded in understanding, sympathetic to how angry and powerless Trig doubtless felt knowing an invisible enemy had besieged the settlement. He waved Elora over and she quickly moved out of her hiding place.

Alysa pulled her into a hug and was soon joined by Trig, who wrapped his arms around them both. He stepped back after a moment, his eyes trained expectantly on the darkness from whence she had just emerged.

"Where are your parents?" he asked carefully a few seconds later, a look of confusion on his face.

Tears sprang to Elora's eyes and she quickly closed them to stem the torrent of emotions threatening to break free. Taking a deep breath, she stepped out of Alysa's embrace and moved to stand beside Asher.

"They were captured," she said, struggling to get the words past the lump in her throat.

Alysa's hand flew to her mouth in shock and she locked eyes with her husband.

"So what do we do now?" Trig asked, looking to Asher for direction.

"We're going over the wall," Asher replied stoically.

"You're just leaving them?" Trig asked incredulously, his face a mixture of shock and disgust.

"We have no choice," Asher answered, his voice hard as he widened his stance and crossed his arms defensively. "They know that. Jonas told us to go."

"And you're going along with this?" Trig asked Elora, his tone accusatory.

"You don't understand Trig," she explained, her voice beseeching, tears trickling down her cheeks. "You know that I would never abandon my parents. But we can't save them. Not yet. Not here."

Trig shook his head with disappointment, looking down at the ground.

"I'm not even sure we can save ourselves," she said finally.

"What do you mean?" Trig asked.

"The Liana are guarding the wall," Asher replied grimly.

Trig's eyes grew wide and he looked at Alysa nervously.

"But there are at least 50 of the Guard on the wall tonight," he said in amazement.

Asher nodded in acknowledgement but shrugged as though it were unimportant.

"They are unaware of the company," he replied.

Trig looked at him with a combination of indignation and alarm.

"How many did you see?" he asked.

"On the stretch of wall near here I saw two Guardsmen and three Liana sentinels patrolling," Asher replied.

Trig grimaced and rested his hands on his hips, sighing with frustration.

"That will complicate things," he said.

"Maybe," Asher said, nodding. "How were you planning to get us over the wall?"

"I brought these," Trig said, pulling his Guardsman uniform and rope out of a satchel at his feet. "Will Holmestead is working the wall over there and I'm going to relieve him. He won't question it. He's been working since early this morning, looking for that attempted horse thief. I'm sure he's probably up there praying for a break."

"I wonder if they found the guy," Alyssa wondered aloud.

"I'm sure they didn't," Asher said bluntly.

"Oh," she whispered, as the realization dawned on her that the horse thief was a member of the Liana.

"Once he's off the wall, I'm going to extinguish one of those torches for a few minutes, just enough time to hook up the rope and get you over the wall," Trig continued.

Asher looked over to Elora briefly before lowering his eyes to study the ground as he silently considered the plan. She stared at him, biting her lip anxiously, gripping the hem of her shirt to calm the trembling of her hands. Her eyes shifted to Alysa and then settled on Trig. Her chin began to quiver as she imagined the horrible consequences that may come from their involvement tonight. What kind of friend was she to put them at risk like this? She looked back to Asher and found that his eyes were trained on her face, his expression unreadable. At last he sighed and turned to Trig.

"It's a good plan," he said, nodding. "Probably our best option."

"Yeah," Trig reluctantly agreed, his eyes fixed on Alysa's fearful expression.

He lifted the Guardsman tunic and began shoving his arm into the sleeve when Asher reached out to stop him.

"No," he said, shaking his head. "I'll wear it. I'll get us over the wall."

Elora's eyes grew wide as she looked at Trig and then back to Asher.

"What?" Trig asked, confused.

"You need to stay here with your bride," Asher replied, taking the shirt from him. "We can do this without you."

Alyssa let out a small cry of relief before covering her mouth with her hand.

"Are you sure?" Trig asked hesitantly moving to wrap his arm around Alysa. "I am willing to help."

"I appreciate that, but it's better this way," Asher said, pulling the tunic over his head. "Is there anything I need to know?"

"There's a key in the chest pocket that will unlock the ladder," Trig said, beginning to fill in the details of the plan. "You can tell Will that Commander Scott sent you."

"Commander Scott, got it," Asher replied as he lifted Trig's rope to take a closer look. "What's this?" he asked, lifting the metal hook on the end.

"There's are rings anchored to the top of the interior wall. Just clip the hook onto it." Trig replied.

"Sounds easy enough," Asher said, looping the rope neatly.

"Use this," Trig said, holding open the satchel for Trig to place the rope inside before handing him the bag.

"Alright, is that it?" Asher asked.

"I think so," Trig answered, his facial expression a combination of relief and guilt.

"Thank you," he added. "For what you've done and for what you were willing to do."

"Anything for Elora," Trig replied.

Everyone instinctively turned their attention to Elora at the sound of her name. She was the reason they were all there, the person they were all willing to sacrifice so much to save. She was staring at Asher, her eyes full of gratitude and admiration. He returned her gaze briefly before fixing Trig with a worried look.

"Elora's parents didn't know the details of our escape but they did know that she was going to ask you for help," he said. "When they aren't able to find us in the coming days, they will come looking for you Trig."

"Alysa and I won't be here," Trig replied, locking eyes with his wife. "I had already arranged for a holiday in the city as a honeymoon. Mr. Redding is taking us to the train station in Sweetwater at first light and we'll be in Red River for a week."

"That's exciting!" Elora said, smiling at Alysa and trying to summon the joyful enthusiasm she would have felt ordinarily at such news.

"I know," Alysa replied, returning an equally forced smile.

"Safe travels, then," Asher said, clasping Trig's shoulder.

"You too," Trig replied soberly.

"And congratulations," he said, smiling kindly. "I wish you a long and full life with your soulmate."

"Thanks," Trig said, turning to smile at his bride. "That's the plan."

"I'll give you a few minutes," Asher said, locking eyes with Elora.

Slinging the bag over his shoulder, he walked outside of the lean-to, offering her a private moment with her two dearest friends.

Elora twisted her hands anxiously as she looked back and forth between Trig and Alysa. Her eyes were wide, as though she were shocked that this were really happening. Her heart was weighted down with fear and sadness and it pulled at her chest, making it difficult to breathe. She dropped her gaze to the ground and tried to calm her racing heart.

"I guess this is it," she whispered.

"I don't know how to say goodbye to you," Alysa said in a small voice, her lips quivering.

"Me neither," Elora admitted, a sob breaking free as she rushed forward to wrap her in a hug.

"Will I ever see you again?" Alysa whispered.

"I hope so," Elora answered. "But I don't know. I don't know anything anymore."

"You'll come back to us," Trig said with optimism. "You have to. Someone has to teach our children how to play in the dirt. Lord knows Alysa won't do it," he teased, circling both women in his arms.

Elora couldn't help but laugh, turning her wet face to bury it in his shoulder.

"Oh God, I'm going to miss you both so much," she blubbered. "I'm so happy you have each other."

"Because of you," Alysa said, taking a shuddering breath and wiping her cheeks.

A resounding crack of thunder rattled the glass in the lantern. They all jumped in alarm as a shadowy figure plodded into the lean-to. It was Mr. Jenkins milk cow, finally concerned enough about the weather to seek shelter. She studied them for a few seconds before dismissing them, dropping her head to graze. Elora exhaled in relief, and the three friends laughed, sharing one last moment of levity.

Asher stepped back into the lean-to, his expression grim.

"I know that wasn't a long enough goodbye, but we have to go. The storm is approaching quickly and it looks pretty bad. We need to get over that wall," he said, seeking out Elora with his eyes.

"We should go too then," Trig said, lifting the lantern from the ground and taking hold of Alysa's hand.

"I love you both," Elora said, giving them one last hug.

"We love you too," Alysa said, her lips quivering.

"Whatever happens, you have a home here," Trig said quietly, kissing the top of her head. He sighed, struggling to let her go. "Be careful," he whispered, his voice thick with emotion.

Elora nodded, unable to speak as she fought desperately to suppress her tears. Stepping away, she turned her back to them, unable to bring herself to watch them walk away. She closed her eyes in one last attempt at denial and a few wayward tears trickled from beneath her lashes.

She heard Asher utter a final "Goodbye," his soft, low voice rumbling in her ears, the sound reverberating in her heart like thunder.

The sound of Alysa's soft crying slowly faded, as did the light from their lantern, until Asher and Elora were left in quiet darkness.

They were gone.

She bowed her head and covered her face with her hands, feeling bereft and alone as quiet tears pooled against her palms. A warm pair of arms wrapped around her, gently pulling her into a comforting embrace. She leaned against him, resting her forehead against his chest and for a moment allowed herself to feel all of the loss and sadness and fear that she'd somehow managed to suppress over the course of this terrible day. He didn't say a word, merely held her close as the muffled sobs racked her weary body.

A few minutes later, she managed to rein in her feelings and stem the flow of her tears. She stood quietly against him, appreciating the comfort of his arms and grateful that he couldn't see her in the darkness.

"Are you okay?" he asked gently.

She felt a lump rise in her throat as she considered how to answer. She wasn't okay. Considering that she was leaving behind everyone she loved and the only home she'd ever known, she wondered if it would ever be possible for her to feel whole again. She felt utterly empty inside.

The question hung in the air uncomfortably until finally Asher sighed.

"I know you're not okay," he whispered, rubbing her back. "I meant, can you still do this?"

Elora took a shuddering breath and nodded her head.

"Thank you for telling Trig to leave," she said quietly. "I know it would have been easier with his help."

"I didn't think you'd come with me otherwise," he replied honestly.

"No, probably not," she admitted.

She sighed and rubbed the tears from her swollen eyes. Lifting her head, she placed a hand against Asher's chest and put some space between them. Realizing that his shirt beneath her hand was wet from her weeping, she wiped at it self-consciously.

"I'm sorry," she whispered apologetically.

"Don't worry about it," he said kindly. "Besides, we're about to get a whole lot wetter."

Elora stopped, suddenly noticing the gentle rap of raindrops drumming against the roof of the lean-to. The front edge of the storm had reached Windom.

CHAPTER 20

Gusts of wind tormented the surrounding trees, bending them low, whistling through their branches and tearing the leaves free of their moorings. It buffeted against Elora and Asher as they walked toward the wall, the flaming torches acting as beacons in the black night. Raindrops pelted down on them, stinging their skin and soaking their clothing. Asher held tightly to her hand, as though he was worried that he'd lose her in the darkness, though it was more likely he was afraid she'd lose her nerve.

"Do you know where the ladder is?" Asher asked, shouting in her ear to be heard over the storm.

She took the lead, pulling him toward where she thought ladder would be; the ladder she'd used only a few short weeks ago when she'd seen beyond the wall for the first time. The wall that used to offer protection but now served only as a prison. The wilderness beyond had once seemed so terrifying but would now be her refuge.

The sky lit up, a bolt of lightning weaving through the clouds like a spider's web. For a split second the wet stones of the wall were illuminated, now only 50 feet in front of them. A few more steps and they would be in its shadow, too close to see the light from the torches any longer. They were nearly there.

Elora's legs felt numb and her entire body trembled with fear. Her terror increased with every step. She stumbled in the darkness, losing her footing in the wet grass. She was unable to catch herself, her body suddenly uncoordinated and her reflexes dull with dread. She would have fallen if Asher hadn't quickly pulled her upright, his grip on her hand steady and firm. He released her suddenly and her heart nearly stopped beating. But hardly a moment passed before she felt his hand at her waist and the strength of his arm at her back. Her hand flew down to cover his and she gripped his fingers, grateful for the added support and comforted by the feel of him beside her. They quickly, but clumsily made their way over the last few yards to the wall. She reached out, her palms resting against the rough stones of the wall.

A faintly flickering square of light danced on the ground 20 feet away where torchlight shone through an opening in the surface of the wall. The ladder was there, mounted onto the wall, stretching from the ground upwards though the opening. Asher began walking towards it, grabbing hold of her hand and pulling her along behind him.

Her feet felt like lead and her breath was coming in short gasps. Was she really going to be able to do this? How would she overcome this paralyzing fear?

At the base of the ladder, Asher stopped and turned to face her. He looked up through the opening, the light revealing the features of his face. He gaze was focused and determined. Elora studied him, marveling at his composure, envious of his bravery. Strangely, his calm seemed to be infectious. She closed her eyes for a moment and took a deep breath.

As they stood beneath the ladder, the wind unexpectedly abated and the downpour eased into a soft drizzle. Though the rain had cooled the night air considerably, the humidity was still smothering, a clear indication that the storm was far from over. They could still hear thunder rumbling in the distance, a hint of what was still to come once the next band of clouds reached Windom. But for now, there was a brief respite from the storm. They could hear the dribble of water falling from the wall overhead, collecting in puddles at their feet. Beneath the overhang they were sheltered from the rain.

She opened her eyes to find him watching her. The light was too faint to see the expression in his eyes clearly, but his gaze was unwavering. She looked away uncomfortably and lifted the hem of her drenched tunic, trying in vain to wipe the water from her face. She ran her hands roughly over her forehead, pushing back her wet hair. Staring at the ground, she nervously avoided making eye contact. After a moment, he gently took her chin in his fingers, lifting her face and silently asking her to look at him again. She at last relented, raising her eyes to his. He leaned down until he was only whisper away.

"You can do this," he said softly.

She stared back at him with wide eyes, her body numb with terror. Her mouth was dry and her heart was pounding mercilessly. A wet lock of hair blew across her face and she tried unsuccessfully to brush it away with fingers that were shaking so violently that they tingled.

"Elora, stop," he said gently. "You have to calm down."

Something brushed against her leg and she jumped, looking down at the ground in alarm. The grass around them had begun to grow and was blowing against their knees as the wind began to gust more forcefully with the coming storm. As she watched, the blades extended another inch.

Elora lifted her hands, at last recognizing the tingling in her fingers for what it was. She felt powerless to control her gift in this moment. She looked up at Asher, her eyes wild with panic.

He took her trembling hands in his and pulled her close. He pressed her hands against his chest, covering them with one of his warm, steady ones. Reached out with his other hand, he gently tucked the wayward lock of hair behind her ear. He lifted her chin, and searched out her eyes with his.

She fixed her eyes on him, trying to focus on something beside the overwhelming fear coursing through her body. Just being near him was soothing and encouraging.

She took it all in; the steady beat of his heart, the quiet confidence of his gaze, his towering frame and strong body. She could see in his eyes that he was nervous, but his determination wouldn't let that stop him. He was going over the wall. He didn't question it. He knew it.

As she stood before him, studying him, she considered what he must think of her. Why was she allowing herself to be controlled by her fear? She was better than this. She was stronger than this. Her parents needed her to be strong. The Claren needed her to be strong. She was the Renascent. She was going to save them all. But first, she would have to save herself.

She took a deep breath, and closed her eyes. She willed her heartbeat to slow. A sense of calm spread throughout her body and the tingling in her fingers subsided. She opened her eyes, no longer wide with terror but focused with resolve. She fixed her gaze on Asher and beneath her hands she felt his chest heave with a sigh of relief.

"I can do this," she said, ignoring the way her voice quivered.

He nodded and released her hands, but the look in his eyes kept her spellbound. He caressed her face once more, smoothing back the hair at her temple.

"You can do this," he repeated once more, though it seemed more for his benefit than hers this time.

His hand dropped from her face and he looked down to the satchel on her hip. Reaching into it, he pulled out the Elysic cloak and shook it out.

"I'm hoping they won't see us at all," he whispered. "But in case they do..."

He fastened it around her neck and pulled the hood up over her head.

"I will go up first and attach the rope," he said quietly. "You wait on the ladder and I'll come for you when I think it's safe."

Elora nodded, taking a deep breath to calm her nerves and steel herself against the fear that threatened to bubble up once more.

The wind began to pick up again and a blinding bolt of lightning illuminated the sky. A deafening crack of thunder quickly followed.

"That was close," Elora whispered nervously.

"I know," Asher replied. "Try not to worry about the storm, Elora. Only one thing at a time."

The gentle drizzle suddenly became a torrent, roaring around them and drenching them completely. Elora pressed her body against the wall and covered her face with her hands, trying to shield herself from the downpour. Sheets of water fell slanted from the sky as powerful gusts of wind propelled the rain sideways. Elora couldn't see or hear, could barely breathe in the onslaught.

She felt Asher take hold of her hand and pull her forwards. Cupping her free hand over her eyes, she squinted in a futile attempt to see him. He firmly wrapped her fingers wrapped around the hard metal of the ladder and let go.

"He can't mean to do this now, in the midst of the storm!" she thought stunned.

She grasped for him with her other hand but only felt the hard leather of his boot as it rose beyond her reach up the rungs of the ladder. Elora froze, unsure of what to do. Should she follow him? She had to be at the top of the ladder when he came for her or the entire escape would fail. But every reasonable fiber of her being was bristling in protest. No sane person would climb onto the wall right now.

As further proof of her point, a knotted rope smacked the ground a few feet away and a Guardsman landed on his feet beside it soon after. He took off in the opposite direction along the wall, unaware of Elora's presence. Even the Guard was abandoning their post in this storm.

But Asher was up there.

"Oh God," she thought, gripping the ladder with both hands. "This is such a bad idea."

One foot after the other, she climbed the ladder, stopping once or twice to wipe the water from her eyes. Her head suddenly and painfully collided against the solid bars of the grate covering the top of the ladder.

"Ow," she whispered, the sound drowned out by the raging storm.

Now, she waited. She dropped down a rung and hooked her arm through the ladder, trying to find a comfortable position. The Elysic cloak was soaking wet and she felt smothered by the fabric around her face.

"No one can see me anyway," she thought, and with her free hand, she pushed the hood back and ran her hand over her wet hair. Her finger touched something unfamiliar and she paused. Patting her updo further, it only took her a moment to recognize the twigs and leaves tucked into the knot of braids.

She returned her grip to the ladder and sighed. Her heart broke a little as she remembered how beautiful the flowers had looked in her hair that morning. Flowers that Trig had gathered to adorn her hair. Wildflowers for a wildflower. What a wonderful life she had been living. She slumped against the ladder, alone in the darkness and soaked to the bone, allowing herself a small moment to acknowledge the abject misery of her current situation.

As quickly as it had begun, the downpour lightened to a sprinkle and the world fell silent. Relieved for the lull in the storm, Elora breathed in deeply and swiped a hand down her face to clear away the water. Thunder rolled in the distance, strong enough to vibrate the ladder beneath her fingers. A gust of wind, buffeted against her, billowing the cloak around her legs. The storm was far from over.

A hand clamped around her wrist and she recoiled in surprise.

"It's me," she heard Asher whisper. "Hurry."

Lightning roiled in the clouds above, casting a dim light all around. Elora looked up and for only a moment was able to see his silhouette, crouching beside the opening. She scrambled up the last remaining rungs of the ladder. As she emerged through the opening, he took hold of her waist and swiftly lifted her the rest of the way, setting her onto her feet and closing the grate.

All the torches had been extinguished by the torrential rain. Elora, blinded in the pitch black night, pressed against the wall, fearful that she would accidently fall. She felt Asher fumbling for her hand in the darkness and reached for him, grateful for the strength of his fingers as they wrapped around hers like a vice. He pulled her along the wall a few feet and then stopped, taking her hand and carefully wrapping it around the thick wet rope he had already attached to the ring and tossed up over the exterior wall.

He cupped the nape of her neck with his free hand, pulling her head close to his and spoke directly into her ear to be heard over the sounds of the storm.

"I'm going first. I'll come back up if I think it's too dangerous," he said. "Use your legs to stay off the wall. I'll jerk the rope when I reach the bottom."

Too frightened to make a sound, she nodded her head, feeling his wet hair brush against her cheek. He didn't move for a moment and she could sense his reluctance to leave her.

"You can do this, Elora," he said again, before abruptly tugging her towards him, tucking her head in the crook of his neck. He held her there for only a moment, before releasing her. She felt a void where he had been standing only a moment ago and felt the rope swaying with his movements as he rappelled down the wall.

"Come back up," she thought. "Please, come back up."

She waited, hoping that he would change his mind, that she wouldn't have to climb on top of that wall in a minute and go over the edge. But he didn't reappear and he didn't make a sound. There was only the subtle movements of the rope, rolling back and forth with his steady descent.

Suddenly, the rope jumped. Her eyes grew wide and she stared down at her hand, her trembling fingers wrapped around the thick, woven cord. It jumped again a moment later. That was his signal. She really had to do this now.

"Please, God," she whispered, pushing the cloak back out of the way and lifting her knee onto the exterior wall. She hoisted herself upwards and laid across the barrier, her heart racing and her fingers like ice. Taking a firm grip of the rope with one hand and holding the back edge of the wall in the other, she slowly lowered her legs over the wall. Something sharp jabbed against her leg and she inhaled sharply.

Jagged and spiked. Trig had been right.

But Asher had made it down and he wanted her to follow. He thought she could do this. She had to do this.

She forced herself to release her grip on the edge of the wall, desperately clinging to the rope, her torso still perched on top of the surface. She wedged her knees against the stones, gritting her teeth against the sharp edges as they dug into her skin, and lowered herself off of the wall. She worked her hands down the rope until she came upon the first knot. Wrapping her fingers solidly around the knot, she shifted her weight, lifting off of her knees and onto her feet. She breathed a sigh of relief, a small sense of victory emboldening her as she slowly inched her hands down the rope.

Suspended in the darkness, she could neither see the perilous wall, nor the ground looming below, making them both more terrifying but also easier to ignore. She focused on the task at hand, carefully dragging her feet along the wall, feeling her way between spikes and finding her footing. Quickly she found a rhythm, encountering the next knot in the rope only a few moment later.

A blinding bolt of lightning darted towards the ground followed almost immediately by a deafening crack of thunder. Elora gasped, startled and disoriented for only a second. Her hands slipped on the wet rope, but she recovered her grip quickly and regained her balance. She needed to hurry. The storm was strengthening.

Larger raindrops began pelting her face as she, inch by inch, lowered herself down the wall. The wind began whipping the cloak around her body, throwing off her balance, forcing her to go even slower.

How far had she gone? How much further did she have to go? She had no way to know. Asher couldn't call out to her without giving them away, not that she would hear him over the sounds of the storm anyway. She had no choice but to continue.

Suddenly a brutal gust of wind knocked her off her feet, buffeting her against the treacherous wall. She couldn't help the cry that escaped as a spike grazed her shoulder, piercing her skin. She felt the warmth of her blood as it dripped down her arm. She struggled to turn her body and plant her feet on the wall, but she was no match for the wind. Wrapping her legs around the rope, she tried instead to support her quickly weakening arms. She swung back and forth, twisting hopelessly, her arms scraping against the rough and jagged rock, her head knocking against the stones, her hands clinging desperately to the rope.

The rain began falling in earnest, drenching the fibers of the rope. Her fingers lost their grip and slid down the rope nearly a foot before gaining purchase against a knot. Too frightened and panicked to even cry, she closed her eyes, holding tightly to the rope and hoping the storm would pass quickly. She had never felt more terrified or helpless in her life. Her hands were numb with exhaustion but still she held on. How would she survive this? She knew how injured she must be, but she felt no pain. Her heart was racing, her body coursing with adrenaline.

Suddenly something smooth brushed against her arm. All at once, she was surrounded by foliage. She could feel the stems weaving and curling around her legs and between her fingers. She heard the gentle thud of raindrops falling against leaves and her body was no longer being battered against hard stone. Had she fallen? But she quickly realized the rope was still there, firmly grasped in her hands. She opened her eyes in disbelief, looking around in wonder but unable to see clearly in the darkness.

Lightning once again illuminated the sky and her mouth fell open in awe. The wall around her was covered in thick vines. They slithered around her like snakes, coiling and thickening before her eyes. Broad, silky leaves burst forth from the stems, unfurling into a soft green carpet, coating the jagged rocks and burying the sharp spikes that dotted the wall.

Elora tried once more to twist around and regain her footing, but the storm had not abated even a little and a fierce gust of wind quickly tossed her back against the wall, now softened by the vines. Though the spikes and jagged rocks weren't as much of a threat anymore, she still couldn't stay up there, dangling defenselessly on the rope. The storm was seemingly tireless and endless, and potentially could get even worse. She had to get down.

Gently, hesitantly, Elora unwound her feet from the rope and shifted her weight onto a thick, woody vine growing beneath her. Slowly, she let go of the rope with one hand, grabbing hold of another vine. They seemed strong enough to support her weight. With an anxious inhale, she released the rope entirely. Quickly, she climbed down the wall of vines, fearful that they would collapse beneath her at any moment.

Suddenly a pair of arms grabbed her around the waist, lifting her off the wall. No sooner were her feet on the ground then Asher pulled her into his arms, nearly crushing her against him.

"Oh God, Elora," she heard him cry, his voice strained. "I'm so sorry. Are you hurt?"

She couldn't speak, so overwhelmed by what had just happened and likely in shock from her injuries. She nodded her head against his shoulder in answer.

"Can you walk?" he asked, shouting in her ear to be heard over the wind.

Could she? A boom of thunder shook the ground and she decided that if it meant getting out of the storm faster, she could find a way to run if she had to.

She nodded her head again, looking up at Asher, only able to see the outline of his head against the stormy sky.

"Yes?" he asked.

"Yes!" she shouted, finally able to summon her voice.

He released her and grabbed for her hand, taking it firmly in his and turning away from the wall. Lightning brightened the sky for a moment, revealing a small barn bordering a wheat field about 300 yards away. He began pulling her towards the field, charging through the knee high stalks, fighting against the wind and rain.

Elora tried to keep up, but kept slipping and tripping, her body unwieldy after the trauma of her descent over the wall. After her third fall, Asher stopped and moved in front of her, crouching down with his back to her. He took hold of her hands and joined them around his neck and then, reaching back, he grabbed behind her thighs and pulled her up onto his back. She barely had time to realize what had happened before he took off at a run towards the barn. She held on for dear life, gripping with her legs and leaning forward to lock her elbow over his shoulder. His arms were hooked behind her knees, clamping down on her legs painfully. She was sure she would be bruised later but she was so grateful to be carried that it didn't even matter. She could feel the strength and agility of his body beneath her, moving them quickly over the rough terrain. Each bolt of lightning revealed that they were nearing the safety of the barn.

A few minutes later he came to a stop and released his grip on her legs, catching her as she slid to the ground. He was panting with exertion, his chest heaving as he tried to catch his breath. Elora took hold of his hand and pulled him the few remaining feet toward the barn. She fumbled in the darkness, feeling for the latch of the door and lifted it, sliding it open and stepping inside. Asher quickly followed and closed the door behind him.

The barn was pitch black. The wind whistled through cracks between the weathered boards, warped by years baking in the relentless sun. Rain dripped steadily through a few gaps in the aged roof above. But the barn was solid and mostly dry.

Elora breathed a sigh of relief, finally protected from the storm raging outside and free of the walls of Windom. She could still hear Asher's labored breathing a few feet away.

"Have you ever been here before?" he asked between huffs. "Do you know what's in here?"

"No," Elora answered. "I've never been beyond the wall before."

Elora stretched out her arms protectively in front of her as she began feeling around the barn, trying to identify her surroundings, hoping she wouldn't encounter anything sinister.

"How injured are you, Elora?" Asher asked quietly a moment later, his voice strained with guilt.

"I'm not sure," Elora responded. "The wind knocked me against the wall quite a few times."

"I should have let you go first," he said with a sigh, his voice throttled with regret.

"It wasn't your fault," she replied, wincing as her injured arm brushed against a post.

Her head hit against something hard and she heard the familiar rattle of glass and metal. Her eyes widened with excitement as she reached up with her good arm to find a lantern hanging from a hook mounted high on the post.

"It's a lantern!" she cried, turning towards Asher. "Do you have any flint?"

She heard him moving towards her. He took the lantern from her hands and knelt down beside her. A moment later, a small spark lit the barn. He had found a small amount of dried straw to catch the flame, lifting it to ignite the wick of the oil lantern. Standing, he stomped out the straw and lifted the now burning lantern, filling the barn with a warm glow. Elora sighed and her spirits lifted, grateful for the comfort of being able to see again after stumbling around in the darkness for so long. She looked around, surveying the contents of the barn. There were scythes, hoes, shovels, and pitchforks sorted in stalls lining one of the walls. A few plows were parked in one corner with leather harnesses hanging on racks nearby. Shelving and a rough workbench were built into a partial wall which blocked off the back third of the barn for what looked like storage. The building was obviously used by the workers who managed the exterior crops. It wasn't a large space, but they weren't nearly as cramped as they had been in the schoolhouse shed. She smiled and turned to Asher.

"Oh God, Elora," he whispered, horrified.

"What?" Elora asked, alarmed.

She lifted her hand to touch her head, finally noticing the dull throb of pain now that things had calmed down. Every part of her body was soaking wet after being exposed to the storm for the past hour, so she hadn't noticed that she was bleeding. But as she dropped her hand, she now saw that her fingers were red with blood. She looked up at Asher with wide eyes, her mouth agape in surprise.

Asher took a knife from his belt and slit the bottom hem of his shirt, tearing off a strip of fabric. He stepped close to her, gently wiping away the blood that was dripping down the side of her face and looked for her injury. There was a cut on her head, hidden in the hair above her temple.

"It doesn't look deep," Asher said, pressing the fabric to the gash.

Elora flinched at his touch and he grimaced apologetically.

"Does it hurt anywhere else?" he asked, his eyes searching hers anxiously.

"It hurts everywhere else," she admitted, sighing.

"Keep pressure on this," he said, taking her hand and placing it over the makeshift bandage.

He pulled at the strings near her throat, untying the drenched cloak from around her neck and pulling it free. It fell to the floor with a soggy "thwap." At the sight of her shoulder, he exhaled sharply. Elora's tan tunic was light red with watered down blood. The spike had ripped a hole through her shirt and left a ragged gash across her shoulder. Asher quickly tore another strip of fabric from his shirt and carefully applied it to her wound.

Elora's eyes were closed and her brows were furrowed as she tried to hold her head still. She knew she had knocked her head against the wall a few times, though she hadn't realize how hard the impacts had been. But now that the adrenaline was wearing off, her head was pounding and her neck was sore.

"Is it bad?" she asked, her lips pursed in discomfort.

"It's not as bad as your shirt made it seem," he said, relief evident in his voice. "But there will probably be a scar once it heals."

He tore another strip from his shirt and wrapped it around her shoulder to hold the bandage in place.

"Your arms and hands are scraped pretty raw, but nothing else seems to be bleeding," he said finally, after looking her over.

"I'm going to be covered in bruises by the morning," Elora said, sighing. She opened one eye to glance up at him. "I knocked my head pretty good," she admitted with a wince.

"You need to sit down," Asher said, taking her by the elbow and leading her to the workbench.

She followed submissively, distracted by the pounding in her head and the ache in her shoulder. The surface of the workbench was relatively high and she looked at it, considering whether having a dry place to sit was worth the effort of climbing up there. Her mouth fell open in surprise when he suddenly gripped her waist and lifted her onto the table. His hands dropped from her sides to brace on either side of her legs as he leaned against the table beside her. He fixed his eyes onto hers and it was all she could do to remember to breathe.

"I am so sorry," he whispered.

The urge to touch his face was nearly overwhelming. She swallowed self-consciously, trying to keep hold of her senses despite the intensity of his stare. A lock of wet hair had fallen over his forehead and her fingers twitched of their own accord, desperate to smooth it back. Finally breaking eye contact, she cleared her throat and scooted her legs back on the table until she could lean against the wall. She clumsily pulled the strap of her satchel over her head, and let it fall beside her.

"It wasn't your fault," she repeated. "If that storm had held off another few minutes, I would have made it down the wall with no problem."

"I just thought, with the torches going out and the storm scaring everyone off the wall, it was an opportunity to escape unnoticed," he explained.

"Well, it was," Elora said, lowering the hand that was holding pressure on her head wound and gingerly touching her injury, feeling for fresh blood. Finding that the cut had stopped bleeding, she dropped her hands into her lap and rested her head back against the wall, closing her eyes.

"But I never considered how dangerous it would be to scale the wall in the storm," he said, shaking his head.

"We're safe now," Elora replied. "And it looks like we did get over unnoticed."

"For now," Asher replied. "Until the morning when everyone sees what you did," Asher replied.

Elora's eyes flew open and locked with his as she realized that the very thing that had saved her would also reveal their escape to the Liana.

"I didn't mean to," she said. "I was freaking out and they just grew."

"It's alright," Asher said, placing a soothing hand on her knee. "It was a good thing. I was about to come back up that rope to get you and I'm not sure either of us would have survived that."

"What now?" Elora asked anxiously.

“You rest here a while,” he said. “I’m going to go get Kit.”

“Kit?” Elora asked, confused.

“My horse,” he replied. “I left her pastured not far from here.”

Panicked, Elora grabbed hold of his hand.

“Wait! You’re leaving me here alone?” she asked, the pitch of her voice high with anxiety.

“Not for long,” he said, squeezing her hand. “I’ll be right back. And once the storm lets up, we’ll go.”

Elora was at her limit. In the wake of losing her parents and saying goodbye to friends, she felt completely untethered. After her harrowing descent down the wall, every part of her body ached. With the storm raging outside and the Liana lying in wait, she had never felt so vulnerable. Asher’s presence, his calm, his kindness was the only thing holding her together. The last thing she wanted was to be alone.

“I don’t like this,” she said, her eyes wide.

“Just try to relax and recover for a little while, Elora,” he said in a tone that brooked no more argument.

“Please hurry,” she said, still gripping tightly to his hand.

“I will,” he said, gently pulling his hand free. “Don’t go anywhere,” he warned. “Don’t come after me.”

Elora nodded stiffly, trying to control her fear.

“Just wait,” he said, leaning forward to look directly into her eyes, the words spoken softly but with emphasis.

Elora stared back at him, the fear evident on her face. He didn't move, waiting for a response.

"Okay," she said, swallowing hard around the lump in her throat.

He nodded and squeezed her hand. Turning, he walked over to the barn door but paused with his hand on the latch. He looked back at her one last time.

"Wait for me, Elora," he said, his eyes fixed on hers.

She froze, caught off guard by the words that had haunted her.

Not lingering for a reply, he lifted the latch and slid the door open a few inches. A gust of wind billowed through the gap and turned the air inside the barn turbulent, making the lantern flicker and sending dust and straw airborne. Elora closed her eyes and turned her face away, startled by the blast of debris. The air settled suddenly and she looked up to find the door shut and Asher gone. She stared at the place where he had stood only a moment ago, her heart thudding in her chest.

Could it be? Could Asher be the man in her visions. It had been weeks since she'd first had that vision and the man had only said those words to her once. Would she even be able to recognize his voice if she heard it again? But the sound of Asher's voice, the way his accent curled around those words, was so familiar.

"No," she whispered to herself, shaking her head.

Asher couldn't be her soulmate. He hadn't been paired yet. He had never mentioned any visions, much less visions of her. And he seemed so desperate to find his soulmate. He believed in the power of the Ever Tree so completely. If he had been paired with her, he would have said something? Besides, she didn't feel the same way for Asher as she did about the man in her visions. Did she?

"Stop it, Elora," she admonished, shaking her head again more vigorously before wincing in pain from her injuries.

"It was probably just a coincidence," she thought, surprised by the disappointment that tugged at her heart. She closed her eyes and dropped her head back against the wall, a small smile playing on her lips.

Probably.

CHAPTER 21

Every crack of thunder made her jump out of her skin. Elora sat on the workbench, acutely aware of every detail of her surroundings, her eyes wide with paranoia. Asher had been gone at least 20 minutes by now and she was struggling to follow his instructions. She stared at the door to the barn, her legs twitching with the urge to go looking for him.

The ache in her head had subsided somewhat and she sat up, sliding her bottom towards the edge of the table. She was too restless to sit still anymore. The Elysic Cloak caught her eye, laying on the floor in a sodden heap. She walked over and picked it up, leaving a small puddle in its place. She began wringing out the fabric, and then hung it from a peg on one of the posts.

Looking for a distraction, she took hold of the lantern and made her way to the darkened storage area of the barn to explore. As she rounded the corner, there was the rustling sound of mice scurrying into hiding. She held the lantern high, looking around at the odds and ends that had been left there over the years. A hopelessly broken plow, a few scythes rusted through, but there was nothing very interesting or useful.

She wandered back to the main area of the barn and peered around, taking a closer look at its contents. Her eyes lighting on a leather water bladder hanging from the corner of one of the tool stalls, she gasped. She hurried over, taking the flask in her hands and turning it over, looking for holes. Perhaps it had just been forgotten and not discarded. She couldn't see anything wrong with it. She smiled, excited to have found something useful. Walking over to the workbench, she placed the bladder beside her satchel and turned to look at the door once more, hopeful that Asher would walk through at any moment. Sighing with disappointment, she continued her inspection of the barn.

After 5 more agonizing minutes, Elora couldn't take it anymore. Something must have happened to him. She had waited long enough.

She retrieved the cloak from where it hung drying and rolled it up, returning to her belongings on the workbench. The leather satchel had kept its contents surprisingly dry despite the torrential downpour. She shoved the cloak into the bag, not caring that it was still wet. The flask went in as well before she lifted the strap over her head and across her chest, tucking the bag behind her hip. She took hold of the lantern and walked with determination to the barn door. Her hand on the latch, she took a deep breath and was about to open it when the handle jerked out of her hands.

The door slid open and Asher was suddenly before her, water dripping down his face. She jumped back in surprise as he walked in leading a brown horse, its coat so drenched it appeared nearly black. She quickly slid the door shut behind him and turned to watch him, breathless with relief.

“Were you going somewhere?” he asked, his back towards her as he fiddled with the straps on his saddle.

“I thought something had happened to you,” she replied, sheepishly.

“I told you to wait,” he said angrily, shifting to glare at her briefly before returning to his task.

“You also told me you’d be right back,” she replied, lashing out, her voice strained with all the anxiety and frustration she’d pent up over the past hour.

“I know,” he said, shaking his head. “Kit was spooked by the storm and it took me a while to catch her.”

Elora approached the horse’s head, holding her hand out to stroke her muzzle.

“I’m sorry I left you alone so long,” Asher said after a long, quiet moment.

Elora nodded, her throat thick with relief.

“I’m sorry, too,” Elora replied softly, hazarding a glance at his face.

He looked over at her, holding her gaze for a minute before nodding slightly and returning his attention to his task. Having unfastened the girth, he pulled the wet saddle from the horse's back and hauled it over to an empty rack near the plow harnesses. He came back to tug the bridle over her ears, gently waiting for her to release the bit from her mouth before he pulled it free of her head. He draped it over the peg where Elora had removed the cloak only moments before. Loose, the horse wandered around the barn, sniffing curiously, occassionally jerking her nose back nervously as she timidly explored her surroundings.

"So this is Kit," Elora said, watching the horse.

"That's Kit," Asher replied.

He was exhausted. She could see the weariness in the lines of his face and the curve of his back. His broad shoulders sagged as he rested his hands on his hips. He inhaled deeply, as though he could finally relax. He lifted his hands to rub the water from his face, pausing to scratch at the stubble on his cheeks before pushing his fingers through his wet hair.

"The storm is still going strong, Elora," he said. "We will just have to sit tight a while. We might as well try to sleep."

He retrieved the lantern and walked over to the workbench. He hopped up easily onto the table, setting the lantern down beside him. He leaned against the wall, letting his head fall back and closing his eyes.

The barn fell into an uncomfortable silence. Elora stood awkwardly, unsure of what to do. Now that they had escaped from Windom and weren't surrounded by the Liana, her fears of being captured had subsided, only to be replaced by a new kind of tension. Asher was a virtual stranger. She was suddenly acutely aware of how alone and secluded they were. She feigned interest in the horse but stole glances at him every few moments.

"They won't come looking for us," he said finally, oblivious to the real source of her unease. "Only an idiot would go out in that storm," he muttered, chuckling at his own joke.

When she didn't respond, he opened one eye.

"Come on," he said, patting the workbench beside him. "You need to rest. We have a hard journey ahead. And I want to put out the lantern already."

She hesitated, but relented a second later as she realized that she truly was exhausted. Her shoulder still throbbed and her arms burned where they had scraped against the wall. There truly was nowhere else to sit and the ground was covered in puddles from the leaky roof.

She walked over to the workbench and clumsily climbed onto the table beside him. Perching on the very edge, she twisted her hands nervously. She snuck a look at Asher and seeing that his eyes were closed again, gave in to her curiosity and studied him. He was strong, and he carried himself with confidence. He had been kind to her friends and was considerate of her needs. He was also uncomfortably attractive, but she no longer found that intimidating. Her hands calmed in her lap and the tension drained from her back as she realized that she felt safe with him. She trusted him. Had she really only met him just this morning? So much had happened since then. And now he was literally the only person she could rely on in the entire world.

She slid the lantern out of the way and scooted back until she could lean against the wall, careful to leave some space between them. Asher's breathing was deep and even. He was so calm. She watched him quietly, his ability to relax so completely soothed her in a way she couldn't explain. Turning down the wick of the lantern, she blew out the flame and the barn fell into darkness. She closed her eyes, letting her head drop back. The roar of the driving rain pounding against the roof and the rumble of distant thunder lulled her to sleep.

The barn was silent when Elora regained consciousness a few hours later. She was still so very tired, it took her a moment to differentiate dream from reality. She was struggling to believe that any of what she remembered from the day before had actually happened. She was content to feign sleep and pretend it had all been a nightmare until she felt something touch her leg. Her eyes flew open in surprise. Her eyes took a moment to adjust to the darkness, but a gentle snuffle put her mind at ease. Kit was pushing against her knee with her velvety nose, tugging at her pants with her clumsy lips. Elora reached out her hand, letting the horse nuzzle her fingers, blowing hot puffs of air through its nostrils.

"She likes you," came a soft voice close to her ear.

She froze, suddenly realizing that she had shifted in her sleep. The feel of Asher's still damp shirt against her cheek finally registered. The heat of his body radiated through his shirt where her arm was pressed against his. She lifted her head from his shoulder and quickly shifted back to her original place a safe distance away.

"Sorry," she whispered, a blush creeping into her cheeks.

"That's alright. I'm glad you were able to sleep," he said, unable to see her embarrassment in the dark. "But it sounds like the storm is finally passed. It's time to go before the sun gives us away."

He pushed off of the workbench and walked over to the barn door, sliding it open to let in the moonlight instead of relighting the lantern. He busied himself saddling Kit in the faint white glow.

Elora rubbed the sleep from her eyes and tucked the hairs that had broken free of her updo back behind her ears. She climbed down from the table and pulled on her satchel. Waiting for Asher to finish, she wandered over to the barn door. The moon was still fairly high in the sky, but the horizon was beginning to lighten with the telltale grays of the early sunrise. She turned and walked back over to Kit, smoothing her forelock while Asher adjusted the straps of the girth.

"Are we going to retrieve one of the horses that my parents purchased?" Elora asked.

"We have to assume that the Liana will know about that," Asher said, shaking his head.

"Right," Elora whispered, dropping her forehead against the horse's wide face. "Because they have my parents."

"For now," Asher replied, pausing to look at her.

She nodded, avoiding his eyes, fighting to keep her tears in check, trying to ignore the painful clenching of her heart. She noticed, for the first time, the bow and quiver of arrows attached to his saddle. Reaching out, she touched the feathered end of one.

"Are Claren usually archers?" she asked, her curiosity piqued.

"Yes," Asher responded, moving to retrieve the bridle from its peg.

"Hmm. Hunters in Windom usually use rifles," she mused.

"A bow is quieter," he said.

Elora nodded in understanding, recognizing that a quiet weapon would be in keeping with their vow of secrecy. She wandered over to the barn door, watching the sky brighten by the second. They only had maybe 30 more minutes before the sun would crest the horizon.

"Are you ready?" he asked, walking up to stand beside her. "We need to start moving."

"I'm ready," she said, nodding with enthusiasm.

She was starting to get nervous. They had taken such pains to escape the wall unnoticed and she didn't want to lose that advantage.

Asher gave a little whistle and Kit walked up to him, nuzzling against his hand. He took hold of the reins and led the horse outside, turning back to Elora and waving for her to follow.

"Let's get out of here," he said.

Elora took a deep breath. Her legs felt weak as she made her way out of the barn, sliding the door closed behind her.

Asher was already on his horse when she turned away from the barn, waiting with his hand outstretched to help her up behind him. She lifted her leg to the stirrup and taking his hand, awkwardly pulled herself up. She winced and swallowed a groan, her sore body protesting the movement. She tried to ignored the ache as she wrapped her arms around Asher's waist and wriggled closer to the saddle.

"Don't let go," he said, pulling the reins to turn the horse and squeezing it forward.

The rain from the storm overnight had turned the ground into slick mud and Kit struggled to keep her footing at times. Elora had to hold on tightly to Asher to avoid throwing off the horse's balance, and to keep from falling off altogether. Her shoulder throbbed in defiance at the way she was using her injured arms. Asher would accidently bump it every so often as he maneuvered Kit through the patchwork of fields. It was very slow going, but at last they reached the far edge of the exterior crops.

In front of them, the open plains stretched all the way to the horizon. An ocean of yellow grass, gently blowing in the morning breeze spread out as far as the eye could see with only an occasional errant shrub to mark the distance. The sun was beginning to rise in earnest, the sky tinted in pinks and oranges but quickly giving way to crystal blue.

As Kit took her first steps onto the wild, untamed prairie, Elora couldn't help but look backwards at Windom, the only place she'd ever been, the only home she'd ever known. It was there, in the small yard behind their sweet little house, that she had taken her first steps. It was there, at a social in the church courtyard when she had been 5 years old, that she'd met a raven haired little girl just her own age and discovered the gift of friendship. She had followed that raven haired girl down the aisle of that same courtyard only yesterday. She had grown strong and smart and confident, safe and content within the walls of Windom, surrounded by her parents and friends. With a pang of sadness, she realized that she was leaving behind her entire life.

They were moving more quickly now, free of the muddy, loose soil of the cultivated fields. The settlement was fading from view just as the sun finally crested the horizon. She turned one last time, fixing her eyes on Windom, committing to memory the last sight she would likely ever have of her home. In the full light of day, she could finally see clearly the wall that had nearly defeated her the night before and she gasped. Even from this distance, she could see the vines climbing the barrier, splashing up against the tan stones like a green wave.

Hearing her gasp, Asher pulled Kit to a stop and turned back to see what had disturbed her.

"Wow," he whispered, staring at Elora's handiwork.

"Yeah," she replied softly, shifting to catch his eyes. "Maybe they won't notice," she said, shrugging her shoulders and giving him a small smile.

He chuckled and squeezed Kit forward, turning them away from the small town and the Liana lurking there.

"Goodbye Windom," Elora whispered, taking one final look.

"You better hold on," Asher said, as he urged the horse into a lope.

Elora tightened her arms around him and pressed her head against his back, trying to move her body with his. They at last settled into a rhythm and Kit found her stride, the ground rushing beneath them, every beat of her hooves taking Elora farther way from everything she had ever loved and saving her from the enemy she had never known to fear.

Tucked behind Asher, in a world all her own, her thoughts drifted to her parents. What must they be going through right now? What were the Liana doing to them? She had to save them. The weight of their love and the burden of their sacrifice made it hard to breathe. She couldn't help the growing feelings of resentment towards the Claren and this cursed Prophesy for the way it had destroyed everything she held dear. If only she had never found that necklace. She could feel it dangling around her neck, the seed gently rapping against her chest with every surge of Kit's powerful legs.

Asher slowed them to a walk, having put a fair bit of distance between them and Windom. She had worked hard, carrying both of them, and her chest was heaving with exertion.

"I'm going to lighten her load and walk for a while," Asher said, pulling the horse to a halt.

He lifted his leg over her neck and hopped down effortlessly.

"I'll get down too," Elora offered.

"No, you should ride," Asher said, shaking his head. "You're hurt."

She could hardly argue with him. After their harrowing ride, her poor body was nearly numb with pain. She nodded and shifted forward to sit more comfortably in the saddle.

Asher took hold of the reins and led Kit forward, allowing Elora to relax and her attention to wander.

She looked around, marveling at the magnitude of the sky overhead. The grassy plains extended to the horizon in every direction, leaving an unobstructed view of the cloudless atmosphere above. It was a breathtakingly deep blue and the vastness of it was both humbling and awe-inspiring.

"I can't believe how beautiful it is out here," Elora said quietly, feeling almost as though it were sinful to talk in the presence of such a view.

"It's pretty," Asher agreed, nodding as he looked around appreciatively.

"That seems like a bit of an understatement," she countered, exasperated.

"Maybe," he admitted. "But you haven't seen Clarendon yet."

"I feel so tiny beneath a sky like this," she said, ignoring his attempt to downplay the grandeur.

"Well, you are tiny compared to this," he laughed, gesturing to the world at large.

"I know," she said, waving her hand dismissively. "But you know what I mean. When you're confronted by how huge the world is, you just realize how insignificant you really are."

"Just because you're small doesn't mean you're insignificant," Asher replied. "You are very significant, Elora Kerrick."

She looked down at him, surprised by his candor.

"Even tiny things can change the world," he said holding her gaze for a moment before shifting his eyes downward to settle briefly on the seed dangling from her neck.

Her hand lifted of its own volition to grasp the seed. That seed had changed everything. It had awakened her powers and set her on the path to her destiny. It had been the instrument of her downfall, bringing the Liana to her door. It had given her visions and stolen her heart. That seed had turned her whole world upside down.

She pictured the seed in her mind with its dull brown shell and ornate ridges, slowly coming to life one bright strand at a time. She wondered what it might look like full of life, silver and shimmering. She pictured it shining brightly, clasped between two lovers' hands. She imagined it being tucked into the earth, a majestic tree sprouting forth and stretching into the sky, a mighty forest spreading outwards from its roots. Hidden within the diminutive form of that little seed was an unexpected power and an unknown promise. It was a secret. It was a beginning. She was holding a forest in her hand.

She couldn't help but think of the other seed, the one on her back. That tiny mark had determined the course of her entire life. It was the source of her gift and the cause of her heartache. But like the seed around her neck, it was only a beginning. It was her beginning. As the mark on her back is growing and transforming, perhaps she too is becoming what she is meant to be. That mark holds the promise that someday she will have the ability to do incredible things.

Elora gazed up at the immense blue sky above an endless ocean of grass and smiled. She no longer felt small. She no longer felt insignificant. Hidden within her was a gift that would change the world. She was powerful. She was destined. She was the Renascent.

END OF BOOK 1

Made in the USA
Monee, IL
01 April 2020